THE DANGEROUS TYPE

THE DANGEROUS TYPE

IN THE WAKE OF THE TEMPLARS BOOK ONE

LOREN RHOADS

NIGHT SHADE BOOKS
NEW YORK

Night Shade books may be purchased in bulk at special
discounts for sales promotion, corporate gifts, fund-raising, or educa-
tional purposes. Special editions can also be created to
specifications. For details, contact the Special Sales Department, Night
Shade Books, 307 West 36th Street, 11th Floor, New York, NY 10018
or info@skyhorsepublishing.com.

Night Shade Books™ is a trademark of Skyhorse Publishing, Inc.®, a
Delaware corporation.

Visit our website at www.nightshadebooks.com.

10 9 8 7 6 5 4 3 2 1

Library of Congress Cataloging-in-Publication Data is available on file.

Cover illustration and design by Cody Tilson

Print ISBN: 978-1-59780-814-9
Ebook ISBN: 978-1-59780-828-6

Printed in the United States of America

*This book is dedicated to Martha J. Allard,
who was there when the story began.*

CHAPTER 1

Kavanaugh had serious qualms about robbing graves. It was
bad enough that the rest of the galaxy blamed humans for
exterminating the Templars. If it were discovered that a
human team was now looting Templar graves, the galaxy would feel
justified in its low opinions of humanity. He didn't like to think
where that would lead.

Still, as Sloane said, it wasn't as if the bugs inside the tombs were
using the weapons and armor and grave goods buried with them.
And it wasn't as if Sloane hadn't paid off every official in the quadrant
who might be intrigued by what the "archaeological" team was doing.
And, yeah, Kavanaugh himself hadn't known anyone responsible for
the Templar genocide: that didn't keep him from feeling bad about it.
It sickened him that he was part of a species who could conceive of
wiping another people out of the galaxy, if those people stood in the
way of humanity's expansionist dreams. Kavanaugh didn't think about
it much, but when he did, he supposed that the kind of humans who
could unleash such genocide probably didn't think of Templars—or
the other sentient species of the galaxy—as "people."

That Sloane could loot the Templar tombs without a second thought
saddened Kavanaugh. And yet here Kavanaugh found himself,
leading the team, wondering how the hell he'd volunteered for this.

The Templars chose these caves for their tombs because the stone was impossibly difficult to cut. They meant for their graves to be sealed for all time. It took Kavanaugh's team hours to calculate how to open each cavern. Unfortunately, Sloane didn't accept facts as excuses. The grave robbers had a quota; Kavanaugh's job was to see they met it.

At least the impossibly hard stone kept the caves' contents incorrupt. The metal was as polished as the day it had been entombed, corpses as fresh. In the past couple of weeks, Kavanaugh had seen more than he wanted of dead bugs contorted by the plague.

Nothing indicated that this cavern would be different from the others. If it had been up to Kavanaugh, he'd have let the men close down the machinery for the night and sent them back to the bunker to get out of the knifing, granular wind. Unfortunately, the boss had made it clear to him that not meeting the quota would cost Kavanaugh his job. He was on the verge of saying, "Fine, I quit," but the boss, long ago, had been a friend.

Lim, the team's engineer, checked input of the measurements once again as they all huddled in the lee of the loader to wait for the calculations to be done. Kavanaugh thought longingly of the flask inside his jacket, but he wasn't about to lift his face screen to sip from it. It wasn't worth losing an eye to the obsidian grit in the wind.

The men were too tired to grumble. They'd already opened one tomb today, stripping it of grave goods and packing the antiques carefully to be shipped off-world.

Sloane had warned Kavanaugh to watch the men closely to prevent pilferage. The memory made Kavanaugh snort. So far they hadn't come across anything to tempt the men. Anything that got stolen wasn't leaving, except on one of the boss's ships. Nobody was stupid enough to risk crossing Sloane.

The computer chimed as calculations scrolled across its screen. "Back to work," Kavanaugh translated.

Lim called out coordinates for Curcovic and Taki to place the charges around the huge stone slab sealing the tomb's mouth. Kavanaugh fingered the flask again, mouth watering, hoping that the tomb would be empty so they could be done for the day and get out of the wind sooner. It wasn't like he was going to sleep tonight, but at least in the bunker he could lie down and rest. The tension of taking these risks for Sloane was killing him.

The men sprinted back toward the loader. The four of them huddled together against the big machine as Taki pressed the switch.

A huge explosion dropped the ground from beneath their feet. Then the blast wave knocked them back against the loader, holding them in place for a moment, air crushed from their lungs, as it boomed through the stone valley. When it released them, Kavanaugh counted the seconds until the echo rolled back down the valley to them.

"Think you used too much," Kavanaugh commented.

"Don't tell Sloane," Curcovic drawled.

"I used just enough," Taki huffed. "Take a look."

The slab had shifted sufficiently that the men could get levers around it and roll it back enough to squeeze past. Lim pulled the levers from the loader and handed them around.

As he bent to work, Curcovic said, as he always did, "Hope there's something good in this one. I'm bored with dead bugs in shiny armor."

"It's not like they're gonna have left dancing girls in any of them," Taki complained. "That's the only thing I wanna find." He turned to Kavanaugh to ask, "When do we get off this rock again?"

"Not soon enough," Kavanaugh answered again. Curcovic laughed, as he always did.

According to plan, they'd wriggle into the tomb one at a time. Kavanaugh always went first. He was the crew boss, hence the most expendable if they tripped a booby-trap. It was a point of honor for him that he didn't ask the men to do anything he wouldn't volunteer for himself. It made him better than Sloane. Besides, Curcovic always joked, Kavanaugh would need the others to figure out how to free him if the slab slipped.

Kavanaugh always had a moment, as he slithered past the edge of a slab, when he feared it would rock back into place and crush him. Or worse, it would rock back after he'd passed it, trapping him inside the tomb. No telling how long it would take someone to die inside one of those graves, how long before the air ran out or dehydration made breathing cease to matter. It wasn't as if Sloane would feel he had enough invested in the team to rescue anyone. Kavanaugh wouldn't put it past the boss to decide it was more cost effective simply to hire new men, leaving the originals behind as a warning to be more careful.

Most of the tombs they'd entered had warehoused whole companies of bugs, the dead warriors of a single campaign buried together. Kavanaugh played his light around the inside this cavern but found only a single catafalque, an uncarved slab of obsidian in the rough center of the room. Whoever lay atop it must be important, he thought. Shouldn't take too long to loot one body. Maybe there would actually be something worth stealing this time.

Kavanaugh peeled off his face shield and lifted the flask, sucking down the last half of its contents. His boot knocked something over. When he bent down to retrieve it, he found a human-made electric torch. Damn. Had someone beat them to this one?

He raised the torch, toggling its switch, but it remained dark.

"What's a human girl doing in here?" Taki asked.

Kavanaugh stopped fiddling with the torch to see his team converge around the catafalque. He couldn't make sense of what they were saying. Why *would* there be a human girl inside a Templar tomb?

"There's your dancing girl," Curcovic teased. "Maybe you can wake her with a kiss."

"'Cept for the dust," Lim commented.

"Well, yeah, 'cept for the dust, Lim. Damn, man, don't you have any imagination?"

"Just what did you have in mind?" Lim asked skeptically.

Kavanaugh started toward them, to see what they were talking about. "Are you sure she's human?"

"I think she's just a kid," Curcovic answered. "No armor. You think she was somebody important's kid?"

"She's the best thing I've seen on this rock so far," Taki pointed out. His hand wiped some of the dust from her chest.

Kavanaugh was halfway across the uneven floor to join them when a low female voice said clearly, "No."

Curcovic stumbled backward, dropping his torch to fumble at the gun at his hip. The corpse sat up, straight-arming her fist into Taki's face. Stunned, he cracked his head on the stone floor when he went down. He lay still at the foot of the catafalque.

Lim backed away, light trained on the figure rising in the middle of the tomb. It was hard for Kavanaugh to make her out in the unsteady light: a slip of a girl dressed in gray with a cloak of dusty black hair that fell past her knees.

Curcovic finally succeeded in drawing his gun. The girl darted sideways faster than Kavanaugh could follow in the half-light. A red bolt flashed out, blinding in the darkness. Lim collapsed to the floor, cursing Curcovic's friendly fire.

The girl rounded on Curcovic, turning a one-handed cartwheel that left her in range to kick the gun from his hand. She twisted around, nearly too quick to see, and cracked her fist hard into his chest. Curcovic fell as if poleaxed. Lim groaned from the floor, hands clasped over his belly.

None of the men were dead yet, Kavanaugh noticed. She could have killed them as if they'd been standing still, but she'd disabled them instead. He suspected that was because they posed no real threat to her. Maybe she needed them alive. He hoped that was true.

Cold sweat ran into Kavanaugh's eyes. He held the flask in his gun hand. He'd have to drop it to draw his weapon. If the noise caught her attention, he'd be headed for the ground before his gun barrel cleared his holster.

"We didn't mean you any harm," he said gently as he let go of the flask.

She wheeled toward him and crouched like an animal. He wondered if she was crazy. How had she gotten into this tomb? Had she been imprisoned here? How had she possibly survived?

"I know you." Her voice was rusty. "Switch on your light. I want to see your face."

With his left hand, Kavanaugh pulled his torch out of its loop. He heard her move, dodging away from where he saw her last, so that he couldn't blind her with the light. Instead, he turned the beam on and held it to illuminate the left side of his face. He closed his right eye, hoping to retain some night vision in case she attacked him… not that there was much he could do against her speed.

"No," she said, her voice desolate. "You only remind me of someone I used to know." She was moving toward the mouth of the tomb. Kavanaugh shivered at the thought that she might knock the chocks aside and seal them in. At least the loader was parked outside—unless she stole it—so that Sloane would know where to start looking for them.

If he cared enough to look for them…

"Where will you go out there?" Kavanaugh asked desperately. "It's a rock. Barren. You can't get off-world without our help."

Somewhere in the darkness, she laughed. The sound wasn't entirely sane. "You're grave robbers. You're going to help me?"

"We're archaeologists," Kavanaugh lied. "We work for Gavin Sloane."

Her response was completely unexpected. "Gavin? Still alive?"

"You know him?" Kavanaugh asked.

She ignored the question. "Is he here?"

"He's on a moon orbiting the planet. I need to report back to him this evening. Why don't you come back to the bunker with us, get cleaned up, and you can speak to him when I check in?"

She paused, just out of reach of the slice of grainy light falling through the entryway. "I do know you. Your voice…I used to know you." There was a pause before she asked plaintively, "How long have I been in here?"

"Can I look at you?" Kavanaugh asked. "Maybe I'd recognize you."

"Your men are wounded. Take them to your bunker, patch them up, and we'll catch up later." She laughed again. "I want out of this hole in the ground."

"Understood. Do you need something to wrap your face? The sand is like slivers of glass out there."

When he shined the light toward the entry, she had gone.

* * *

The dream was so vivid that Jonan Thallian woke shaking. He roused Eilif, sleeping beside him, and sent her to bring him a carafe of coffee. He intended to sit vigil through the remainder of the night.

In the dream, he'd stood in the throne room at the heart of Earth. Stood and did not pace. Stood at attention, as the Emperor catalogued the expense Raena Zacari had put the Empire to: officers and soldiers killed, ships destroyed or disabled, an Imperial mining prison in ruins. That was in addition to the time Thallian himself had wasted pursuing the girl. Clearly, Thallian was not to be trusted in matters concerning her. The Emperor was deeply disappointed.

Thallian remembered the boom of the Emperor's voice, the conversational way he detailed Thallian's failure.

Eilif pulled Thallian out of his memories when she returned, carrying a carafe of fragrant coffee. She poured a cup, blew across its surface, and then sipped from it. Thallian watched her. When nothing happened, he took the cup from her and drank.

His wife didn't ask what had woken him. She sat on the floor at his feet, leaned her back against his chair. Thallian stroked her graying hair.

Sipping his coffee, he sank back into memories. The video transmission had been poor quality, but the Emperor had watched it avidly. A squadron of human engineers used a sophisticated anti-grav feedback system to roll back the large wheel of black stone that sealed a tomb. When the grave's maw finally gaped open, Marchan emerged from his shuttle. He carried Raena's slight body down the ship's ramp toward the tomb. Her limbs dangled. She was unconscious or drugged.

Thallian remembered how he'd studied her, instead of his rival. Her face was turned toward Marchan's chest, so that Thallian saw only the white column of her throat. He remembered its warm strength under his fingers. Locks of her long black hair thrashed like tentacles in the wind. Her tiny feet in their absurdly high-heeled boots were alternately hidden and revealed by the flapping edge of her cape. One hand had fallen out away from her body, its palm just visible behind her unconsciously curled fingers. That seemed so childlike, so innocent, it tore at Thallian to remind himself she had betrayed the Empire. She had betrayed Thallian himself.

Turning away from the playback, the Emperor had said, "As a favor to you, my friend, I am not condemning her to death."

Thallian understood exactly what the Emperor left unspoken. If Thallian proved his loyalty to the Emperor's satisfaction and beyond, perhaps one day Raena would be set free. As if she would be sane then. As if she would thank anyone for sparing her life.

Thallian finished the cup of coffee. Eilif roused herself and poured him another. They repeated the tasting ritual. Then Thallian said, "Go back to bed."

"I don't mind sitting up with you, my lord."

"Go," Thallian repeated. "You'll be no use to me tomorrow if you're exhausted."

"As you wish, my lord."

The dream had called the memories back full force. Thallian remembered the sour, medicinal smell of the old Emperor. He remembered the tearing ache he'd felt in his chest as he watched Marchan walk alone out of the tomb and give the order for the engineers to replace the stone slab.

He'd heard Raena scream, "No!" Felt it.

Then he'd fallen on his knees at the old man's feet and swore once more, "I live only to serve you and the Empire, my lord. I beg you to command me."

That was when he agreed to commit genocide in the name of Humanity.

What else could he have done? Any other action meant death.

If he was lucky.

If he was luckier than Raena had been.

He sipped the synthetic coffee, savoring its artificial bitterness and remembered every inch of Raena's flesh. He knew which of her scars he had inflicted. He knew the stories she told about the others, how she had really come by them. He knew the smell of her, the taste, the sound of her breathing. Twenty years had done nothing to dim the memory.

Even so, he was surprised to see her in his dreams tonight. It had been a while since he'd thought of her, longer since he'd missed her as intensely as he did now. The ache returned to his chest, the hollowness, as if something had been torn out. He'd thought he had finally outlived all that.

If she had survived very long in her tomb—and Thallian honestly did not know—she would have been emaciated, frail, and quite, quite mad by the time she finally died. He wondered if he would recognize her corpse.

Kindness was a gesture Thallian seldom considered. However, in Raena's case, it would have been a kindness to end her misery once the War was over and the Emperor executed.

Nothing had prevented him from doing just that, except—and this was difficult to admit even in his own thoughts—fear. He had been afraid of what time and captivity and claustrophobia had wrought. He feared seeing Raena twisted and broken. He could not bear the thought of contaminating his memories with the horrible truth.

The unattainable perfection of the past mocked him. He would desire her always, and she would never, ever, be his.

As always before, Thallian resolved to let the past remain buried.

He finished his coffee and returned to bed to wake Eilif once more.

* * *

When Taki came around, his pupils were uneven. Curcovic was still out cold. Lim was bleeding, but it didn't look too bad, more a flesh wound than anything else. Lim was lucky: if Curcovic had caught him in a kidney, Sloane would be looking for a new engineer. Kavanaugh wondered if they would have buried Lim here, amidst the looted tombs. He never mentioned any family that might claim his body.

Then again, none of them had anyone who cared about them, or they wouldn't be working for Gavin Sloane.

Kavanaugh shifted the men out of the tomb and settled them on the loader. He drove to the bunker, carried everyone inside, and set about doctoring them as best he could. Seven Earth years on a tramp medical ship as a kid had taught him everything he needed to know about battlefield medicine.

Thinking about the past made him suspect who it was they had just rescued. He hadn't thought about Raena Zacari since he'd seen her walk away from a bounty hunter twenty-some years ago. But what she was doing here on this gods-forsaken world, locked in a tomb? And why did she still look the same as she had twenty years ago?

✳ ✳ ✳

Across the galaxy, the comm beeped as soon as the hour could be considered decent. Eilif's hand dropped on it, stifling the second beep. She said softly, "Yes?"

"I must see my lord at his earliest convenience, regarding the long-range scan he commanded."

Thallian reached down to the comm and covered Eilif's hand with his own. Hollow sickness twisted in his stomach. "Five minutes. My office. Bring Revan and Jain."

Releasing the comm, Thallian stepped out of bed and pulled on a robe. Eilif glanced over her shoulder at him, then hastily tugged on the leggings she had worn last evening.

Thallian took her chin in his hand. "This information isn't for you. Yet."

She froze at his touch, except to turn her eyes up to him. "How long-range was this scan?" she wondered.

"Outside the system."

Eilif frowned. "Are we at war?"

Thallian smiled at her, but his heart wasn't in it enough to make it truly menacing. "Not yet. Perhaps not at all."

He swooped down to kiss her, purposefully cutting her lip on his teeth. The familiar taste of her blood steadied him a little.

"Bring breakfast to my office," he ordered as he stepped through the door into the internal corridor.

Eilif left his thoughts before the door closed behind him. So someone had tampered with Raena's tomb. The thought made his eyes feel strange, as if he might cry.

In the solitude of his office, Thallian reconsidered the haste of calling this meeting before he had properly dressed. Would they read his eagerness as weakness? *Was* it weakness, sentimentality, paranoia? If the dream hadn't woken him in the middle of the night, his feelings would be clearer now.

He settled into his chair and keyed in the command to unlock the door.

Thallian's oldest brother entered first and took the comfortable chair. Revan ran his fingers through graying hair still tousled from sleep. His clothing was rumpled, but at least he'd dressed. He smiled at Thallian and said nothing.

Fourteen-year-old Jain quivered with barely contained energy. He was Thallian's favorite son, the fiercest. He wore loose black exercise clothing and the sidearm Thallian had helped him to build. He'd teased his blue-black hair into standing straight up this morning and his gray eyes shone with excitement. It always pleased Thallian to recognize his own facial structure and coloring echoed in his sons.

The scanner tech came last. Nerves drew his mouth into a grimace. He stepped forward to place a handscreen on the edge of the desk, then retreated behind Revan's chair.

Thallian didn't move forward to retrieve the screen yet. "When did this information come in?" Galaxy-wide FTL communications might be commonplace, but the flow of information still slowed and bunched up around the shoals of Humanity's limited capacity to examine and act on it.

"My lord, as you know, the Templars' tombworld is not under constant surveillance. We spot-check the data once each month. Last night, during the scan you requested, I noticed that the scanner had gone offline."

"When?"

"I estimate that it cannot have been more than three weeks, my lord."

Jain repeated, "Three weeks!"

Thallian silenced the boy with a glance. "Revan, take Jain and a well-armed escort to the Templars' tombworld. I want to know what happened to my scanning equipment. I want to know if anyone dared meddle with the Templar Master's tomb."

Revan pushed himself to his feet. "At your command, my lord."

"Are we going to war?" Jain demanded exuberantly.

The scanner tech protested, "It may be only a malfunction, my lord. The equipment was antiquated and due for replacement."

"Perhaps," Thallian agreed smoothly. The speed at which he'd convened this meeting demonstrated that he thought not. To Revan, he added, "I want to know if anyone has been on that planet. I want to know if anyone has opened that tomb. I want to know if they removed anything. I want to know where they've gone. I expect your report in four days."

Revan bowed. Jain echoed him. With less grace, the scanner tech jerked down to follow them. Thallian opened the door, but did not watch them leave. Instead, he turned his attention to the data screen.

CHAPTER 2

Night was drawing in when Raena appeared outside the bunker's hatch. Kavanaugh couldn't guess where she had been in the intervening hours—other than checking to see if she could steal their formerly operational hopper. Sloane had wrecked the little ship in a fury when he decided the men were likely to steal from him. Luckily, Kavanaugh had been able to salvage enough parts to build a backup transmitter, in case Sloane left them behind when he hauled his loot away. Which assumed, of course, that Sloane left them alive when he abandoned them.

No wonder he couldn't sleep, Kavanaugh thought. Maybe Raena would let him come with her when she ran away this time.

She stood outside the hatch, black rags tied around her face against the gritty wind. Kavanaugh recognized her stance, her slight angular body, and the heeled boots she wore to give herself some height. She was thinner than he remembered—she'd been pretty thin then—but that could be expected. They hadn't found much to eat in any of the Templar tombs. Which begged the question: how she could possibly still be alive?

The Raena he had known had been fleeing an Imperial special envoy, who had sent a string of bounty hunters after her. It was a safe bet that he hadn't gotten a hold of her. Whatever Raena had thought Thallian wanted do to her, she expected it to be worse than being buried alive.

Or maybe there wasn't anything worse than that.

As he palmed open the lock, Kavanaugh thought about all the night creatures and tomb denizens he'd heard about across the galaxy: things that survived on flesh, on brains, on creatures slower and weaker than themselves. Kavanaugh checked to make sure his gun was charged before he opened the hatch, for all the good that would do him.

She halted in the doorway, looking both directions down the hallway to the cabins and the galley. Then she began to peel the rags from her face, dropping them to the deck. Kavanaugh watched the unveiling with curiosity. What would the fragile, high-strung girl look like now?

Her black eyes met his gaze. She looked sane, more serene than she ever had, but weary. As the bunker's harsh lighting revealed her arched black brows, Kavanaugh remembered the scar that ran between them, where, save for luck, Raena would have lost an eye. Above the scar, her forehead was still surprisingly unlined. No crow's feet surrounded her eyes. When at last she unwrapped her mouth, she looked exactly like the girl of his memory, twenty-odd years in the past.

Kavanaugh gasped. "You haven't changed a bit, Raena. I mean, you haven't aged a day."

She raised her hands to her face, slowly exploring her features like a woman woken from a coma. Her hands were smudged and raw from being out in the wind. Her knuckles stood out beneath the skin. Then she focused on him again. "Who are you?" she asked. "How do you know me?

"I'm Tarik Kavanaugh. I use to be on the *Panacea* with Doc and Skyler. We rescued you from a bounty hunter's ship, more than twenty years ago."

"Twenty years," she echoed.

After a pause, he asked, "Are you dead?"

"I don't think so. Being dead wouldn't hurt so much." She held her hand out. After a moment, Kavanaugh took it. Her skin felt cool and dry, but it seemed alive.

"We should run the med scan over you anyway," he said.

"What do you expect to see, other than malnutrition and dehydration?"

Whatever the hell had kept you alive, unaging, for twenty long years. Instead of saying that, though, Kavanaugh asked, "Want some stew? I made it a couple of days ago. It'll warm you up inside."

"That sounds good. It's been a long time since I felt warm."

Rubbing at the grit that always seemed to find its way into his beard, Kavanaugh led the way to the galley. He noticed she hadn't commented on his name or their shared history. He had a moment of doubt. If this was Raena, wouldn't she recognize him? Acknowledge him somehow? Maybe it wasn't her after all. How *could* it be? But if it wasn't her, it was a damn good facsimile. Why would anyone bother to make an android that looked like Raena Zacari? Why would they shut it in a tomb? Why would they whittle the weight off of it so that it looked starved half to death? It had to be Raena. Unaging or not, she looked like hell.

Kavanaugh's first thought was that this was a problem that he'd be relieved to turn over to Sloane. Then, horrified at himself, he hoped he could think of a way to smuggle her off-world without Sloane ever finding out about her. *That* would be a favor worth thanking him for.

"Are your men all right?" she asked.

Kavanaugh glanced back at her, wondering that he was so comfortable with her behind him. "They've had worse hangovers."

She smiled. That made him certain this truly was Raena. There had always been something sad about her smile, something apologetic for who she was and what she felt forced to do to survive.

For the briefest instant, Kavanaugh felt like the tongue-tied adolescent he had been all those years ago, awed by the mysterious drifter.

He busied himself with taking the pan of stew out of the fridge and setting it on the burner to warm. That didn't fill enough time, so he asked, "Want some coffee?"

Kavanaugh swirled the murky liquid around the bottom of the coffee pot, frowned, and dumped it down the drain. While he busied himself with making a fresh pot, Raena lit on the corner of the mess table, arms wrapped around her ribs. She didn't look too good in the harsh artificial light.

"No, thanks." She gestured at a swivel chair, its stuffing leaking out. "Come talk to me, Tarik. You can't imagine how starved I am for the sound of someone else's voice."

He took the chair. "I used to work for your sister."

"Sister?" She seemed surprised.

He frowned. He hadn't realized she had more than one sister. Ariel never mentioned that. Brushing it off, he said, "The War dragged out for a long time. Ariel did what she could, shipping materiel for the Coalition, trying to change the balance of power. I ran deliveries for her for a while."

"Do you keep in touch?" Raena asked. "How is she?"

"She's good. She's got a swarm of kids now...."

"And how many husbands?"

Kavanaugh laughed as he got up to pour the coffee. When he returned with two mugs, he said, "No, they're all adopted. There were a lot of orphans after the War. Ariel bought them out of slavery, like her family did you."

Raena's smile was more enigmatic than usual. She held her coffee in front of her heart, gratefully inhaling the steam.

"Drink it. It'll warm you up while the stew is heating."

She shook her head. "I'm enjoying it just like this. Hope you don't mind."

"Nah. I woulda made a pot anyway."

"Where are your people?" she asked.

Kavanaugh shrugged. "Around here someplace. They're all on the mend. Thank you for going easy on us in there."

"No, I'm sorry about that. If I'd been paying more attention, it wouldn't have been necessary to hurt anyone. Believe it or not, you startled me."

Kavanaugh didn't know what to say to that. He looked down into his coffee, around at the jumble of equipment on every flat surface, at the rusting, slapped-together walls of the converted cargo container. Avoided looking at her, because she could've come out of that tomb like a caged animal and killed them all.

Raena asked, "What do you need to tell me about Gavin Sloane?"

Caught off guard, Kavanaugh looked straight at her. He'd never been certain if Raena could read minds, or if she just found it effective to act as if she could. Her gaze was level and non-threatening. Something about her—her stillness, her calm—was so out of character for the Raena he remembered, the hairs crept up on the back of his neck.

"It's just—" Kavanaugh started "—well, you knew Sloane a long time ago." How to say this? He finished lamely, "Sloane's changed. He's not like he was during the War."

"Changed how?"

Kavanaugh shook his head, unprepared to say more.

Raena set her coffee on the tabletop and leaned forward. "Tarik, I appreciate your discretion, but I owe Sloane my life now. I need to know what sort of bargain I've made."

Sipping his coffee, Kavanaugh tried to frame years of disappointment into one careful phrase.

Not content to wait, Raena said, "Tarik, you and I both know that I can make you tell me. I'd much rather you'd simply be honest with me, as a friend who needs your help."

He stared at her, amazed at how easily the threat passed her lips. He didn't doubt that she could force him to do anything she wanted. "It's just that … a long time ago, I thought of Sloane like a brother. I was just a kid, and he was just a smuggler, a pirate—space trash—but I felt like I could rely on him. Probably it was just luck, but he was always there when I needed help. I thought he was a good friend...."

"And then?"

"I thought working for him would be fun. But he's not Sloane any more. Everything I liked has been systematically replaced by this businessman I don't know. And I don't want to know. He's cutthroat now. Dangerous to cross. And he doesn't have any friends left."

"What changed him?"

"I don't know. Ariel warned me not to take the job an' she was right. It's like he thinks money will make me forget the past." He looked up at her, finally realizing what it was he needed to say. "You'd be safer if I didn't tell him you were here."

She gave him that sad smile again. "No," she said firmly, "I need to see him. We have some things to work out."

Kavanaugh gulped his coffee and went to stir the stew. After a pause, he said as seriously as possible, "Get away from him as quick as you can."

Raena nodded. "Thank you, Tarik. I'll try."

The comm beeped. Kavanaugh sighed. He'd been expecting it. He got up to answer, taking his coffee with him.

A young woman on the comm screen asked, "How'd things go today?"

Kavanaugh drank deeply before answering. "We found something."

"You're supposed to find things," the voice on the monitor teased. "It's your job."

"Yeah," Kavanaugh drawled. "This is something special. I'd like to bring it up to show him."

"Can I see it?"

Kavanaugh turned toward Raena. "Are you sure?"

She nodded and presented herself before the comm.

The young woman on the monitor was blond and hazel-eyed, absurdly pretty like a doll. She always reminded Kavanaugh vaguely of Ariel. He wondered if Raena saw the resemblance, too.

Zilla gazed at Raena appraisingly and said, "Welcome back."

Kavanaugh watched Raena standing before the monitor. He'd used to think he had a crush on her, but he didn't feel any of that any more. He recognized that a lot of what he'd felt had been envy. Raena was quick and lethal. Remorseless. Kavanaugh had been awed by her ability not to care who she killed. As a scared kid in the middle of a war, he had found that inspiring. Now as an adult, he was horrified by her callousness.

He wondered what had happened to Raena back then that made her so broken. He didn't expect he'd ever know. Those who had been closer to her—Ariel, Sloane—didn't seem to know. Or care, for that matter.

Raena smiled at something Zilla said. "I'm looking forward to seeing your boss again."

Kavanaugh touched her shoulder gently and Raena faded back out of his way. "Send a shuttle down, would ja, Zilla?"

"All right, Kavanaugh. Give me fifteen to get things arranged up here. You okay down there?"

"We'll keep."

*　*　*

After she signed off with Kavanaugh, Zilla Olangey commed her boss. "Kavanaugh's coming up."

"I don't fuckin' want to be bothered," Sloane growled back.

"You want to be bothered by this." Zilla waited while her boss scrolled through the comm record she'd made. She wished she could see his face, but as usual he hadn't turned on the screen. "That's the girl you're looking for, isn't it?" she asked.

"The girl I'm looking for," Sloane growled bitterly, "would be old enough to be that girl's mother. I don't know who this impostor is, but I'm sure as hell going to find out who put her up to it. Send them in as soon as they land."

Sloane turned back to the spreadsheet on his monitor. This whole boondoggle had been extremely expensive: hauling the equipment out to this rock, buying his employees' silence, bribing the right galactic officials to look the other way as his crew looted the Templar tombs. Sloane had hoped to find enough collectibles to subsidize the excursion, but two decades hadn't been enough to make Templar mementos very rare. If he could have afforded to hang onto things another lifetime or so, he might have made a killing.

Still, bankrupting himself would have been meaningful if he'd solved Raena's disappearance. He'd tracked her, in the years since the War. The decades-old trail, while intermittent and icy cold, eventually led to the Templar tombs. The most he'd really expected to find was a corpse he could lay to rest somewhere less desolate. Raena deserved that. And Sloane anticipated that seeing her dead would break the chokehold her ghost had on him.

He punched some numbers into the computer and scowled at the calculations. A few more keystrokes and he had readied a series of bank transfers. He'd take a look at this impostor, cut his losses, and dismantle the whole fiasco. If the men had figured out whom he was looking for and had gone so far as to set him up, it was time to dump them. And probably time to realize his obsession couldn't be trusted to anyone else. He would have to find her alone.

* * *

The muscle never fit the décor, Kavanaugh thought. This time their props were carefully chosen: the thermal blanket draped over a bulging forearm to conceal an automatic, the medical box undoubtedly packed with sleep grenades. Sloane's bodyguards looked pricey, professional, and out of place in the dusty "archaeological" encampment.

Kavanaugh watched Raena clock them as they entered the bunker. The goons scrutinized her, too. Her face gave nothing away, but between her small stature and the gray in her pallor, she could not have looked less threatening. Kavanaugh remembered the bounty hunter who'd been holding her the last time he'd rescued her, back when they were kids. She hit the man once, hard enough to shatter his skull. Kavanaugh had few illusions about what Raena could do when pushed.

At least the muscle seemed well-trained. They'd wait for her to make the first move, before they took her down. Kavanaugh wondered if they'd heard about her single-handedly disarming his whole team. He hadn't reported it, but someone else might have.

Raena stood to follow her escort. The bodyguards fell into step, one in front of her and one behind, spacing themselves to present two targets. The economy of their movements said more than the size of their shoulders. Disarmament wouldn't slow them down. They wouldn't be bullied into dropping their weapons. These two she would have to kill. Kavanaugh guessed she would kill the one behind them first, then take the sleep grenades from the other. He'd have to be careful not to get caught in the crossfire.

Instead of attacking the bodyguards and stealing the shuttle, as Kavanaugh fully expected, Raena leaned against him as they left the bunker. The incessant wind whipped her tangled hair into Kavanaugh's face. In apology, she slipped her small hand into his as they crossed a moment of wasteland to Sloane's sleek yacht. A rush of affection flooded him, followed by pity. Had Raena lived her whole life in the wrong place at the wrong time?

* * *

Every morning, Eilif got up, saw that Jonan's food was safe for him to eat, got the boys up and dressed, checked their food, and then went down to swim.

Mostly, she went by herself. No one wanted to join her in the gelid water very often. She actually treasured her time alone. It was the best part of her day: when no one shouted at her, no one struck her, and she didn't have to taste anyone else's favorite food to check it for poison.

The water flowed in from the ocean outside the city. Its current was fast as it flooded into the city's circulation system. The concrete basin hadn't been meant for a swimming pool, but Jonan insisted that Eilif exercise every morning in order to keep herself strong.

She could have done fight training with the boys—or on her own—but Jonan preferred it if she couldn't fight back. So Eilif swam every day and watched the fight practices, when she thought she'd be unnoticed.

Eilif rounded the catchment basin to the outer wall and dove into the flow. For a second, as always, the cold stole her breath. She felt the current wash her toward the culvert into the city. If she had the luxury of drowning, she might have been tempted. Being shredded through the grill was less appealing.

She gulped in a breath and forced her legs to kick.

* * *

While Sloane daydreamed, time slipped. Before he was prepared, Zilla commed him again. "They're here."

"Send them in."

The new girl followed Kavanaugh through the office door. She wore an old black jumpsuit, practically threadbare with age. The exhaustion in her expression pinched the beauty from her face. Black hair hung in dusty tangles past her knees, echoing the cape she used to wear. The hair looked real, not like extensions, and unloved, as though she endured it rather than cherishing it.

Beyond those superficial differences, the likeness to the girl in his memory was uncanny. Sloane shut down the balance sheet and rubbed his face. This girl's dark skin looked as hard and opaque as stone, with an underlying silvery tone that was completely unnatural.

Her eyes remained as black as he remembered, but the sharpness of her gaze was blunted. He remembered the fierce girl, fast as lightning and twice as lethal, that he had tried to rescue so many years ago. She hadn't aged a day; yet, looking into her eyes, he saw that the years had passed for her, too. Excruciatingly so.

The half-smile he remembered, the smile that had disturbed his sleep a thousand times, the faint scimitar curve of her sweet soft mouth, warmed her eyes as she acknowledged his scrutiny. "I knew you'd come someday, Gavin."

He had far too many questions, so many things he wanted to tell her… He didn't know where to start.

She preempted him. "Could I have some water?"

Laughter burst out of Sloane's chest, loosening the tension of too many hours of work, too many hours of worry. "If you're really Raena Zacari," he promised, "you can have a feast."

"Just a drink of water, for now."

Sloane got up from behind his desk to open the refrigeration unit in the wall. As soon as his back had turned, doubts overwhelmed him. It couldn't be Raena. In the unlikely event she had survived the War's end, she would have aged. Time was inescapable. This girl had to be an impostor.

At least her story might be amusing. He broke the seal on a bottle of water. "Where have you been all this time?"

"In that tomb, waiting for someone to let me out."

"It's been, what?" Sloane asked casually as he poured her a tall glass of water. "Twenty years? What'd you do for entertainment?"

"The claustrophobia burned itself out after a while. Thank the Stars for that. After that, I had my memories for company."

She appeared at his side. Her hand brushed his on the glass. Startled, Gavin sloshed water onto the chrome bar and the fur carpet below. She caught the half-empty glass and drained it, eyes closed, savoring the feel of the water across her tongue.

"You're first-class," Sloane snapped, taking the glass away. "Who put you up to this? One of my competitors? One of my ex-wives? Kavanaugh? Ariel?"

The shadow of pain passed over the girl's face, wrinkling her perfect, unlined forehead. Raena had been twenty when the galaxy swallowed her. This girl, whoever she was, could scarcely be more than that.

She looked up at him. "I relived the memory of our first kiss a million times," she said. "It helped me to stay sane. You hauled me into your lap in that sleazy bar on Nizarrh. You crushed me in your arms. You kissed me like you'd known me forever, Gavin. You fixed something in me that was broken."

She dropped her gaze, dismissing him. "Your life has gone on." She waved at his ludicrously spacious office, implying the entire base around them, the encampment below. "How could I have expected you to recognize me?"

Some nobility kept her shoulders square as she turned back toward Kavanaugh and Zilla. Zilla's hand was on her gun, just as Sloane would have ordered it to be.

Kavanaugh, though, stared at the waif with the long black hair, his hand half-extended toward her. Something in Kavanaugh's guileless brown eyes surprised Sloane. Kavanaugh accepted the girl's impossible story. His certainty was more persuasive than anything the girl might have said.

If you let her go this time, Sloane thought, you won't find her again.

It's not her, he told himself. It can't be. Raena *must* be dead. And Kavanaugh had always been a credulous kid.

Even so, Sloane pursued her. Years of dust dimmed the black shimmer of her hair. When he reached for her, her arm felt warm and solid beneath his fingers, a young woman's muscles hard beneath the tattered black jumpsuit.

She turned back toward him. Her face tilted up, lips parted as if she wanted to lean toward him, kiss him once before she vanished forever.

Sloane engulfed her in an embrace.

She smelled like the passage of time, like a body grown cold in the grave. She was real, solid and strong, warm and alive. Sloane wanted desperately to kiss her, but their whole glorious romance had existed in his imagination for so long, he wasn't sure how to initiate the real thing.

Raena twisted in his arms until she could look up at him. With a smile, she rose up on tiptoe. Sloane found himself bending down. Their lips met so softly Sloane thought he'd imagined it.

Then she pressed against him. She was shorter than he remembered. He lifted her feet from the floor without really intending to. Her small hands held the back of his neck like a vise. He felt her smile against his lips.

Eventually they separated a fraction, enough to look wonderingly at each other. Raena made a long exhalation that might have been a sigh. She stroked his beard with the palm of her hand, traced the lines that creased his face, pushed a lock of dirty blond hair back toward his bald spot. "I've lost so many years."

Sloane gazed at her. Tears sparkled in her eyes. The crystalline shimmer against the black depths of her eyes was possibly the most beautiful thing he had ever seen, in a lifetime of coveting beautiful things. How could he have ever doubted this was Raena herself? Then he remembered to put his thoughts into words: "I can't believe I've found you again."

"Let's go," Zilla said, herding Kavanaugh out of the room.

"I knew you'd come," Raena repeated. "I didn't know it would be so long." Then she forced a smile and asked, "Could I have a little more water?"

Sloane picked up the bottle, tilted it against her glass. "I am serious about the feast," he said. "Not on this base, of course. What would you like to eat? Anything in the galaxy…"

"You know what I'd like?" Raena asked. Sloane found himself eager to guess, but she surprised him by saying, "A bath. A bubble bath. I don't suppose your base has a tub."

Sloane frowned. "A shower won't do?"

"I can wait 'til we make planetfall."

The thought that she would have to wait for anything was intolerable. Sloane mentally ran through the base's stock, trying to think what might be large enough to use as a bathtub. He remembered an old rocket casing. With some spot-welding, it should be watertight. If they cycled the coolant to the reactors and rationed washing up, there should be enough water for a satisfactory soak. He commed Kavanaugh and got him sealing up the tub.

"Tell me everything that happened since I saw the soldiers overwhelm you," Sloane demanded.

"Ancient history," Raena said dismissively. "I'm not interested in the past anymore. You can't imagine how many times I relived it, just to have something to think about."

Another twinge of doubt stung Sloane. Why would she duck the question? He went at it from a different direction. "Who locked you in the tomb?"

"Marchan. He did it on the Emperor's orders, to spite Thallian. I think it was a test of Thallian's loyalty, to see if he'd come rescue me. Of course, I always knew where Thallian's loyalties lay. He left me to rot."

She circled the desk and sank into one of the leather chairs facing it. She looked so very tired, as if drawing each breath drained her strength. Sloane wondered why she wasn't more ecstatic at her release.

"He'll come after me, you know."

Sloane shook his head, trying to follow her train of thought. "Who? Marchan is dead."

"Thallian."

The name drove a cold shudder up Sloane's spine. He counted himself lucky that he'd never met Raena's former boss, but over the years, he'd done enough reading to loathe the man. Sloane forced a jovial tone and said, "Thallian must be dead now, too. You don't know how it was. After the War was finally over, there were reprisals, tribunals... It seemed like the accusations would never end. If anyone deserved to be caught up in all that, it was Thallian."

"Jonan would have hidden out somewhere. Too many people were loyal to him to let him be captured. He's out there. He'll come for me."

Sloane didn't have any answer for that. On the face of it, it sounded like paranoia. But Raena sounded so resigned in the face of her certainty that he couldn't come up with any plausible denials. No wonder she wasn't thrilled about being out in the galaxy once more, if she thought she'd have to face Thallian again.

If there were any sort of justice in the galaxy—which Sloane seriously doubted—he'd get a clear shot at Thallian's head before the monster laid another hand on Raena.

Before Sloane could promise that, Kavanaugh commed them to say, "Tub's ready, boss."

* * *

Jonan Thallian walked into the center of the gym and closed his eyes, awaiting the familiar sensation as the anti-grav switched on. He felt sudden buoyancy in his chest and jumped lightly. The hop propelled him upward faster than was possible within the constraints of quotidian planet-bound life. Thallian had spent the first half of his life aboard starships, playing assassination politics. He'd fought in Zero G more than once.

As he neared the ceiling, he turned a lazy flip and pushed off hard, diving fast back toward the floor.

Eight of his sons entered the room. Most of them quickly reacted to their father's trajectory, leaping out of his path to handholds on the walls. The last boy should have entered at a run, but the older boys had dawdled and obstructed his view of the playing field.

Thallian barreled into Jimi at full speed, knocking him off his feet and into the doorframe. Something crunched. The boy collapsed without another sound.

Two of his brothers leapt down belatedly to aid him. Thallian pushed off the doorframe at a steep angle that catapulted him beyond the reach of the metal staves they carried.

The point of the game, as always, was teamwork. The game only ended in two ways: Thallian disabled all of the boys and walked alone to the showers, or they devised a group strategy and overcame him. Thallian hadn't lost yet, but he foresaw a day in which that might be possible. In that eventuality, he trusted that their sense of filial duty would keep them from killing him. Still, if ever he fell to a mob of teenage boys, he deserved whatever they dished out.

All the same, the boys wouldn't win today, without Jain here to play. He wasn't the most agile or the most cunning of Thallian's sons, but he was the most brutal. All the other boys feared the punishment they'd receive each time Thallian declared the game. Jain alone bore his scars with pride.

The eldest twins—Jozz and Jamian—launched themselves toward their father. Each held the end of his brother's staff so that the metal formed a barrier between the boys. Thallian flashed them a grin as he bounded upward. Two of the other boys—Jaden and Jarad—quickly moved in to block that space by holding their staves between them.

It was too late to change trajectory. Thallian turned his body so that he could land his feet on the staves and bounce away. The change of position showed him that the remaining boys had moved to box him in. "Good!" he cheered.

Before his feet touched Jaden's staff, the boy spun it upward out of his brother's hand. If he'd been an instant faster, it would have landed hard on Thallian's shin. Instead, the older man caught it between his knees and held fast. He hurled himself into a somersault, pulling the boy out of position. Jaden lost his grip and spun into his brothers' staves.

Now that he had a weapon, Thallian made short work of the boys. It was tempting to take his anger out on them and show them the sort of damage a quarterstaff could do in determined hands, but Thallian refrained from blows to the head when he could, striking instead at ribs and arms, breaking bones that could be quickly mended.

The children took their punishment stoically. The only sounds to interrupt the silence were labored breathing, the crack of bone, and the squeak of rubber shoes on the gym walls as the battle wound to its foregone conclusion.

Thallian piled the staves on the floor as he collected each one. After he stacked the last one carefully, so the pile wouldn't shift in Zero G, he turned to regard the wounded children clinging to handholds around the room. He bowed to them, then touched the control clipped to his belt to cut the anti-grav. He was proud when no one groaned as gravity dragged on his wounded limbs.

As always, Thallian walked alone to the showers.

Eilif and Dr. Poe slid into the gym behind him to tend the wounded.

CHAPTER 3

While Sloane fussed over the temperature of the water, Raena peeled out of her jumpsuit. As he turned, she balled up the tattered fabric and pitched it toward the incinerator. It fell short. The black jumpsuit lay on the deck in a spill of ragged shadow.

She'd been nude beneath the garment. Her small breasts probably didn't need much restraint. At the junction above her thighs, the hair was thick and black. Sloane savored his first glimpse of her body, ending his appraisal when he reached Raena's eyes. Did he read condescension there?

Raena defused the moment by asking, "Help me with my boots?"

Sloane didn't question the eagerness with which he knelt at her feet. His knees protested loudly. His mouth unaccountably went dry.

Raena leaned back against the lockers, gripped an edge with her bony fingers, and lifted her foot into his lap.

How long had she been wearing these boots? How long had it been since she'd washed her feet? Sloane had a moment of dread, then had to laugh at himself. Her body didn't smell, except of dust and darkness.

Gripping the boot at the heel and toe, he eased it off.

Raena wriggled her toes, flexing her foot past the angle of the boot, then pressing her sole flat against the floor. She sighed. "I may never wear shoes again."

Sloane reached for her other leg. He wanted to make her so many promises that they stopped his throat. He wanted to kiss her feet, to take away every discomfort she might feel.

Raena's low laughter raised goosebumps across his skin. "Wash me first," she said.

Had she read his mind? Sloane had never known the limits of Raena's abilities. Whatever they were, they hadn't been enough to keep her from being captured by the Empire time and again. And even though she'd engineered escape after escape, nothing but the Templar tomb had kept her safe from Thallian.

She slipped past Sloane to sink into the makeshift tub.

"Let me wash your back," he said.

Raena dutifully rolled over in the water. Sloane's breath hissed sharply. Long stripes ridged her skin, where burn marks had been forbidden to heal smoothly. Sloane touched her very tenderly, rubbing foam across her scar tissue with the flat of his palms. As gentle as his hands were, his emotions seethed white-hot. The possessiveness of his anger startled him. "For fleeing the Empire?" he asked in a low, tight voice.

"In service to Thallian."

"We'll get them removed once we get back to civilization. I'll get you the best plastic surgeon in the galaxy…"

"I don't want them removed," she said. "They're badges. They remind me what I've survived."

"All I see is him hurting you…" Sloane couldn't bear to speak the name again, to have Thallian come between them.

Raena twisted to face Sloane. Bubbles sloshed out of the tub onto the deck. "See me instead, standing up to him. Exhausting him.

The only way he could express his love was after he hurt me. The pain bound him to me. It kept me alive."

"Why would you want to remember?"

She smiled bitterly. "Because I thought I loved him."

She traced her fingertips lightly over the faded scars webbing Sloane's knuckles. "We don't escape the past," she reminded. "If I sanded away my scars, I'd lose the talisman that prevents the past from happening again."

"No one will ever hurt you like that again," Sloane swore.

"Really?" She smiled again, grinned wider when she saw him flinch. Then she promised, "Some tortures leave no marks."

She pulled herself up against him, pressing her wet breasts against his dry tunic. She caught his lips in her kiss and twined her limbs around his, crushing Sloane against her.

When she finally allowed him to breathe again, she whispered, "Join me?"

He peeled off his wet clothing as she settled back beneath the bubbles. She watched him undress. Sloane was self-conscious in a way that he'd never been with other partners. He felt old enough to be Raena's father.

She noticed his sudden loss of ardor, but only smiled.

He shivered where the ventilation blew across his damp skin. The water in that tub wouldn't stay warm forever. "Where are you in there?" he asked.

She bent one knee so it broke the surface of the bubbles. Sloane placed his hand on it and used it as a landmark as he slipped into the water beside her.

She snuggled over against him, curling her head down under his chin where he couldn't study her face. Sloane held her close, caressing her arms with his hands. He tried to analyze the feelings battling in his chest. Raena was naked beside him. She'd kissed him, clearly wanted to kiss him, and then stripped for his examination and invited him into her bath. But she wasn't pursuing him or even making particularly suggestive gestures. She was just clinging to him like a grateful slave might hug her master: willingly, without being aroused or otherwise invested in the consummation. Sloane found the realization repellant.

Once again Raena seemed to read his mind. "Don't you want me?" she whispered.

"With all my soul."

"Then take me. You deserve it. You rescued me."

Sloane pushed her back far enough that he could meet her eyes. "Don't you love me?"

Raena allowed him to look at her, gazing back with black eyes that revealed nothing. "Of course," she agreed.

"Tell me."

"I love you, Gavin."

"How much?"

"More than air." She thought a moment, then added, "More than light. More than freedom. More than life."

He watched her perform the litany. The gap between her promises and his doubts was excruciating.

Raena smiled at him, mocking and heartless. Then she pushed herself out of the water and bent over the tub's edge. Sloane stared at the view she presented. She rummaged around on the deck, then slithered back under the bubbles. She held his boot knife above the water. With a grin, she caught hold of a handful of her black hair and hacked it savagely from her head.

"Careful!" Sloane warned. "That's sharp."

"I can handle a blade," Raena teased. "When I've taken some of the edge off on this mess—" she raised another handful of hair "—I intend to give you the closest shave of your life."

Sloane raised a hand to his beard. "I'm not sure I want you that close to my throat with a knife."

Raena laughed as she sawed off more of her hair.

* * *

After she'd shaved him and let him escape from the tub, Sloane led Raena to his bunk, watched as she slid over to make room for him. He turned his back to pull on some slacks before he lay down. She only watched him, saying nothing.

He touched her face, marveling at the smoothness of her skin. The scar that had missed her eye was familiar from years of studying her wanted posters and images he'd stolen from Ariel, but so much time had passed, he couldn't accept she had not aged.

Sloane knew the stone of the Templar tombs kept their contents from decay, just as moist and fresh as the day things were sealed inside. That was great for the antiques: the armor remained untarnished, the nectars and fruits juicy, the fabrics bright and crisp. He didn't understand how it had kept Raena's body alive for twenty years.

"Did you eat the grave offerings?" he asked.

"There weren't any. The tomb was ready for the Templar Master, but he was never buried in it."

"Weren't you hungry?"

"For a while. Then I had the memory of hunger to torment me. Eventually, though, I had to let it go."

"How did you survive?"

"I don't know," Raena answered. "I didn't want to. I expected— hoped—to starve to death. If the Empire had left me anything I could've used as a weapon, I would've killed myself in the first hour. But when I shredded my cape, it never knit itself back together. The damage was irreversible. After that, I was terrified to injure myself. What if I broke my neck by accident or lost an eye or even just gave myself a concussion—and I had to live like that forever? I didn't know if I would ever heal."

He saw the horror of living permanently damaged reflected in Raena's eyes and flinched away.

"I don't know how I survived, Gavin. I don't know why. I don't even know if the Emperor knew that was what would happen to me when he had me imprisoned there."

"Fucking Templar tech," Sloane said. He pulled her into his arms so he no longer had to look at her face. "I'm just glad you did survive."

"Me, too," she whispered. In the space of a handful of breaths, she dropped off to sleep, unaware of—or unconcerned by—his scrutiny.

*　*　*

Rather than fidget beside her and keep her awake, Sloane retreated to his office where he could watch her on the monitor.

She curled up around his pillow, a faint smile on her lips. The feelings he had for her were tangled, beyond the reach of words. Never one for much self-analysis, Gavin watched her sleep and tried to figure out what he should do next. So much of his life had been consumed by searching for her. What did he need to do now?

He felt at a loss. He couldn't figure out why he hadn't made love to her in the bathtub, when she was so obviously willing. Of course she would want to celebrate her return to the land of the living with sex. Who wouldn't? But as much as he wanted her—or believed he did—he realized that she didn't know *him*. He'd had twenty years to obsess and study and research her. He'd learned everything he could about her: poring over medical records and her Imperial service and watching her trial, interviewing everyone he could find who had met her or served with her or had survived trying to hunt her down. He'd analyzed Ariel's memories and even quizzed her mother, although Ariel didn't know about that. Sloane knew as much about Raena as she did herself.

But to Raena he was little better than a stranger. They'd met twice, briefly; both times ended with Raena taken into Imperial custody. She knew nothing about Gavin's life before or after she vanished from it. He was forced to wonder if her declarations of love—however desperately he wanted to hear them—were only an act.

He would have to woo her, to make certain he could win and keep her.

The way to do so would be clearer with some help. He reached down to pry loose the box hidden on the underside of his desktop. Once he opened the lid, his hands knew the drill, setting out the vial and needle and kit. He had the shot set to go when Raena turned over in his bed. One of her hands stretched out as if reaching for him.

His body made a decision and contradicted his brain. He stood, crossed two steps to the disposal unit, and dropped the needle inside. The rest of the paraphernalia followed. Then, with the vial in his hand, he halted. The blue oil was valuable: expensive and hard to find. He should sell it. Send it to Ariel as a peace offering. Find some other kind of use for it...

That was the danger. If he kept it, he'd use it. And he didn't want anything to come between him and Raena. Funny, how the thing that had kept him focused on finding her for so many years was persuading him to part with it. Dumping the Dart was the logical thing to do.

He opened the disposal and pitched the vial in, but turned away before he had to watch the drug incinerated. It was exactly like money going up in smoke.

* * *

When Kavanaugh stepped into the office, Sloane sat behind his desk studying his monitor. Kavanaugh debated whether he was meant to stand until noticed. In the old days, Sloane would never have kept him waiting.

Sloane looked terrible. It shocked Kavanaugh every time he saw him—the eyes sunken into pits in his skull, his nose shaved away to a beak. Sloane was just a handful of years older than Kavanaugh, but his face had set into a mask of determination, all traces of humor sloughed away. Only the muddy green eyes remained the same, although nothing ever warmed them any more. Kavanaugh wondered if the older man was dying. It made him cut Sloane slack when anyone with any sense would have refused to take his abuse.

Kavanaugh scuffed across the thick fur carpet and flung himself down into one of the chairs.

At the sound of Kavanaugh's worn trousers hitting the expensive leather, Sloane looked up. "Thank you for coming."

"Sure, boss."

Sloane nudged the monitor around to face Kavanaugh across the polished steel surface of his desk. The screen displayed Kavanaugh's numbered account and a startlingly high balance.

"I've appreciated your service, Kavanaugh. I could always rely on you to get the job done."

"You're firing me?" Kavanaugh asked.

"Now that I have what I was looking for, I'm closing down the archaeological team. Your men have all received generous severance packages, too. Once you've broken down the encampment, packed up everything salvageable, and loaded it onto the shuttle, give them the numbers. I'll have Zilla drop you all off somewhere civilized."

Kavanaugh looked up from the bribe in his account. There was so much that he wished he could say, for the sake of old times. Instead, he said the first thing that came to mind: "Raena asked you to shave the beard, huh?"

Without the beard, Sloane looked older, vulnerable and uncertain for the first time in a decade. Sloane made an aborted gesture toward his chin. "Thank you for helping me find her, Kavanaugh. I—"

"I knew her first," Kavanaugh said quietly. "When I was a kid, I saw firsthand how dangerous she was. I still count myself her friend, Gavin, but I'm no rival to you. You don't have to buy me like this."

"You got a problem with the money?" Sloane growled.

"It's insulting. You don't need to bribe me to keep silent about her. You, of all people, should know you don't need to buy my loyalty."

"I'm trying to cut you a break," Sloane snapped. "Raena thinks that she still has enemies living, that he'll come after her..."

"Thallian is alive?" Kavanaugh interrupted. "So...what? You're sending me away as a decoy?"

"I'm giving you enough money to get good and lost so that anyone looking for her doesn't find you instead."

"I'm good in a fight," Kavanaugh protested.

Sloane's laugh was mean. "She doesn't need you to protect her, Kavanaugh. You know you'd only be in her way."

* * *

Three days later, Sloane landed the yacht without a bump on the planet Brunzell, pleased that he could still fly so well after hiring Zilla to pilot for him. She'd taken her firing with more grace than Kavanaugh had. Sloane wondered if the girl was simply relieved to be free of his temper. Or maybe she had a good use for her hush money.

The yacht could've made the trip more quickly if he'd used the gate system, but Raena was freaked out about being traced leaving the Templar cemetery world. The yacht's tachyon drive wasn't as fast as the new tesseract drives on this year's ships, but it was nice to have some time alone in transit. They'd put the days to good use, getting to know each other better. Sloane smiled to himself, wondering if he had any secrets left from her.

Sloane looked across the cockpit. Raena slept in the co-pilot's chair, curled up in the crash web. Even in sleep, her face didn't relax. Some worry drew her arched brows together. The frown emphasized the old white scar that just missed one of her eyes. In the yacht's panel lights, Raena's pallor had a shifting gray tone, like mercury. Shadows pooled in the hollows of her cheekbones and in the circles under her eyes.

Then again, he hadn't actually seen her eat anything since Kavanaugh brought her out of the tomb. Water, sure. She'd drunk bottle after bottle of that, but as far as Sloane knew, nothing solid had passed her lips. He didn't think she was frightened of food, but after twenty years in the grave, she seemed to have lost the habit of eating. He'd see what he could do about that. After all the years on the Dart, he had no place to criticize her eating habits. He could stand to put some weight back on himself.

He powered the yacht down, then went to collect the gear he'd need to settle in on Brunzell. When he returned, Raena was still asleep. He reached out cautiously. He hated to shock her awake, but the everyday sounds he'd made had no effect. Sloane touched her shoulder with his fingertips, ready to jump back as soon as she flinched. Raena didn't react at all.

Gathering courage, Sloane shook her just a little. Again, he received no response. She was dead to the world, in Zilla's oversized clothing.

This complicated things. If he had to, he could carry Raena home, but he had hoped to be inconspicuous enough that even the door system at his apartment complex wouldn't notice his arrival. Raena jeopardized that if she refused to play along.

Sloane stomped out of the yacht to deal with the port authorities. He wanted to arrange to have the ship restocked and to schedule all the routine maintenance he'd deferred. If Raena was right about Thallian still being out there, it would be worthwhile to have the yacht ready to go in case they needed to run.

* * *

Raena kept her eyes closed a moment longer, listening to the hum of the yacht around her. From the sound of the engines, they had landed somewhere, probably on the planet Gavin had been trying to get her excited about. He didn't appear to be moving around the ship: off bribing the port authorities to ignore them, mostly likely.

She disentangled herself from the crash web and lay her hand on the computer terminal. It chirped, recognizing her. She silently thanked Zilla for her rushed tutorials.

Bit by bit, in every spare moment, Raena had been catching up on the galaxy. There was a lot she needed to adjust to. The human empire had been smashed. What was left of humanity had scattered across the stars. Gavin's strictly human organization seemed to be an anomaly.

The thing that interested Raena the most was the extermination of the Templars. It didn't surprise her that the Empire had conceived of something as horrific as a genetically targeted plague. What did surprise her was that her former boss was generally accepted to have been the key disseminator of it. Raena couldn't believe she'd had no clue about that before she fled Thallian.

The more expert testimony she listened to, the more certain Raena became that her betrayal of Thallian somehow led to his part in the genocide. Either the Emperor had blackmailed him into participating—or Thallian had volunteered, figuring he had little else to lose. He'd hated everything that wasn't human anyway.

Raena didn't want to be responsible for genocide, however tangentially. The further she dug, the more the evidence accrued. It made her feel sick, but why should she feel guilty for something that happened after she was erased from the galaxy? She was sure Thallian had no such qualms.

* * *

Jain Thallian bounded from the *Raptor*, exhilarated to be allowed away from home on this rare adventure.

Revan Thallian followed more slowly, surrounded by a cluster of the family guard. It had been five years since he'd last been sent off on one of his younger brother's errands. On that excursion, three of the guards had been shot. Another defected. Of course, Merin had hunted that one down before the family could be sold out. Revan had never been so relieved to be home as after that journey.

This trip shouldn't be as eventful, but Revan was by nature cautious. Jonan's chief order was to reconnoiter a deserted Templar world and report if anyone had been there. He'd given Revan the coordinates of a specific tomb and asked him to make certain it was still sealed. Revan didn't know what had been in the tomb. It didn't matter. He'd see what he could, report back, and return home gratefully as soon as he was allowed.

They had arrived in the target system without incident. The family's ships, though antiques now, were meticulously maintained. Jain's orbital scans of the planet showed that it was as uninhabited as reported. Revan had ordered the transport set down outside the bunkers being abraded by the gritty winds. The way the airlock door hung open made it clear that whoever had been camping on the cemetery world had abandoned the place.

The encampment had been pretty thoroughly ransacked, Revan observed. The bunkers had been emptied of everything small enough to carry away, except for broken and worthless odds and ends: an armchair leaking its stuffing, a torque wrench with stripped gears, miscellaneous flywheels missing teeth.

The guards fanned out between the buildings looking for evidence that might identify the looters. Revan didn't expect to find much, aware the thieves would hardly leave a calling card. But they'd left in enough of a hurry that they hadn't scoured the site clean. A direct hit from space would have done the job handily. Either they'd known they'd attracted Jonan's notice and panicked or they'd found what they were looking for—whatever Jonan was looking for—and everything left behind was inconsequential.

One of the guards inched forward, studying the broken airlock of the largest building with a forensic scanner. Revan's chief hope was that one of the thieves had had a record in the Empire. If one of them could be identified, Revan would be able to track the rest. It was a straw, but Revan was hopeful enough to grasp anything that would get him home sooner. He never felt safe out in the galaxy.

The bunker's internal air smelled singed. The power feed from his transport's generator must be overloading the bunker's less-than-standard wiring. Revan grinned without mirth as he checked the charge on his hand torch. The guards would have to be cautious, or they'd accomplish the demolition the looters hadn't bothered with themselves. It'd be all too easy to burn this place down and leave no trace.

Jain came hustling back, his taciturn guard in tow. "They were robbing graves!" he announced, titillated and horrified simultaneously.

Revan smiled affectionately at his nephew without pointing out how obvious that assumption was. "How can you tell?"

"Well, they put the tomb slabs back when they were done, so the looted tombs look untouched. But there are loader tracks all over. They're filling in with sand, but they're not erased in the shadows of the mountains, where the wind doesn't reach."

"Well done, Jain. Can you tell which tomb they opened last?"

"I'll figure it out, Uncle Revan."

"Good. If we know where they stopped, chances are we'll know what they were looking for—whatever was important enough to bring them, and us, to this rock."

* * *

When Sloane returned to the yacht, Raena sat at the comp terminal, one foot tucked under her, unconsciously spinning a stylus in one hand. She smiled up at him, not the least bit guilty about being caught poking around.

"What are you up to?" Sloane asked as he crossed the cockpit to plant a kiss on the top of her head.

"Spying." Raena pulled him down so she could kiss him, hard and fierce.

He held her face in his hands as he straightened, gazing down at her as if he could capture her image on his retinas and hold it there. Her hair rayed out from her head in an uneven corona, black as space. Her dusky skin seemed polished, unlined by time. She barely looked twenty.

Sloane's gaze slipped past her shoulder to the computer screen. He'd never seen Thallian in person, but he'd heard enough about the man's exploits when he was tried in absentia. The wanted poster was old, although apparently still valid. The bounty hadn't been collected at least. Enough zeroes trailed the number that even Sloane was impressed. Wanted for war crimes, it said.

The man on the screen was strikingly handsome: angular face, spade-shaped beard, silver eyes surrounded by lines that implied a love of life, a sense of humor, things not borne out by the list of offences for which he had been sentenced to death.

"Why wouldn't he erase himself entirely from the historical record?"

"Because he's vain," Raena said with certainty. "He wants to be certain he's remembered."

Sloane didn't know how to answer that. Instead he asked, "Any clue where he's hiding?"

"Not yet," Raena said seriously.

"Must be somewhere deep and dark," Sloane said. After the words left his lips, he regretted them.

"Not as deep or dark as it ought to be," Raena threatened. Without looking away from the screen, she added, "It's strange to think that the War is over."

"War's been over a long time, darlin'." Sloane's answer came out more flippantly than Raena deserved, but it was too late to recall it.

"But the Templars—don't you feel bad about what happened to them?"

Sloane sank into the pilot's chair and started locking the yacht down. "The plague was fast, targeted. Something engineered. It wiped the bugs out within the course of a year. The Emperor was implicated in its dissemination. Everybody else in the galaxy—all the non-humans—rose up, banded together. They would have exterminated us…"

"So humans turned on those responsible for the plague," she guessed.

"It was horrible. Everyone was under scrutiny. It was risky to travel, hard to find work . . ." There was more, much more, but Sloane knew he'd have time to share it with her later. "You're lucky you missed it," he said, meaning to joke.

"Yeah," she agreed seriously. "Since I'd been Thallian's aide, I would have been on the wrong side of the purge."

Sloane left the silence alone while he finished locking up. Then he changed the subject. "I'm glad you're awake. A taxi's coming for us."

"Where are we going?" Raena stood and stretched, indifferent to how ridiculous she looked in the oversized clothes. Even wearing her high-heeled boots, she'd had to turn the cuffs on the cargo pants back enough times that the pant legs hung awkwardly. The gray-green sweater she wore drooped off one shoulder. Its hem fell most of the way to her knees, which made Sloane smile. He reached out to ruffle her soft hair.

"I've got a city place, kind of a hideout. As far as anyone here knows, I'm a legitimate dealer in Templar artifacts."

Raena frowned at that, but didn't comment.

Sloane continued, "We can hang around here a couple of days, until I sell some of the stuff I brought along. Then when we're flush again, we can go anywhere in the galaxy you like. So think about where you'd like to go."

"I will." She seemed more serious than the situation warranted, but Sloane didn't pursue it.

She went down the gangplank first and waited at the bottom while he closed up the yacht. When he turned, it felt bizarre to see her standing there, still as a statue, dressed in borrowed clothes, and gaunt to the point of concern. He'd been searching for her so long and there she was, smaller than he remembered. She still looked deadly. Something about her—her stance? her stillness? the muscles obvious beneath her ill-fitting clothing?—marked her out as dangerous. The pedestrian traffic of the busy commonway between the docking slips swerved around Raena as if they sensed her otherness. She watched the variety of life forms with an intensity that seemed focused on potential threats.

Sloane moved to join her before somebody started something that Raena didn't have the strength to finish.

* * *

After they'd settled into Sloane's apartment, the doorbell rang. Sloane checked the monitors and saw the building's concierge android waiting outside with an armload of shipping cartons. Sloane palmed the locks open and reached out for his packages without a word to the machine.

Raena came to help him bring the boxes in. "This one's for you," Sloane told her, gesturing with his chin to the one on top.

She set the others on the sofa, then drew his knife from the top of her boot to open the one he'd indicated. Folded inside lay an evening gown of indigo silk.

"Hope you like it," he said as she held it up.

"It's lovely. I'm going to try it on."

She grabbed the hem of Zilla's sweater and tugged it over her head. Amused, Sloane noted that modesty was a concept foreign to Raena. It apparently didn't occur to her that she could go into the bedroom to change.

He hoped the dress would fit. He'd had to guess her measurements, settling at last on the smallest of the standard sizes. He turned back to opening his other packages—food and other necessities—while Raena fussed with fixing herself up.

Finally, she drew his attention back by saying, "It's beautiful, Gavin."

The floor-length gown he'd chosen for her fell from diamond clips at her shoulders, leaving her sleek, strong arms bare. The draping of the low neckline implied more cleavage than Raena actually possessed, but the way it shifted when she leaned forward pleased Sloane.

The color might have been a mistake. The deep blue lured his eye in the designer's catalogue, evoking the emotions he felt for her. Now, seeing her wear it, he wondered if he should have chosen something brighter. On Raena, the indigo looked chemical and harsh, emphasizing the steely component of her coloring. It made her look dreamlike and unreal.

Raena smoothed the skirt over her hips and looked up at him with shining eyes. "I've never had anything so nice," she said.

Another man would have something magnificent to say to that. Sloane managed, "You look good enough to eat."

"Hungry? I could be on the menu." She grinned up at him. He remembered that she was scarcely tame.

"Later," Sloane promised. "You should eat something first before we hole up, and there's nothing in my cupboards. What are you hungry for?"

She turned the question around. "What do you recommend? You must have had someplace in mind when you ordered this dress."

He smiled at her. "Let me call them to see if we can get a reservation."

She laughed, honestly amused, as he crossed the room to the computer screen.

"What's so funny?"

"Pirates … excuse me, grave robbers … making dinner reservations. How the galaxy has changed."

Sloane wondered if she saw it as an improvement. Still, his credit was good and she deserved a special meal. He concentrated on the computer screen as he pulled up the city directory.

*   *   *

Kavanaugh felt glad to be back on his own ship, even though the air smelled weird after it had been in storage for so long. He leaned back in his pilot's chair and propped his new boots on the console.

He stared out the view-screen at a quasar flickering in the distance. There was a time when he'd spent so long in space that ground felt strange beneath his feet. In the months he'd been working for Sloane, he'd spent more time on the dirt than in the air. It felt odd to be alone again. And to have enough money to buy company, if he wanted it.

He scooped the Templar jewel casket off the console and held it in his lap. His fingers traced its edge, searching for the hidden catch. The dark brown box was formed of some kind of Templar metal buffed smooth without a hint of sheen. It swallowed light.

Kavanaugh's thumb found the catch. The lid irised open soundlessly. He looked inside, not ready to touch the blackness coiled within.

Sloane hadn't noticed when Kavanaugh snuck in to the makeshift bathroom and collected a lock of the hair Raena had sawed off with the knife. Kavanaugh swept the strands together as best he could, pulled a lace from his shirt, and knotted it around a sheaf that was easily as long as his leg.

He thought he remembered Raena's hair being as black as space. Now with space to compare it to, her hair was clearly blacker. Space, at least this corner of it, had enough ambient light to brighten it.

It was hard to admit that it never occurred to him to look for her after she'd disappeared. When Raena stepped off of Doc's ship into the storm twenty-some years ago, she'd said she knew how her story ended. Thallian was looking for her and absolutely wouldn't stop until one of them was dead.

Raena had convinced Kavanaugh that she would die before being taken captive. He'd always believed that was what had happened. He knew her wanted posters had gone down, anyway. He'd hoped that meant she took Thallian down with her. Now, thanks to Gavin, he knew that wasn't true either.

Without touching the coil of Raena's hair, Kavanaugh closed the casket. He'd save the evidence of Raena's survival for when he needed it. If he needed it.

He leaned forward to switch on the comm. This wasn't going to be an easy call to make.

CHAPTER 4

"R eady?" Sloane asked, offering the crook of his arm. Raena clasped it and pressed close against him, feverishly warm. "You'll have to help me remember how to behave in public."

"You'll do fine," Sloane said as he swept her through the door.

"Like falling off a wall," she agreed. "How hard can it be?"

She sat beside the door of the taxi, head leaned against the window, staring out at the darkening city with devouring eyes. Everything interested her. She even followed the self-propelled street sweepers, nosing into every cranny. Sloane had never paid much attention to their rodent-like scurrying.

Sloane fought down the urge to chatter, filling her up with details of all the years since she'd walked free. He wanted to share with her, to cheer her, but feared that the catalog of everything she'd missed would only depress her. He tried to convince himself that Raena would question him when she was ready to know more about his life or the galaxy at large.

Pedestrians of every species jostled along the walkways. Raena stared at their feathers and finery, their furs and fashions, absorbing it silently. Sloane knew she had been on the run long months before her capture. Surely, she had seen some of these peoples before. Then he reminded himself that she'd been imprisoned a long time. Perhaps she'd forgotten that humans were the minority in the galaxy. Especially now, after the War.

As the taxi found an opening and accelerated upward, Raena studied the other vehicles around them. Sloane didn't even know if she could drive. Maybe that was something she'd like to learn. It would give her a measure of freedom though, and the thought made his chest cramp. If she could drive, she might leave him.

He'd have to be certain she'd stay before he gave her the means to go. That was important.

In the channels where the sky was visible beyond the high-rises, it burned a bluish violet, lambent and achingly beautiful. The light reflected in Raena's eyes, lending their blackness a soft glow. Sloane darkened the taxi's windows so that Raena would turn her attention to him.

"This is a lot to get used to," she said.

"Understatement of the year," he teased.

She smiled and slid across the oversized seat to lean against him. Sloane realized how much he took for granted now: that the taxis were built to accommodate creatures larger than humans, that it was unusual to see another human face on the street. Raena couldn't disappear here. She stood out by virtue of her species, her size.

The taxi made a sudden swoop upward when it reached the correct building. It connected to the external elevator track, which lifted them up the outside of the tower to the correct floor. When the elevator halted, the taxi's doors peeled open.

Raena took Sloane's hand and allowed him to help her from the car. He wasn't sure if her trembling was from the shock of being out in the world again or if she was faint with hunger.

The maitre d' led them to a quiet table. Window tables were exorbitant on an hour's notice. Raena turned her chair away from the view so she could watch the room: force of old habit. Sloane wondered if she would ever live it down. He hadn't, personally, but until now, he hadn't had Raena to watch his back.

She appeared overwhelmed by the menu. Nothing suggested by the fanged waitress tempted her. Most of it was alien and unfamiliar, so Sloane took over and ordered for them both. Raena smiled gratefully. Then she concentrated on sipping the glass of water set before her, savoring each icy mouthful. A delicate purple flower floated in it.

"I could live forever on floral water," she said quietly.

Sloane tried the water himself, but couldn't taste the flower.

When the salad came, flowers garnished it as well. Raena didn't move forward to help herself, so Sloane served some onto her plate. She trailed her fork through it.

"You must be hungry," Sloane observed as he speared a bite.

"I guess so." She looked up from her plate. "The way the red sauce streaks the greens is pretty. Don't you think?"

Swallowing quickly, Sloane encouraged, "It's good."

Raena scooped up a forkful of food and put it into her mouth. Her teeth closed on her lip and she winced. The food went down with a gulp. What color she had drained from her face.

"We shouldn't have come," Sloane said hopelessly. "It's too soon…"

She shook her head, sipped the water again, then speared another forkful of salad and put herself through the whole painful process again. After she'd choked that bite down, she said, "Eat to thrive: Ariel's father drilled that into me."

Both of them were relieved when the meal was over. Sloane helped Raena into a taxi and wasn't surprised when she fell asleep. So much for getting lucky after their big first date. This time, now that the apartment complex was familiar with her, he didn't have any compunction about lifting her in his arms and carrying her home.

* * *

When Sloane woke, Raena was gone. Maybe he'd imagined her presence. Maybe he'd dreamed they'd found her in a tomb.

Sloane touched his lips with his right index finger, remembering her kiss.

"Gavin?" Raena called.

"Where are you?"

"Out here."

He heard something in her voice, some unfamiliar tone that hurried him over to the window. When he swept back the billowing curtains, rain blew into the room. The raindrops stung, cold and sharp against his bare skin.

Facing the storm, Raena stood barefoot on the balustrade, naked, arms flung wide, head thrown back. She looked as though she might lean forward and take flight on the storm wind. Water ran down her narrow brown back, broken into rivulets by her scars.

Sloane shouted over the storm, "What are you doing out here?"

"Isn't it beautiful?"

He wasn't sure he'd heard her right. He wanted to yank her back from the precipice, but he lifted his hand and froze, unable to reach for her and unable to step away. Startling her might be deadly. The rounded balustrade looked slick.

"What are you *talking* about?" he asked, more calmly than he felt.

"The rain. The feeling of the rain on your skin. Isn't it incredible?" She turned to face him.

The light trickling over his shoulder highlighted her against the black night sky. Her raw-boned body looked terrible and inhuman. Her collarbone looked like he could snap it between his fingers. Shadows outlined her ribs.

Sloane pulled his gaze up to her face. Her eyes swam with sadness as deep and dark as her captivity. Sloane stepped forward into an ankle-deep puddle and raised his arms toward her.

Rather than take his hands, she leaned onto his shoulders. Her small breasts hung in front of his eyes as she jumped down.

Sloane caught her weight before her feet touched the puddle. He held her hard in his arms.

She wrapped her legs around his waist, hugging him with her thighs. She rested her wet head against his neck.

Sloane carried her back into the bedroom and set her onto the bed. She submitted docilely enough. He pulled the comforter from the mattress and bundled it around her.

When he returned from closing the window, he repeated, "What were you doing out there?"

"I heard the rain and got up to watch it. I'd forgotten how beautiful rain is. Raindrops were falling into the puddle hard enough to toss up a spout of water." She held up her fingers, measuring. "Each drop cast a circle around itself, all the circles expanding and flowing into each other . . . I had to feel it on my skin. I can't believe I'd forgotten about rain."

Sloane joined her under the comforter, snuggling close against her back. He rubbed his shaven chin against her shoulder and kissed the bare nape of her neck. "You might've caught your death," he chided.

"A little rain never hurt anyone."

"I'm more worried about the chill."

"Was it cold?" She scooted around and crawled into his lap like a child. "I don't really notice cold any more." Hanging her arms around his neck, she buried her face against his chest.

Though her nearness aroused him, Sloane simply held her, stroking her back, tracing her scars. Gradually he realized that the wetness of her face pressed against his chest had grown hot. Raena's weeping had been so silent he felt heartless not to have noticed it sooner.

Sloane tilted her chin up. He licked her eyelids, feeling the fringe of her eyelashes even as he tasted the startling tang of her tears.

She moved so he could feel the heat growing in her groin. That realization set up a feedback loop. He ran his fingers up under her hair, holding her head in place as his kisses grew more passionate. Raena met his mouth, impaled it with her small pointed tongue.

She leaned backward to the mattress, drawing Sloane down atop her. She hooked her ankles together at the small of his back. During the transition, she pressed against him, wet and hotter than her tears. Sloane required no further encouragement.

She made no sound as he entered her, but her whole body clenched around him, so that he couldn't breathe. Then her hips thrust up against his and Sloane gasped. All he could do was try to keep his balance while she writhed beneath him.

Throughout it all, she remained completely silent, too deeply focused to make a sound. Sloane found that unnerving.

Raena caught his earlobe between her teeth. Sloane wanted to turn his head and watch her face, but feared she'd bite his earlobe off if he moved. The mere thought sent him over the edge.

* * *

Halfway through the night, Raena suddenly pushed off Sloane's arm and struggled to her feet. Scarcely awake, Sloane heard her trip, hit the wall hard, blunder onward. It sounded as if she barely reached the toilet in time.

"You all right?" he called hopefully after her.

"No."

The unfamiliar tone in her voice—panic? Raena?—galvanized him. Sloane snapped on the bedroom light and came after her.

"Go back to bed," Raena commanded, not looking over her shoulder at him. "It's just dinner fighting back."

Sloane didn't point out how little dinner she'd actually choked down. He opened the apartment's cabinets, searching through the designer-chosen things until he found the liquor. He poured himself a stiff whiskey and downed half of it without pausing for air.

Everything Sloane had on this world was in another name, even the bank accounts. He was as anonymous here as possible,

masquerading as a legitimate dealer in Templar artifacts. He'd
envisioned settling down with Raena, showing her the nightlife,
such as it was, and getting to know her.

Now he wondered if she'd survive the night. The sickness barely
let her rest.

The toilet flushed once more and he watched her curl up on the
bathroom floor. He knew she didn't want a witness or a nursemaid
or any fucking company. All the same, he stripped the silk-covered
duvet from the bed and bundled it into his arms. He carried it to
the bathroom and flung it out over her where she curled on the
cold tile.

Her bony hands clutched the blanket under her chin and she
smiled. Through a throat scorched by stomach acid, she whispered,
"Thank you."

When he came back into the bedroom, he lurched toward the
comp terminal. Once he had the concierge on the line, he asked if
the building had a doctor on staff.

From the bathroom, Raena shouted, "No doctors!"

Sloane muted the connection and said in a normal tone, "You
need to get checked out, Raena. We ate the same meal. This isn't
food poisoning. Something is seriously wrong..."

She came to stand, shaking, in the doorway. "No doctors, Gavin.
I don't have any ID. If I show up as an unknown—on a civilized
planet like this—they'll scan me. Sooner or later, some computer
will ID me. He'll find me, Gavin."

Sloane didn't have to ask who. "We'll be gone by then," he promised.

"Right now Thallian doesn't know I'm out," she argued. "That's
only a matter of time."

"Is that what you're worried about? Look!" He broke the link to
the concierge, input a string, and waited.

The screen filled with a familiar labyrinth of black stone and
wind-blown sand. "Someone had rigged up a surveillance system

around the Templar tombs. I rewired it, so I could keep an eye on things after we left."

He shuffled through the cameras.

"There," Raena said. "Stop."

Sloane's fingers stuttered to a halt. A view of the bunker complex flickered onscreen. An antique black diplomatic transport parked far enough away to be out of the blast radius if the grave robbers had left things booby-trapped. Sloane kicked himself for not think-ing to order that.

"Who is that?" Sloane wondered, before he thought the better of the question.

Raena gave the predictable response: "No doctors, Sloane. I mean it. We'd better start packing."

"I've got to go out, do some business, once it's light," he pro-tested. "I need to get us some traveling cash."

"Fine." She went back to the bed and hunkered down on it. "Give me a gun before you leave."

"Fair enough."

* * *

Sloane had lived his life bluffing from one action to the next. He'd never given much thought to where he was going or how he'd get there, just kept moving. Kept running, actually, from the mem-ory of Raena and how she'd been stolen from him the first time, how she'd bolted from him the last. Until Ariel started him on the Dart, that is, and he found himself able to pursue long-term plans.

He finished his drink and poured another. Twenty years ago, when he'd first located Raena in that bar on Nizarrh, she was a slip of a girl in a swirling black cape. He hadn't been much older than her himself. He'd thought she was shit-faced drunk, since her head kept drooping over her glass, but after he got her onto his ship, he realized that it had literally been days since she'd slept. He'd hovered over her sleeping form, fascinated by how delicate she looked, how scarred. She looked like she'd walked through Hell in nothing but the clothes on her back.

She'd been on his ship—which one had it been back then? they never lasted long—less than a standard day before the scanners melted down. He'd practically sailed *through* another ship before Raena persuaded him to drop back to real space. And the *Arbiter* was right there, waiting to pick her up.

Over many sleepless nights since then, Sloane had puzzled over that. Had Thallian known she would fall into his hands? Had it just been bad luck? Had Raena guessed he was there and simply quit running? If there'd been a trace on her, why had Sloan been able to get her off Nizarrh at all? Had there been any way he could have outrun Thallian or out-maneuvered him or hidden her better?

If the story had ended there, maybe Sloane could have chalked it up to rotten luck and moved on. But once he'd tracked her to Thallian's custody and learned what that meant, he bought a forged med ID, got himself into her cell, and saw what Thallian had done to her...

The memory made him shiver even now. She'd been strapped into a metal chair, electrodes inserted all over her skin. At random intervals, she got a shock so fierce the restraints left bruises.

If anything, Raena looked more alive under torture than she'd been, fleeing on Sloane's ship. Some nights, the vision of her arching up under the current, galvanized by Thallian's device, woke Sloane. Made it impossible to find sleep again. The memory of her in the torture machine guaranteed that Sloane would do everything in his power to find her again.

He swore to himself that he didn't want to hurt her like that. But she'd looked so beautiful then, like an engine stripped down to racing trim, like a brand-new gun shiny from the manufacturer. His hands ached to caress her. He wanted to taste her bruises and feel her tears on his fingertips. The craving shamed him and drove him for decades. He hoped to make it up to her for even thinking those thoughts.

Sloane perched on the bedside, watching Raena sleep. He'd killed enough creatures to know what death looked like. Raena barely looked alive. In the valleys between each breath, he strained his ears, waiting for the pause that must most certainly come.

Sloane remembered how she was before when he'd rescued her the second time. They almost made it out of Thallian's clutches and off his ship. Then Raena ran out of the lift right into a squadron of soldiers. She'd obviously hoped someone would shoot her down and put her out of her misery. Instead, they'd taken her prisoner and marched her back to their master.

Had Sloane freed her this third and final time only to have her die in his arms? He wondered if all the years held at bay by the stone tomb ate at her now. Would she turn to dust if he waited beside her long enough? Would that take days, a week? He couldn't run away from her or the sickness or the memories. He couldn't just sit and watch her die. He had to call someone. If she wouldn't let him take her to the doctor, he'd need to bring a doctor to her.

He dragged the portable comp over and began searching the human interweb. This would be easier if he hadn't burned his bridges with Kavanaugh.

* * *

Revan ordered the guards to collect all the abandoned equipment. He wondered if any of it would prove useful. Most of the large pieces seemed to have had their serial numbers erased with acid. All in all, what was left of the encampment looked like junk, worthless and untraceable. Still, it was his job to find out who had been on the planet and what they'd taken off-world.

It would have helped, of course, if Jonan had been more forthcoming. Then Revan could have narrowed the scope of his search. Ultimately, though, it didn't matter. Revan had served his younger brother long enough that he knew the consequences of asking too many questions. Jonan was clearly spooked. That was enough to stir Revan to action.

As he watched a technician dismantle what was left of a vandalized scanner, an enormous explosion went off nearby. The blast wave, rumbling like an avalanche toward them, knocked Revan into the mountain and pushed the technician from his perch on the extensor ladder. The man hit the ground hard.

Revan spun to see a cloud of debris, driven by the relentless wind, headed his way. He had no time to duck before it engulfed him.

He pushed off the wall and fought his way through the vortex of grit. The radio at his hip squealed and shouted unintelligibly. He would have recognized the cadence of Jain's voice, but he didn't hear it.

Whoever had abandoned the grave robbers' camp had set a booby trap. They'd known they would be tracked.

Thanks to the planet's unceasing gale, the debris cloud cleared enough that Revan could see again. He found Jain slumped against a loader, coughing hard as if he'd inhaled a stone.

Revan put his hand on the boy's shoulder, meaning to extend a measure of comfort. Instead, the boy swallowed his weakness and snapped to attention. His chest betrayed him, heaving with restrained coughing.

Behind the boy, beyond the loader, it seemed as if the entire face of the mountain had come down. A boulder larger than their transport had rolled to a stop a meter away. A guard's arm protruded from beneath it. Jain's other guards had vanished.

"It was a trap," the boy said needlessly, his voice too loud.

"Did it damage your hearing?" Revan shouted over the wind.

Jain, looking at the devastation for the first time, didn't respond.

The explosion must have deafened him. Revan shook his head, dreading to report the news to Jonan. Still, the trap solved one problem. Now they knew where to focus their search for traces of the grave robbers.

* * *

Jonan settled into his office before he opened the comm. Revan stood in front of an avalanche of broken black stone.

"We don't know who the grave robbers were yet," the elder brother said without preamble. "They opened a number of tombs before they found the one they wanted. They left a fair amount of broken equipment spread around their encampment. We're trying to trace it now. Your scanners were reconfigured. I'm tracking the feed. I'll find out who's viewing it and where."

"Report to me before you proceed there," Jonan answered.

Before Jonan could cut the connection, Revan said, "There's more. This disaster behind me is the Templar Master's tomb. Jain's team set off a booby-trap."

Revan paused, as if unsure how to deliver the rest of his report.

Grimly, Jonan asked, "How many casualties?"

"Jain lost his hearing in the explosion. One of his guards is dead. Two more are missing."

"Presumed dead?"

"I'll make certain," Revan assured.

The brothers had no other words of comfort for each other.

Jonan closed the comm and sat back, more alive than he'd felt in years. Raena had survived. She was free in the galaxy. Soon they would be reunited.

Was she on her own or had she co-opted the grave robbers into aiding her? He wondered if his men would find a pile of bodies somewhere. What would it mean if they didn't?

That she'd hurt Jain was disappointing. Thallian had hoped that she would learn affection for the boys. Start to think of them as family. If things had gone differently in the past, they might have been her sons.

He shook the thought away. It didn't really matter. What mattered was that she had not forgotten him. She'd known he would come for her and she'd set a trap. Jonan was touched. He'd have to think of a suitable welcome for her in return.

CHAPTER 5

In the morning, Raena looked even worse. She managed to pull herself out of bed and into the bath he'd run for her, but Sloane noticed she walked like her bones ground together. He rummaged in the cabinets for some painkillers, but the only candidate for the job was whiskey. Not what she needed on an empty stomach.

"Stop fussing," she groused. "You make me nervous."

Sloane laughed, as she'd intended him to. He came to sit on the polished stone ledge around the ludicrously large tub.

"I feel awful," Raena confided, lifting one bony hand above the sea of bubbles.

"What can I do?" Sloane asked.

Raena shook her head.

Half to himself, he muttered, "I shouldn't have fired Kavanaugh. He spent enough time on that med ship that he could cobble together medicine out of space junk and leftover food."

"You wanted me all to yourself," Raena reminded. "That was sweet."

Sloane shook his head, doubting she really felt his possessiveness of her was sweet.

"Maybe you could have me skinned," she offered. "Make a robot of me. She could be the companion you want."

He sputtered, "I can't believe you'd even joke about that."

She bared her teeth. "All I wanted was death, Gavin. The Emperor refused to have me executed. Once I was in that grave, I spent years waiting to be rescued. I would even have been glad to see Thallian. And for twenty years, Thallian knew I was in that tomb and he *never* came. But as soon as his scanners went off-line, he sent a transport to find out why. If he finds out I survived the tomb, he'll want me back. You saw what happened the last time he got his hands on me."

He wondered guiltily if she knew he'd been thinking about that in the night.

"I will die before I let him touch me again," she promised.

"How do you even know for sure those men were his?"

She cocked an eyebrow.

Sloane sighed. "All right. I need to go out and unload some of this stuff. You asked me to leave you a gun."

"At least one."

He helped her out of the water, settling her on the edge of the tub so he could dry her off. It surprised him how gentle his old scarred hands could be. He wrapped Raena in the robe he'd found behind the closet door.

Once he'd tucked her back into the bed, something terrible occurred to him and he shuddered. "You're not planning to use it…"

"Gavin." She reached for his hand. "I won't do that to you. I'll be here when you get back. I just want the gun in case anything comes through that door that you didn't order."

"If they find anything on the tombworld—which they won't—they couldn't get to us before I get back from my errand. Unless that antique shuttle can warp time. And if they possessed that kind of tech, they would be ruling the universe. So don't worry." He bent down to kiss her forehead and laid a laser rifle on the bed beside her. "Want a lesson before I go?"

"Gavin, *please*. It's a rifle. I was firing these when I was a kid."

He ruffled her hair. She felt like a soft little animal. "Just don't blow a hole in the door. We're trying to lay low here."

"Got it." She fiddled with the safety switch, checked the power pack, and sighted down the barrel.

"I'll leave you two to get acquainted," Sloane teased.

She snared him again with her black eyes. "One more thing."

"Anything."

"Do you remember when I gave you my medallion?"

"Of course." Last-second bravado barely covered his wounded tone. Did she think he had forgotten? She'd given it to him when she'd kissed him goodbye. He lifted the flap on the breast pocket of his jacket and pulled it out, laying it in her hand.

When she smiled at it, he saw a whole new girl, one he didn't recognize. This was a child, thrilled to have found something precious, something she'd thought lost. The joy in her expression shocked him.

He watched her skeletal fingers stroke the silver disk. The years had tarnished the cheap metal. He'd always thought the medallion's engraving of the crossed swords silly or pretentious, but now he understood that the girl she'd been had thought it dramatic and serious. He wondered if he would have liked that girl if he'd known her before she was broken, before Thallian chased her halfway to hell and back.

"It's smaller than I remember," Raena said softly. She placed the medallion on the comforter beside the gun and activated its holo player.

The woman in the recording looked tiny, built like Raena. Ragged black hair streamed down her back. Her face was hollow-eyed and paranoid. Her left thumb rubbed up and down the length of her forefinger, clenching her fist again and again. The gesture was unconscious, obsessive.

"I know it won't make sense to you now, Raena," the recording said. "You might even doubt that I love you, but that's not true. I have to do this, for your own good. If love were protection enough…"

Recording span maxed, the litany looped, began again.

"Sometimes when I watched this," Raena said over the recording, "I used to concentrate on her hands. What was it she wanted to grip?"

To keep Raena talking, Sloane asked, "Who is she?"

"My mother." Raena shook her head. "I'd forgotten her eyes were brown. Who forgets the color of her mother's eyes?"

Sloane didn't give a damn about the color of his own mother's eyes. "What's she talking about?"

"This was her farewell message as she sent me away. I was supposed to go to a chapter house, continue my training. I was good with computers, fascinated by them, but I was always getting into fights. Fiana couldn't control me. She was crazy then… You can see it. I'd forgotten that, too."

"What happened?"

"Slavers. The transport crew took me to the chapter house, where it was meant to be, but it was gone. Burned to the ground by the natives. What did transporters want with a kid? They were just space trash, living from job to job. Fiana had already paid them to transport me. Job done. So they sold me to the first slave ship they came across. Viridians," she spat.

"You're lucky you ended up with Ariel," he said.

Raena's smile was hard to read. Not entirely happy memories there, Sloane would have said. "You know Ariel, then?" she asked.

Sloane's mouth twisted into a grimace before he could stop it. "We have a history, let's say."

Raena touched the rifle beside her. "She's clearly not selling you guns."

"Not any more."

Uncomfortable with the way the conversation had turned, Sloane stood up from the bed. He leaned through the hologram to kiss Raena again. "Stay out of trouble while I'm gone," he directed.

"If trouble doesn't come here, there will be no problem," she promised. "I'm not going anywhere else." She watched the hologram play again.

* * *

On Station 23—neutral territory—Kavanaugh hadn't really decided what to say to Ariel Shaad, even as he wove through the crowded bar to meet her. He'd intended to come straight to her and say that Raena was free again, albeit in Sloane's clutches, but with every step he took, he couldn't imagine how that knowledge might work out well for anyone. Raena wasn't a slave; if she wanted to contact her sister, she could undoubtedly manage it. If Ariel thought Sloane had thwarted her again—over anything—she might go on such a rampage that someone would end up dead. As much as Sloane might deserve it, he had once been Kavanaugh's friend, closer even than Ariel or Raena. Out of friendship, Kavanaugh decided to hold his tongue.

Just another untenable position Sloane put him in.

Ariel sat at a scratched-up table toward the rear of the tavern, her back against the wall like any other veteran. She'd run weapons for the Coalition during the meltdown, but her family's money had come from manufacturing guns for the Empire. Kavanaugh had thought Sloane lucky when he started dating this rich girl. Kavanaugh might even have been jealous, except that Ariel was a good decade older than him and consistently treated him like a kid brother.

All these years later, she remained stunning: graying blond hair still pulled back in a long braid to emphasize her cheekbones, blouse unbuttoned far enough to showcase the upper curve of her breasts.

She'd always liked her clothes tight enough not to get in her way if she got in a fight. With Ariel's short fuse, a fight was rarely far out of reach. Unfortunately, between her and Sloane, Ariel was the reasonable one. It had always been a simple matter of time before they combusted.

She grinned when she saw Kavanaugh checking her over. She scooted over to give him room to get his back against the wall, too. "I was surprised to hear from you," she said diplomatically.

"No, you weren't." Kavanaugh grinned back. "You knew he'd fire me eventually."

"Yeah." She avoided Kavanaugh's eyes by waving a serving android over. "What will you have?"

"How's the house ale?"

"Good. But have anything you want."

"I can afford to," Kavanaugh said, gently rejecting her offer to get the tab. There were times he'd taken her up on it and been grateful, but now, thanks to Sloane's severance, Kavanaugh intended to pay back some of those free rounds he'd drunk. "Refill?"

Ariel smiled again, pleased and not a bit condescending, and ordered another Rocket Fuel. The android filled their glasses and bustled off to the next table.

"How is the old bastard anyway?" Ariel asked.

"I don't know what's wrong with him." Kavanaugh sighed. "He trashed our hopper at one point, to make sure the men didn't loot anything without him knowing about it." Or so Sloane had said at the time. Now that the words left his lips, Kavanaugh wondered again if Sloane had suspected Raena was alive in her tomb, if he'd wrecked the hopper to prevent her from escaping him. Escaping him hadn't even seemed to occur to Raena. Instead, she went to her meeting with Sloane like it was fate.

Ariel was watching Kavanaugh when his gaze returned outward from his thoughts. "I don't know what's wrong with him," he repeated.

"Nothing a shot to the head wouldn't fix," Ariel said, but not as seriously as she once might have.

There was no way to bring the reason for this meeting up naturally, so Kavanaugh said as casually as possible, "Remember that guy who was chasing Raena?"

Ariel took a shaky sip from her glass. "I still have nightmares about him."

"Sloane disbanded our operation overnight," Kavanaugh said. "He had some kind of warning that guy had the job site under surveillance."

"What could Thallian be watching on the Templar tombworld?"

When Kavanaugh twitched, Ariel grinned. "Yeah, I keep tabs on Gavin. I know he had you robbing graves."

"Well, I've done worse things for a buck," Kavanaugh conceded, swallowing more of his ale. "But Sloane thought Thallian was coming after him."

"You looking for a place to hide?" Ariel asked.

"Worse than that. I'm warning you to run, too."

Anger sparked in Ariel's hazel eyes. "What has Gavin done?"

"My silence has been bought and paid for," Kavanaugh said, lips curling into a grimace. "These days, he'd probably shoot me for saying as much as I have. But you've got more to lose than I do. You've got to get those kids into hiding."

"There aren't many of them still at home," she said hopelessly. "I mean, they're all trained and armed as well as I could manage, but they're adults. Or as adult as we were when we went away to war." She drained her glass. "If Gavin's crossed Thallian, the devil won't bother to come after my kids. They've got no connection to either of them."

"You're right," Kavanaugh hurried to assure her. "But you're the only one of us who's faced him. Who knows firsthand what he's capable of."

The color drained from Ariel's golden skin. Kavanaugh ordered another round of drinks, handed over his card—in an alias, natch—to give her a moment to pull herself together.

"If that monster is still alive in this galaxy," she said after a long swallow, "someone really ought to do something about it."

"Thought I might try," Kavanaugh answered.

"You'll need arming," Ariel observed. "Someone to watch your back."

"I'm not volunteering you for this," he clarified. "It's quite likely gonna get me killed."

"If it comes down to getting captured by that psychopath, you'll be glad to have me along to put a bolt between your eyes first."

He clinked his mug against her glass. "Comforting. Thank you, Ariel. I could always rely on you for that."

She grinned, showing off her perfect teeth. "Sorry. But at least you can rely on me to tell you before I shoot you, unlike Gavin."

Kavanaugh wondered if she'd ever forgive Sloane for that. No real reason why she should, he supposed. Not when "for old times' sake" included as many bad memories as good.

* * *

For the next couple of days, Raena continued to fade before his eyes. Sloane started drinking, only to be interrupted by the computer's chime.

He examined the woman on the security monitor. Doc had aged rough. Her shoulders stooped, as if Brunzell's gravity dragged on her. Deep lines etched across her forehead and around her mouth. Her hair had gone steel gray, threaded with pure white. Appearance had never concerned Doc, so Sloane wasn't surprised she hadn't bothered to have herself fixed up. He was amused that, as always, she wore sturdy clothes in shades of brown that wouldn't stain.

Doc lost all her family fighting with the Coalition during the War. Afterward, her companion Skyler succumbed to some alien disease that had eaten him from the inside. Kavanaugh was the closest thing to a son she'd ever had. Sloane braced himself for the tirade, figuring that, no matter what the payoff, Kavanaugh had already spilled to Doc what it was that Sloane needed a doctor off the grid to examine.

Doc ambled out of the lift. "How's the universe been treating you, Sloane?" she growled, surprising him with a hug.

"I'm getting by," he said, unwilling to go into the details. He knew she'd see the wealth displayed in the room behind him, so unlike the Old Spacers Home where she worked these days. As an afterthought, he added, "You?"

"Not much call for battlefield medicine these days." She filled her eyes with the shiny Templar artifacts in the crate by the door. "Since I had to hock my ship, I don't get my feet off the dirt so much any more."

Abruptly cutting off the reminiscences, Sloane said, "She's in here. She's probably asleep. She's most comfortable when she's asleep."

"Who?" Doc asked, but Sloane palmed the door open and went into the darkened bedroom.

The medic followed haltingly, waiting for her eyes to adjust to the dimness.

"Raena," Sloane called gently. When the girl didn't stir, he reached unwillingly down to her shoulder. His fingertips slipped into the well beneath her collarbone. Her skin felt like cold leather.

Doc put her bag down on the bed. "She looks like hell," she snapped, deeply shocked. "When did you find her?"

"About a week ago. She hasn't been able to eat. She could keep water down for a while, but…"

"Have you given her anything?"

"She wouldn't let me."

"All right. Leave us alone and I'll look her over."

*　*　*

Sloane had barely left the room when Raena's eyes opened.

"Awake?" Doc asked quietly.

Raena nodded.

"Remember me?"

"It's been a long time," Raena rasped, "but I remember. Kavanaugh send you?"

Doc frowned. "I didn't know he was messed up with Sloane, but I don't suppose it should surprise me." She rubbed her hands together to warm them, then began her examination. Raena endured it without complaint, even though the abdominal prodding had to be painful.

"Sloane called me," Doc explained at last. "Actually arranged fast transport for me. Didn't tell me what he wanted, but he made the offer lucrative enough." She watched the woman's face, but didn't see the condemnation she expected.

"It's good to see you again," Raena whispered. "You took good care of me before."

"You look terrible," Doc said. "How long since you ate?"

Raena chuckled. It sounded like bones grinding together. "Too long."

"Well, that's not doing you any good." Doc scribbled on a battered handheld. "I'm gonna give Sloane a shopping list. You know what my nutri-shakes are like. Won't taste good, but you need to get it down. And keep it down. If you can't do that, then I'll put a line into your stomach."

Doc finished the list and set it aside. "For now, I'm gonna give you an IV. It's just fluid, but it will make your joints ache less. Should help with the headache and other pains, too. It'll be easier to eat later, if you have some spit to swallow with."

Raena was out again by the time Doc had the IV set up and the needle flushed. She picked up the woman's hand and turned it gently. Sunken skin draped every bone. Doc shook her head. Hard to believe the woman wasn't dead.

It took some looking, but she finally located a vein that would take the needle. Then she pulled the blankets up around the woman and went after Sloane.

* * *

"The deal is this," Doc said. "She's completely dehydrated. That's what's causing her pallor, the dry skin, the sunken flesh. She's malnourished enough that I'd be surprised if she could stand. At one point or another, every bone in her body seems to have been broken, but they're old injuries and, for the most part, have healed well. There's been a lot of tissue damage, but it's old, too."

"About what could be expected," Sloane said, "with the life she led."

"That's right. The thing that's weird is that she doesn't seem to have aged. At a guess, I'd say she's still physically about twenty." Doc locked her gaze on Gavin's eyes. "How can that be?"

He weighed whether to tell her Raena had spent the last two decades trapped in a Templar tomb, but decided, on the spur of the moment, to hold back. Pragmatic Doc wasn't likely to believe the truth. "The Templars had her in some kind of stasis," he lied. "After we found her, Kavanaugh broke her out. I'm surprised he didn't tell you about it."

As he expected, Doc fell for the change in topic. "I'm surprised, too," she said, sarcasm icing her words. "Then again, Tarik's always been a man of his word. I'd guess that your payoff, however much it was, bought his silence."

Sloane winced, point taken. "Drink?"

"Hell, yes," Doc said. "I was afraid I'd need to break into my medicinal supply if you made me wait much longer."

He poured her a glass, even delivered it to her after she'd sunken into a leather-wrapped armchair and propped her scuffed boots on the fringed hassock. She sipped the whiskey with eyes closed, like she was accepting a sacrament. "Been a long time since I tasted the real thing," she said softly.

Surprising himself, Sloane said, "It's nice to have someone to share it with again."

Doc squinted at him. "I haven't given you the rest of my diagnosis," she warned. "It's good that you have that drink in your hand."

"Don't sugarcoat it, Doc." He collapsed into the matching chair across from her.

She smiled grimly. "What I don't see is whatever is killing her now. There's no sign of infection. No disease. But if she can't start to keep food down, I'd give her a week at most. Probably less. If she has any family left," Doc advised, "this would be the time to contact them."

Sloane felt like she'd stabbed him. "Less than a week?"

"With Raena…I don't know. I've seen her do some amazing things in the past. But she's a long way gone. I don't know if she can pull herself back from this."

* * *

Once Doc had gone back in to sit with Raena—fortified with a fresh glass of whiskey—Sloane sent a message via the Shaad family's priority channel. It was the sort of call that Ariel could not ignore. Without a doubt, she'd overheat when she found out who sent it.

Sloane broke the connection and got up to pour himself another drink. If not for Raena, he and Ariel would have never spoken again. He wasn't sure how he felt about that. Ariel Shaad wasn't a woman who forgave, although she'd made excuses for him the first time he'd undercut her. When Ariel's employees died mixed up in Sloane's business, *that* overloaded her circuits. To Ariel, employees were as good as family. She had probably even considered homicide: that wouldn't have been out of character. Still, despite her family money, Ariel had always been honorable enough to handle the worst work personally. He'd known she wouldn't put a bounty on him. When she didn't come herself, he knew he was safe.

Back then, the Dart made him not care. Business had been business, and Ariel, though hotter than live plasma, had been in his way.

Raena's reappearance could go a long way toward healing that damage. Ariel would forgive him anything, if Sloane delivered her sister healthy and safe. But if Raena died in his care…

Sloane drained the whiskey from his glass. His hand trembled the slightest bit as he remembered the silk of Ariel's hair, the softness of her skin. Her scent. Her laughter. God, the taste of her. They'd had good times.

Until she'd introduced him to the Dart. Maybe she could forgive him, if she found out that the Dart was the reason he'd been able to track Raena into that tomb.

* * *

After the booby-trap went off, Revan wasn't about to venture closer than the nearest ridge until he knew it was safe. He knew he'd been right to be cautious earlier. At least Jain had listened to him enough that he hadn't been crushed by the avalanche.

Apparently, whoever set the explosive charge had been hurried or over-confident or their supplies were low. Whatever the reason, nothing else exploded. Leaning against the black rocks for balance, Revan watched through his macroscope as the workmen removed the last of the boulders tumbled down around the tomb's entrance. He saw them enter the tomb.

Hardly any time passed before the men radioed that they'd found evidence of the tomb raiders they were hunting. Revan strolled back to his cart and let it drive him to the tomb. Circling in his thoughts was a prayer: *Let this be all the information he needed. Let it be enough that he could identify the grave robbers. Let him be able to report to Jonan and return home.* Revan was sick of the gritty wind slicing at him every time he bared an inch of flesh.

The reorganized bombsite looked completely different than the last time he'd visited. The broken stone stood in neat piles now. The Templar inscription scrolling around the tomb's doorway had been revealed. Revan didn't pause to examine it.

Just inside the tomb, out of the wind, one of the men handed him an electric torch. Revan pointed it up high, admiring the size of the lofty cavern. All around him, the black stone swallowed the light without reflecting it.

"Here, sir."

Revan followed the voice to the catafalque in the center of the tomb. He waved the light over the stone to read the words scraped into the hard black rock: "You knew where I was. Now you don't."

"That's it?" he asked.

"Yes, sir." The man held up something else between his gloved fingers. "And this. Someone coiled it in a circle around the message."

Revan angled the torch to see what the man held: a single strand of long black hair. He pulled a vial out of his pack and carefully plugged the hair inside. Now he wanted to race back to the ship and run a DNA test. Who was he chasing?

And what did she mean: "You knew where I was"? Was she addressing Jonan?

On his way back through the archway, Revan commanded, "Copy down the tomb's epitaph and have someone translate it. And search every inch of this place. I want every scrap and crumb logged for study."

✶ ✶ ✶

As soon as Sloane answered her return call, Ariel Shaad said, more reasonably that he'd expected, "I don't want to get mixed up in your business again, Sloane."

Sloane filled his eyes with her—still built for speed after all these years—but didn't make her wait too long. "This isn't business, Ms. Shaad. This is family." Funny how that word always got Ariel's attention. "I've found her," he said simply. Raena's name need not even be spoken.

Ariel's choked whisper was almost swallowed by the distances crossed by the transmission. "Oh, Gavin…where?"

"Still imprisoned…"

Fury ignited in Ariel's voice. Sloane saw sparks in her hazel eyes and felt a moment of vertigo. Even with Raena in the next room, he was startled to discover how much he'd missed Ariel Shaad.

He spoke carefully, cutting across Ariel's tirade against Imperial butchers. "She's alive, Ariel."

"I'm coming. I can leave as soon as…"

"No," Sloane said.

"Gavin, I'm the only…"

"No. Not yet. Doc is here now, seeing to her. She's very weak and disoriented." He let those shocking, unlikely words sink in, and then said, "I know this isn't the way you want it to be, but that's how things have fallen out." Surprised by the lone tear that trailed down Ariel's face, he softened his tone. "I'll contact you as soon as she wants visitors."

"All right," she said, but it really wasn't. Ariel rubbed away the traitorous tear. "Is there anything she needs? If I can help in any way…"

"Clothes would be good. You know that sort of thing better than me." He stroked his chin, missing the beard Raena had shaved off. "She's about the same size as she was. Just don't buy black. She's tired of blackness."

"I'm on it. And tell her—"

"I will," Sloane promised, sparing Ariel from having to tell him.

"Thanks, Gavin. And hey," she paused, weighing whether to continue, then added, "it will be nice to see you, too."

He grinned, relieved to know she'd felt the old charge as well. "You, too, Ari. I'll let you know as soon as I can."

Just after he broke the connection, Doc passed through the lounge on her way to the bathroom. "She wants you," she said.

Sloane gulped down his drink and went back into the bedroom.

Raena lay propped up, doll-like, in the middle of the huge bed. He recalled what she'd said about making a robot garbed in her skin. Just thinking about it made him feel sick.

Raena's voice rasped with dehydration. "What did Ariel say?"

Sloane poured her a glass of water and brought it to the bed. He held it for her as she drank. It was easier to lie when she wasn't watching him. "Ariel's got business she needs to wrap up. She'll come when she can."

Raena put her feverishly warm hand over his and steadied the glass against her lip. She finished the water in two long gulps, then nudged the glass away. "You don't want her to see me like this," Raena accused.

"*I* don't want to see you like this," Sloane corrected.

Raena shifted against her pillows, seeking comfort. "If I told you I was dying, would you let her come?"

"You're *not* dying," Sloane protested.

"Not yet." Raena smiled, amused at herself. "But I want to see Ariel before I do."

"She'll come," Sloane assured. "For now, just conserve your strength."

Raena nodded. "I'm tired of sleeping, though. Could I borrow a terminal and cruise around the interweb?"

"Of course."

* * *

Ariel closed the comm down and took a deep breath as she sat back from her desk. A forest of holo frames displayed the smiling faces of her kids. Usually, seeing them all made her smile in response. Now even they couldn't improve her mood. Kavanaugh knew—had to have known—about Raena. And Gavin's money bought his silence on the only subject Ariel really cared about.

She rubbed her forehead, temples, eyes. Really, she couldn't blame Kavanaugh. She knew Sloane too well, knew that he'd fight to the death with friends over things that meant less to him than Raena did. To be honest, Ariel wouldn't trade Kavanaugh's life for news that Raena was hanging around with Sloane. That was scary and wrong on too many levels to contemplate.

Ariel took another deep breath, steadying herself like she'd do if she were taking her best shot. Then she opened the comm again and messaged Kavanaugh. She wanted to let him know she knew now. She wanted to find out everything he knew. Then she needed to pack, so she'd be ready to fly to her sister's side whenever she was allowed.

* * *

Even in the privacy of his cabin on the transport, Revan stood at attention to make his report. "The tomb was empty," Revan said. "Its occupant left you a message." He repeated the phrase they'd found scratched into the catafalque. He watched his brother for a reaction, but Jonan merely blinked. Nonplussed, Revan continued, "There was a single black hair, one hundred and twenty-six centimeters long. We're running a DNA trace now."

"You needn't bother," Jonan said calmly. He typed something and the screen filled with a three-dimensional image.

Revan studied the hologram. The woman was delicately built and slightly smaller than Eilif. Maybe she'd been conventionally pretty before life took her in hand. Her face was a long oval with outsized black eyes. She was wiry, taut with muscles, and scarred in face and spirit.

"That's who I'm looking for?" he asked, just to confirm it.

"Her name is Raena Zacari," Jonan said. Unfamiliar emotion tightened his throat and made his voice strange. "She was my aide before the galaxy went mad."

Revan tried to imagine how she would have aged. Was her hair still black, still knee-length like the one she'd left behind? Did she still wear those ridiculous stiletto-heeled boots to give herself the illusion of height? Once she knew she was hunted, would she change her face, alter her body, try to hide?

"I want her found, Revan. I want her back."

"I'll see it done," Revan assured. He knew the cost of failure.

*   *   *

Kavanaugh answered her call within the hour. By way of hello, Ariel told him, "I just heard from Gavin. He told me you'd found her."

On the comm, Kavanaugh looked like the sheepish teenager Ariel met so many years before. She was amused to see he'd finally stopped blushing to the tips of his ears. The years had carved interesting lines into his face, but his hair was still strawberry blond.

"I'm not mad," Ariel said. "I wouldn't put it past Gavin to kill you for discussing his business around the galaxy. I'm just that much more surprised that you would come warn me about her ex-boss, in light of everything."

"I don't suppose Gavin mentioned him."

"Seemed to have slipped his mind," Ariel said.

There was a pause while Kavanaugh searched for some way to defend Sloane. So predictable, Ariel thought fondly.

With a sigh, Kavanaugh changed the subject. "I wish we were drinking again."

"Time enough for that. For now, though, I think we should hold off on our other plan. I don't want to go looking for trouble, if trouble is likely to come looking for her."

"Understood," Kavanaugh said. "I'm not hurting for money, so I don't need to get right back to work. But if you find yourself needing a pilot and a cargo ship…"

"I won't hesitate," Ariel promised. "I appreciate it, Tarik."

She signed out of the comm program and turned to do some shopping. Of course, Gavin hadn't given her a shipping address, but shopping passed the time. Ariel wanted to find something wonderful to welcome Raena back to freedom.

* * *

A day later, Doc sank into the chair Sloane had left by the bed. It was a nice chair, comfortable enough to sleep in, upholstered in some kind of soft tan leather that smelled brand-new. She suspected he didn't spend much time in this bolt-hole. Probably rented it already furnished, just waiting for him to need a hideout.

Raena was asleep again, looking pretty much like the dead. The gray tone hadn't left her skin, even though she was managing to keep liquids down now. Doc got the feeling that something might be dead inside the girl, but without real equipment, there was no telling what. And Raena had scared Sloane badly enough that he was prepared to let her die, rather than drag her to a hospital.

Doc pulled the flask from her bag and sipped from it. Clearly, grave robbing served Sloane well, if this was the quality of liquor he drank these days. She'd have to fill the flask again before she left. Might be a long time before she tasted anything this good.

She jumped when she realized that the girl's eyes had come open. "You awake?" she asked cautiously.

Raena nodded.

"Sloane's out, up to some kind of no-good," Doc said. "There anything you want to talk to me about while we're not gonna be interrupted?"

"What makes you think that, Doc?" Raena's voice sounded like the raggedy edge of torn paper, but Doc remembered the fatalist sense of humor behind it.

"I remember you as somebody who fought every step of her way," Doc said. "Why are you giving up now?"

"I don't have a lot of strength left." Raena shook her head. "There was a moment, the other night, when I thought about dying. Something woke me and I was going to throw myself off of the balcony while Gavin was asleep. I just couldn't face living. Things were much easier in my tomb. No one expected anything from me. I didn't have to please anyone. There was no one but myself to fight."

"What stopped you?" Doc asked quietly.

"It was raining. The raindrops were little prisms, catching the city lights. The beauty trapped me—and then Sloane came out to talk me down. I couldn't make him watch me die."

Raena didn't seem to want to say more, so Doc sipped her whiskey and said, "I wonder if you've been thinking about all you have to live for. I don't mean Sloane, of course, 'though he'd prefer if you decided to live for him. But you, personally. Don't you have some unfinished business you'd like to settle?"

Raena gazed at the older woman. Doc knew she should meet the girl's eyes, but she just couldn't do it. There was too much pain there, and darkness, and death. Heaven knows that Doc had had enough of those in her own life. She was getting too old to take on anyone else's.

"Of course," Raena said quietly. "He's still out there, Thallian, the man chasing me all those years ago. He's sent men to look for me already. He knows I'm out." She didn't elaborate and Doc didn't ask. Wherever she had been held, escaping it had just about killed Raena. The old woman knew she'd sleep better if she didn't know any more about it than that.

Raena finished, "I don't have the courage to run any more."

"You could always take the fight to him," Doc said, opening her flask to check its level. "That's what we did in the old days."

The girl laughed. "I can't even get out of bed, Doc."

"I can give you stuff for that. I can put the weight back on you, the muscle. I can give you your strength back. I can save your body, if you decide that's what you want. But I can't give you the reason to live. And if you decide you'd rather die than run or face him, hell, I can't tell you you're making the wrong choice."

"What are you saying?"

"This guy was bad news, right? Evil? Doesn't he deserve to pay for that?"

Raena gave her the same empty laugh she'd used when Doc tried to recruit her to the Coalition all those years ago.

Doc took a different tack. "No one else knows he exists any more, do they?"

"No."

"Then no one but you can put him down."

Raena shook her head. "I'm scared. I've been out of the chase too long."

"So has he," Doc argued. "And he's old now, older anyway, and probably getting slow. All I'm saying is: think about it."

CHAPTER 6

The recording of Raena Zacari's trial was remarkably easy to find. Of course, it hadn't ever occurred to Revan to look before this. He hadn't concerned himself with the War or its aftermath since Jonan came home…eighteen years ago? Although Revan was hazy on the date, he remembered that day very clearly: the day his successful younger brother, pride of the family, crawled home like a whipped dog.

Watching Jonan at Raena Zacari's trial brought Revan's emotions flooding back. In the recording, Jonan's hair was still black as obsidian. He stood at strict attention throughout the trial and listened intently to the catalog of wreckage the little woman in black had accomplished: Demolition of an Imperial mining prison. Destruction of a quasar-class ship with all hands aboard. A large number of soldiers, broken down by ranks, permanently out of commission. For such a youngster, the devastation was quite impressive.

In fact, Revan was surprised they hadn't gone so far as to calculate the civilian casualties for which she was undoubtedly responsible. No one in the Imperial courtroom seemed to care. Revan supposed it didn't much matter.

The girl took full responsibility for her crimes. Clearly, she hoped for swift military justice. Execution should have been inevitable.

Revan watched the recording several times, just to observe the play of emotions across Jonan's face. His brother adored his aide, if that's really all she was to him. His eyes never left her unless the court addressed him directly. He felt the guilt that she did not, the shame, the regret. She was proud of what she'd done if for no other reason than because it hurt him.

The recording ended before her sentence was handed down. A notation appended to the video said that she had been executed by the Imperial government, but that couldn't be true if—and it remained to be proven—she had really been imprisoned alive in the Templar Master's tomb.

Jonan believed she had been in the tomb. To understand why, Revan was going to have to ask him about it. Revan dreaded that more than any assignment his brother had ever given him. Jonan's judgment regarding this girl was questionable. Now Revan understood that had been true for decades.

* * *

When Sloane finally came home, hours later, Doc was stretched out asleep on the sofa, boots crossed at the ankle, gun in one hand across her chest. She cracked one eye, saw him in the doorway, and went back to sleep. Good thing he was paying her to doctor and not to guard.

Raena had propped herself up in the bed, pillows supporting her joints to prevent them from gouging into the mattress. She looked as if they'd gotten her into the shower, which was an improvement over recent days.

"Feeling better?"

"Doc's a miracle worker, but you knew that. That's why you're paying her the big bucks."

"You've been discussing her pay?" Sloane asked, surprised.

"Maybe we should be," Raena shot back. "One more day of gagging down those protein shakes of hers and I'll be ready to go back to that restaurant for another flower salad."

He grinned and sat down on the bed to pry off his boots. "That sounds like a vast improvement."

He leaned over to kiss her. Her lips met his eagerly. She set the computer screen out of her lap so she could wrap her arms around him. Sloane basked, happy in a deep way that had eluded him... for how long? All his life?

Somehow, eventually, the kiss dissolved. Sloane turned the screen to see what she'd been up to that put her in such a good mood. With a shock, he recognized the gray wasteland of the Templar tombs.

"I copied some video before I destroyed your connection to Thallian's spyware," she said. "It was only a matter of time before they traced the feed, so I scrambled it up pretty well. Thought you'd like to see this, though."

The camera faced a sealed tomb. A handful of men in black uniforms milled around, wandering in and out of frame, carrying things that weren't quite recognizable in the driving wind.

"Makes you homesick, doesn't it?" Raena teased.

"I never spent much time down on the planet," Sloane admitted.

She announced abruptly, "Here's the good part."

Without any more warning than that, half the rock face suddenly sheared off and came tumbling down. The feed hadn't included sound, so the avalanche unfolded in silence. The graininess of the recording made it seem like something that had occurred a long time ago, to people whom the years would have killed anyway.

"Would have been nice if you'd programmed in a focus," Raena said. "I'd like to confirm the fatalities. Two or three that I'm sure of." She pointed at an arm sticking out from beneath a boulder.

Sloane didn't know how to respond. He'd known she was a killer back in the day. For that matter, so was he. But this was more plea-sure than he'd seen her take in anything since she'd walked into his office and asked for a glass of water.

She shifted, too happy to sit still. "Oh, it gets interesting again here."

A man ran into the frame. He halted beside the loader, leaning over someone the camera couldn't see.

Something about the man echoed the wanted poster she'd been looking at when they first came to Brunzell. "Is that him?" Sloane asked.

"No. But alike enough to be related. And watch…"

The man put his arm around the other person and led him around the loader toward the camera. The wind-blown debris cleared enough to reveal the similarities between the man and boy.

"That's Thallian's big brother," Raena said, "and probably his nephew."

"Do you think *he* was there?" Sloane asked. "At the tomb when it came apart?"

"That would be too lucky." Raena rolled the screen up and pushed it between the supplement bottles on the nightstand. "If Thallian was under the rubble, they'd be more upset about the avalanche. If he were on the planet, they'd be hustling to assure him they're all right. No. He's holed up somewhere, sending his minions out into danger because he's too cowardly to go himself." She smiled grimly. "People just don't change that much, do they?"

✳ ✳ ✳

Head injuries weren't so quick to heal as damage from training. Revan wished again that Jonan had allowed him to bring the family doctor along on this jaunt. He had faith that Jain's hearing would return, but the computer could only give time frames and advice, not actual aid.

While Jain was on the mend, it made sense to give him the computer searches to run. Now that Revan knew they were looking for Raena Zacari—if she'd truly survived the fall of the Empire *and* the witch-hunts at the end of the War—it would be worth looking into any of her known accomplices. Perhaps one of them had rescued her.

It was a long shot, but the examination of the grave robbers' camp was turning up little else. The only thing Revan knew for sure was that after the grave robbers opened the tomb where Zacari had been imprisoned, they'd pulled up stakes and fled the planet. Had the little woman driven them away? Buried their bodies in another tomb? Or had she been what they sought all along?

Revan spelled out exactly what he wanted. Jain rolled his eyes; he was a teenager, after all. Of course, being a Thallian, he knew his duty. He agreed to see what he could find.

It didn't take too long. "Before the end of the War, Father captured Zacari aboard a tramp freighter called the *Bluesong*," Jain reported. "Its captain was Gavin Sloane, smuggler, drug runner, and more recently, quasi-legitimate dealer in Templar artifacts."

"That's interesting," Revan encouraged. "Where do you suppose those artifacts came from?" He looked through the viewscreen at the windswept gray planet outside. "Any word on where Sloane is now?"

"He seems to have dropped off the face of the galaxy a month ago," Jain said. "I'll keep looking."

"Good boy. Check to see if Zacari has any living family, too."

* * *

"We're almost ready to travel," Sloane told Ariel over the comm. "Where should we meet you?"

As expected, Ariel smiled, flattered to be asked. It lit her up and Sloane saw the mouthwatering beauty he'd fallen hard for years ago. With a couple of strokes, she sent him a brochure that opened on his screen to reveal pictures of casinos, swimming pools, indoor skiing, ocean sailing.

"Kai's a pleasure planet," she explained unnecessarily. "Weapons are banned."

That struck him as funny, coming from a former arms dealer.

"Safer for everyone," Ariel said over his laughter.

"All right. We'll get in touch when we make planetfall," Sloane said. "Give us two days' travel time."

"See you then."

Maybe this would be okay, Sloane thought as he signed out. If Ariel couldn't bring her guns, she'd be less apt to lose her temper and shoot anyone.

The place looked expensive, which might prove a problem if they stayed long. Sloane hoped the concierge could find a buyer for this hideout apartment to refill his accounts a little. And maybe Ariel could get most of the tab on Kai. She could certainly afford it.

Sloane went into the bedroom to tear Raena away from the other screen. She'd been obsessed with catching up on the galaxy now that she'd decided to live in it and was even teaching herself to speak Galactic Standard. Sloane couldn't get over the miracle Doc had wrought. Every day Raena looked healthier, strong like she used to be. Her appetite for him had improved, too.

She smiled up at him, blanking the computer screen before he could see what she'd been up to.

"Ariel's ready to meet us," he reported. "It's a pleasure planet that's outlawed guns."

"Where's the fun in that?" Raena teased as she got up to dress.

✳ ✳ ✳

Two days later, as they settled into life on the pleasure planet, Raena led Sloane into a beachside bar on the edge of Kai City. She kept her sunglasses on. The light on this desert planet hurt her eyes.

The caterwauling over the bar's sound system was meant to pass as music. Raena sang along, half under her breath, as she stared around the bar. The place was jammed with creatures who'd come in off the beach. There were so many different species in the bar that Sloane only recognized a fraction of them. He noted that he and Raena were the only humans. No one paid much attention to them after a few desultory glances.

Ariel would be easy to pick out here. So would Thallian's men, if they showed up.

Of course, Sloane told himself sharply, that was just paranoid. No way could Thallian trace them to Kai.

It had been so long since he'd taken any downtime that Sloane barely knew what to do with himself. He couldn't tell if anyone here was conducting business. Most of them watched a sail race on the monitors. The only money he saw changing hands seemed to be bets of some arcane nature. He couldn't begin to guess how to get in on the action.

He glanced at Raena. After an application of logic, he'd persuaded her to wear a blouse outside the hotel room. He still had not grown accustomed to the scars striping her back; they were guaranteed to attract notice on a resort planet where everyone was wealthy or young or could afford the pretense of both. While some people chose to go around topless or nearly so, traffic would stop if anyone got a look at Raena's back. That was the last thing she wanted.

She managed to find a flowing jacket, lightweight but opaque, to throw on over her loungewear. The turquoise color was a shock, since Sloane still expected to see Raena wearing black, but turquoise suited her better than the ill-fated gown he'd chosen. He paid the delivery robot without demur.

Sloane rubbed his eyes. He felt as if he'd spent altogether too much time lately watching her. He half-expected she would vanish as soon as he turned his head.

Her chin came up suddenly, startling Sloane. For a moment, he feared that Thallian had found them. He reached for the gun no longer strapped to his thigh.

A smile lit Raena's face: pure girlish joy. "Finally," she said.

A familiar figure stood in the doorway, eclipsing the bright beach outside. The years had carved away Ariel's softness, but the proud stance remained unchanged. Ariel Shaad still wore her blond hair in a braid and her stark white blouse partially unbuttoned. Her pearly gray trousers fit like a second skin. Sloane found it weird to see her unarmed.

Ariel lingered on the threshold. Sloane guessed, "She can't see us in the darkness," but Raena had already slipped out of the booth. Before he registered her disappearance, she appeared in the doorway, petite beside Ariel's gaunt height. They might be mother and daughter now, but could no longer pass for sisters, if they ever had.

Ariel recognized Raena immediately, unquestioningly, and clutched her in a hug.

Sloane found he had been holding his breath and sighed. An orange-furred waitress smiled at him as she sauntered by.

Sloane nodded back. "Bring us a bottle of your best green. For old times' sake."

Still in the doorway, Ariel leaned on Raena. Her shoulders convulsed like she was crying. Raena whispered to her and petted her back.

The green arrived. Sloane cracked the seal on the bottle and poured himself a tall glass.

Before he swallowed his first bitter mouthful, Ariel said, "I need some of that." Her voice sounded huskier than he remembered.

He poured her drink silently, without looking up. Things had ended badly between them: his fault, yeah, but she hadn't helped. Sloane didn't feel like apologizing. Listing his transgressions might take the rest of the day.

Raena slid into the booth beside Sloane and chose a glass from those on the table, the one that had been Sloane's. She lifted it silently.

"What are we drinking to?" Sloane asked.

Raena waited until their glasses joined hers to say, "Old times."

The glasses chimed prettily against each other. Ariel held her drink in both hands, turning her face down to it as if she would cry again.

Raena waited until Ariel had drunk as deeply as she wanted, then took the glass away and set it back on the table. The kiss Raena gave Ariel was definitely not sisterly. Sweet surprise warmed Ariel's hazel eyes before they slid closed. She returned the kiss.

Sloane shifted awkwardly, horrified and aroused at the same time. This was not the relationship he had envisioned between them. He knew that Ariel claimed Raena as a sister, even though she'd been bought from a slaver.

When the kiss continued, Ariel purred low in her throat. Sloane decided to make himself scarce.

As he slid out of the booth, Raena's hand snagged his wrist. She tugged, using an inexorable pressure that would be painful to fight. He didn't wait to see if she'd hurt him to prove her point. He gave in unwillingly, letting her haul him up behind her.

Raena placed his hand on Ariel's breast. Sloane squeezed, just to be friendly, and was about to escape when Raena turned to kiss his jaw. Ariel moved her attention to his lips. One or the other of them reached for the front of his trousers, applying a steady pressure that sent sparks up his spine.

"This is a public place," Sloane muttered.

Raena asked, "You have a reputation to uphold?"

"As a matter of fact..."

Ariel knocked back the rest of her drink and thumped the glass on the table. "Let's go, then. Bring the bottle."

Sloane's smile felt mean. "You know, Ms. Shaad, I really hate it when you order me around."

She relented with a shaky smile. "Sorry, Gavin. Old habits and all. Could we *please* get out of here?"

Raena drained her glass and turned it upside down on the table, looking at him expectantly.

"Fine." Sloane grabbed the bottle as he stood.

As they stepped out into the glare of the afternoon, Raena wrapped one arm around Ariel's waist and captured Sloane with her other hand. "No arguments," she said softly. "No blame. Mistakes were made; let's leave it at that."

No one protested.

Raena put a little bounce in her step.

After they strolled a short distance up the boardwalk, she asked Ariel, "How was your flight?"

"Fast. I've added a new drive to my racer. You'd like her, Gavin. She's built for speed." Ariel met his eyes over the top of Raena's head.

He tried a smile on her. She smiled back. Maybe this wouldn't be *so* bad.

Ariel's gaze returned to Raena as if magnetized. "What did you do to your hair? Looks like you lost a knife fight."

Raena shrugged. "Thought I might set a fashion."

Ariel rubbed her hand over Raena's head, which led to another round of kissing.

This time Sloane laughed. "Take it back to the room, you kids."

"You're coming with us," Raena told him.

"Wasn't planning on it. Looks like you need some time alone."

"Please, Gavin?" Raena asked, like she was normal. Like she was tame.

Ariel had sneaked around behind him and hugged his back. "Come on, Gavin," she purred into his ear. "Where's your sense of adventure?"

* * *

They shed their clothes without looking at one another. The women wrestled Sloane onto the bed, one on either side of him. Ariel held his face in her hands, kissing him with intensity that—while it didn't forgive him anything—was meant to remind him what he'd been missing. One of her long legs hooked over his hip.

Raena snuggled against his back. Her feathery hair tickled the nape of his neck.

Just as he was getting accustomed to that, Ariel pulled Raena up over Sloane into a kiss more enthusiastic than the one he'd been enjoying. The position suspended Raena's breasts in just the right position. He used enough of his teeth to ensure she'd hold still.

Someone's hand slipped between Ariel's hips and his own to grasp him hard enough to be just below the threshold of discomfort. He jumped. The kiss above him dissolved. Everyone leaned back to steady their breathing.

It was Raena's hand. Should've guessed that. And she hadn't let him go.

Ariel asked, "You want him first?"

Ariel's thumb—it had to be Ariel, he was mostly certain—kept a steady rhythm, up and down, the slightest range of motion. The pressure was constant, never hurried. Not being able to see whose hands held him spooked him.

Raena shrugged. "Why don't you go ahead? I've had him more recently."

"Hope he's showered since then."

Sloane complained, "You two talk too much."

Raena slid away as Ariel shoved him onto his back. She looked like she was feeling mean. Sloane reached for her, hoping to gentle her, slow her down.

Raena got to her first. With Ariel's braid wrapped in her fist, Raena drew Ariel's head back for a kiss. From the awkward angle of her throat, Sloane wasn't sure how Ariel could breathe. He hoped Raena knew what she was doing.

Apparently, she did. Sloane felt the fight go out of Ariel's body. She settled against him, slightly askew and thoroughly distracted.

Sloane shifted, aligning her better. Determined to be gentle, he pressed up into her. Her body opened for him, welcoming him with that familiar shudder. He was amazed at *how* familiar it felt. He had missed her so long that he couldn't remember the last time they fucked. He sort of wished she'd punish him for that.

* * *

Thallian seemed to wake up as the last cuff snapped around his ankle. At least, it felt like he opened his eyes. The sleep chamber was so dark he couldn't see a thing.

He tugged experimentally and felt metal bite around his wrists. The bonds had almost no give. His limbs were stretched to their full extensions so that, if he struggled, he would break his own skin. He thrashed anyway, until he smelled his blood on the air.

How had his assailant gotten through the family's security? Why, after they had him immobilized, did they abandon him? In the total darkness, the room echoed as if empty.

Something cold struck his chest. Wetness soaked his pajamas until they clung clammily against his skin. The liquid lashed out again, drenching him.

Fear threaded through him. "Eilif?" The tone of his voice embarrassed him.

"She's dead," an all-too-familiar voice replied. Raena Zacari struck a match. Twin flames sparkled in her black eyes. She hadn't changed, hadn't aged a day: still twenty years old and too thin for her tiny frame, with black hair hanging straight down her back.

A smile slipped across her face like a knife being eased from its sheath. Thallian felt his body respond to that smile. He shifted his hips to draw her attention.

She flicked the burning match at him. It tumbled through the air, arcing slowly above his sodden clothing. The fumes ignited with a whump that crushed him down against the bed. A rush of intense heat stole the air from his lungs. As his flesh began to burn, Thallian jerked awake.

Moon-colored light filled the sleeping room the way water would fill an aquarium. Eilif sighed gently at his side.

His reaction to the bondage hadn't been a dream. Uncomfortable, he looked down at his wife. She slept like a child on her stomach, one knee drawn up, her fist curled softly beside her cheek. In the fifteen years she had been his, Thallian watched the lines etch around her eyes, watched her body grow lean as it outlasted its youth. She was no longer the beautiful girl he'd taken for his own. Still, she was his. She was here.

His mind whispered, if only Raena had touched him before the flames woke him...

He shook the thought away. He crawled between Eilif's open knees, grasped her hands in his, and worked his way into her body.

Eilif woke, every fiber aquiver. Thallian rode her, using her counterthrusts to his advantage.

She managed to gasp, "My lord ..." before he released her hand to cover her mouth. He pinched her nose as well, allowing her to understand the consequences of breaking her silence.

Raena never spoke to him during sex. She merely gritted her teeth and set herself against him, taking pleasure unapologetically no matter how he used her.

Eilif began to panic as her brain starved for oxygen. Thallian released her at the last moment of consciousness, savoring the flavor of her terror. She was, in so many ways, Raena's inferior.

* * *

Raena woke Sloane by nipping his ear. He opened one eye enough to squint at her. She grinned wickedly. Sloane's heart jumped.

"It's nearly dawn," she said throatily. "Ariel and I are going out to run. Wanna come?"

He groaned and turned his face into the pillow. Raena rubbed her cheek against his neck. He felt her crawl off the mattress. When he turned to look, Ariel braided her hair in front of the mirror. Both women wore leggings and hand's-breadth bands to bind their breasts. They'd tied windscreen jackets around their hips.

Ready to go out, he realized. They'd never expected him to want to come along. Raena woke him merely as a formality, so he wouldn't wake alone and worry.

The light cast by Ariel's mirror struck Raena's back, highlighting her scars. She felt Sloane's gaze on her and turned to meet his eyes with a smile so fierce and sweet it made his heart stop.

Ariel joined her, slipped an arm around her sister's shoulders, and grinned at him, too. Her smile was more complicated. Then the women traded an amused look and stepped out into the hallway.

Sloane tossed in the too-big bed before he finally got up and poured himself a drink. The image of the two of them, arms around each other, backlit by the mirror, would not leave him alone.

* * *

By the time Ariel and Raena reached the beach, Sloane had already been forgotten. The horizon had lightened to mauve. The white curls of the breakers reflected the ambient light of the casinos up on the palisades overhead, but the beach itself sprawled out, dark enough to be featureless. Ariel pulled up, expecting Raena to halt, too. When she kept running past, Ariel called after her, "I can't run in the dark!"

"It's not that dark, is it?" Raena called, her voice moving farther away.

"It's too dark to be sure of my footing," Ariel answered.

"It'll be light soon," Raena promised. "Wait for me."

Ariel stormed back up the boardwalk to the bench beneath the final lamppost. She adjusted the knife sheath tucked into the waistband of her leggings and sighed. She wished she had her holdout pistol, but like all her other sidearms, it was safely locked on her ship. Carrying a weapon on Kai was punishable by death. Still, a girl couldn't be too careful. Ariel would have felt naked if she went anywhere completely unarmed, especially with Thallian lurking around the universe.

Then again, no one but Raena would be foolish enough to come down to the beach in this murky light. Ariel wondered how dark it had been in that tomb, if Raena wasn't afraid of blundering around now.

Her pity faltered as anger swept up over her again. It figured Raena would abandon her; Her sister was definitely trying to prove something, Ariel thought furiously. She ought to go back to Sloane's bed and give him something to wake up for. Let Raena come back when she got good and ready.

Her hand rose to touch her lips where Raena's wake-up kiss still lingered. Under the covers in the hotel room with Sloane's familiar snore on the far side of the mattress and Raena's small warm body pressed against hers, Ariel had a moment of the kind of happiness she hadn't known in a long time. Running on the beach at dawn seemed like a wonderfully romantic idea.

Instead, here she was, alone again.

The first sunlight gilded the clouds. Before Ariel worked herself into too dark a rage, Raena doubled back. She lengthened her strides until she practically flew across the damp sand. Her body looked like a top-flight machine, every element and system in tune. Her grin spoke of pure physical pleasure, the deepest enjoyment of freedom and movement.

Ariel tried to imagine what freedom must feel like for her sister. Raena seemed to have been frozen in time. Of course, only her appearance remained unchanged. The spirit inside had been caged for twenty years. Ariel remembered Raena's childhood nightmares, the shouting horrors that woke her with the sensation of being buried alive. How could Raena have survived the reality? Ariel shuddered, unable to envision it.

As the dawn began in earnest, Ariel stretched to warm up before she jogged down onto the beach. Raena pulled up, grinning. "Enough light for you now?"

"Some of us can't see in the dark," Ariel said, meaning to tease but getting the tone wrong.

"I'll remember." Raena seemed unfazed by Ariel's rebuke. "How far do you want to go?"

Ariel decided to let it go and answered the question. "Up to the arches?" That was a good couple of kilometers, about as far as Ariel could see in the dawn mist. Three stone arches, little more than fingers of rock offshore, pointed out to sea.

"You set the pace," Raena said. "I'll keep up."

They ran in silence. Ariel dodged the incoming waves, trying to keep her shoes dry, but barefoot Raena splashed happily through the water. She seemed childlike now, hardly the jaded teenager Ariel remembered. This Raena seemed excited by everything: the growing light, the incoming surf, the feeling of running…

Raena said, "It's beautiful here. Did you pick it or did Gavin?"

"I came here with my mother just after the Templars died, before the War ended. The city was smaller, less built-up then."

"I'm glad they left the beach alone," Raena said. "Race you to that rock."

You'll win, Ariel thought, but she dug in and sprinted with all her strength.

* * *

They reached the end of the beach. Ariel leaned over, hands on knees, to catch her breath. Raena stretched, twisting in a slow-motion dance. Her sister's joy in simply being alive made Ariel feel maternal. It was like something Ariel's kids would try to express, something they could only convey physically. She felt overcome with longing for them, a desperate wish to confirm that they all were safe. Better not to draw attention to them, though.

Bending back to look up the cliff face, Raena asked, "What do you think is up there?"

"A hotel pool," Ariel guessed. "That's the way this place is: an ostentatious pool overlooking the perfectly vacant ocean."

"Wanna find out?" Raena dusted her hands off, looking for a crevice into which she could hook her fingers. Lean arms knotted with muscle, she pulled herself upward until her pointed toes left the ground.

Ariel ached. There was a time when they were young that she would have attempted anything Raena did. She wouldn't have cared about wrecking her manicure or tearing up her fingers. Her muscles would have been in condition to climb a bare cliff without suffering for it later.

"Go on up," she encouraged. "I'll spot you from here."

"You want me to come back down?" Raena asked. She looked poised to jump, even though she'd already shimmied up twice Ariel's height.

"If you think you can make it to the top barehanded, I want to see you try." Ariel backed up another step so she could look up without craning her neck. Didn't want to get a cramp. "I can't wait to hear what they say when you creep up on them up there."

Raena concentrated, looking up no farther than her next handhold, never looking down. Her bare toes served mostly for balance when she reached upward. Her arms and shoulders did all the work. Ariel tensed just watching her.

Just then, Raena's fingers slipped. She swung by her left hand, both feet off the rock. Ariel felt time stop. If Raena fell from that height, Ariel couldn't break her fall without the chance that they'd both be seriously injured.

As Ariel watched, Raena strained upward and wedged her free hand into the cliff face. She didn't glance down to gauge Ariel's reaction.

Ariel shivered. Raena had clearly returned to fighting trim. Ariel wondered why that scared her so badly.

CHAPTER 7

The medical robot trundled backward and Jimi flexed his fingers. The healing left behind a twinge of pain, but Jimi was used to that. His bones were a map of injuries inflicted by his father. Each repair left a little more pain behind.

Even though he was only twelve, he knew he had to get away. This would be the time to do it, while Revan and Jain were gone, while his father was distracted by his latest obsession.

It would mean keeping out of the way of Uncle Merin, the family watchdog. Jimi didn't underestimate his danger, but in this chaotic time, avoiding Merin's notice should be easy enough. Merin preferred the boys who were warriors like himself. He had little use for the handful of boys who opted for mental over physical challenges.

Jimi hopped down from the examining table. *Choosing* to leave home was the easy part. Figuring out how to do it was the problem.

* * *

By the time Raena reached the top of the cliff, Ariel craved a drink. She summoned a taxi to bring her up to casino-level, which saved her the jog back down the beach. When she found the right hotel, Raena was waiting in a restaurant with lush vines concealing its Templar-stone walls. Electronic birds sang from hiding places near the ceiling.

Raena had pulled on her windbreaker to cover her back. She wasn't the most underdressed patron in the place, but she was by far the most awake. She'd tucked the lily from the table decoration over her ear. She grinned as Ariel slid into the booth beside her, both their backs to the wall.

Before she could lose her nerve, Ariel asked the question that was foremost on her mind, "What happened between you and Gavin?"

"Originally?" Raena asked.

Ariel fidgeted with the menu. "Yes."

"Didn't he tell you?"

Ariel shook her head. "You know how he can be. I've never known anyone less likely to give a straight answer. He said Coalition command sent him to get you. He said you were coming in."

So full of amusement that it bubbled over, Raena asked, "Did you believe that?"

"Were you?"

"That wasn't my plan. I was stranded on Nizarrh. Imperial troops were everywhere. You remember how it was. I knew I was running out of time. Then Gavin showed up, claiming he'd been sent to rescue me. I planned to ditch him as soon as he got me off-world. I expected to have to kill him."

Pitching her voice to be more lighthearted than she felt, Ariel asked, "How'd that lead to romance?"

Raena sipped her water and grinned at some private joke. "We got off Nizarrh all right. We were somewhere in the void when Gavin's ship started acting up. When he kicked us back to normal space, the *Arbiter* caught us. Thallian's men boarded Gavin's ship and recaptured me."

That was nothing like Ariel had imagined the story to be. Sloane's veiled admissions over the years had led her to envision something grander. "So when did you two have time to fall in love?"

Raena met her sister's eyes. "Who says we're in love?"

Ariel frowned, trying to sort it out. "Why did you give him your medallion then?" She noticed Raena was wearing it this morning.

"Well, there's more to the story, between my capture and the tomb."

Ariel signaled the waiter and ordered a bottle of xyshin. The saucer-eyed marsupial checked its chronometer, then thought the better of remarking on the early hour when Ariel placed a fifty-credit chit on the table.

Raena waited until the drinks arrived and she'd had a good swallow. "Gavin came after me with some half-considered plan about smuggling me off the *Arbiter*."

Ariel sucked down her own xyshin with a shiver.

Raena took Ariel's free hand and continued, "When Gavin appeared in my cell, it was a total surprise. I know he came after me simply out of pride, since he'd given me up without a fight, but that made me realize he was crazy enough to survive the War. I didn't know if you were still alive. I didn't know if your parents were alive. Who else knew me? I was afraid to vanish without a trace. So I gave Gavin the only thing I had, in hopes that someone, somewhere, would remember me."

"What did you do to him?"

Raena gave her a blank-faced look. Ariel had known her long enough to know such innocence wasn't an act; it was just Raena's expression of surprise.

"Gavin always believed that you witched him somehow so he'd never be able to forget you."

Raena filled their glasses again. "I know he thinks I did. I guess that's easier for him to believe than to believe that he imagined the whole grand romance. I asked him to remember me. That was all."

"And the message you left on the medallion?"

"There wasn't any message for Gavin." She pulled the medallion out from inside her top. "It still has the holo of my mother on it."

"So this great love…"

"We kissed twice. Once was goodbye before I gave myself up."

That was so entirely opposite of what she'd expected that Ariel was grateful for her own glass of xyshin.

"If we're going to drink heavily," Raena observed, "we'd better order breakfast."

*   *   *

The apartment on Brunzell was opulent despite its shades of beige and chocolate. Jain walked around the perimeter of its sitting room, trailing his fingers from leather to suede to fabric so soft he didn't have a name for it. It seemed a very long way from the spartan barracks he shared with his brothers.

Uncle Revan and the guards moved methodically around the apartment, checking for anything that might confirm the identities of the people who'd stayed in there. Jain knew he should help with the search, so he began opening the cupboards built into the sitting room's wall.

His first find was a bottle of Old Kentucky Home whiskey. The words didn't mean anything to Jain, but he guessed the nature of the contents. With a glance over his shoulder to confirm that no one was paying any attention to him, he slid the bottle into his satchel and cinched the top shut.

He continued poking around, hoping for some other contraband. Anything he brought home for the other boys would be vastly appreciated. They led such sheltered lives, eclipsed by their father's shadow.

His fingers brushed a wall panel that seemed no different than the others, but triggered a hidden door. When it slid open, a sheath of indigo silk hung inside. Without knowing why he did it, Jain held the fabric to his cheek. He caught a warm, wild scent that brought a flush to his cheeks.

He swallowed hard. "Uncle Revan?" he called. "I found something."

* * *

Ariel gave the server a businesslike smile as he slid a platter of raw shellfish onto the table. She noticed his attention linger over Raena and felt a hot flash of jealousy before reason reasserted itself. Of course he was more interested in Raena; she looked closer to his age. She had the crazy knife-shorn hair. The breast band she wore revealed the corona-shaped scar where she'd once taken a bullet for Thallian. Undoubtedly, the waiter had heard that she'd climbed up the cliff face from the beach, too. For someone lying low, Raena wasn't passing very well as an average tourist.

The boy, who sported an exuberant topiary of facial hair, offered Raena an appreciative nod, then backed off.

"How come we have a human server?" Raena wondered. "All the other waiters have been aliens."

"We don't call them aliens any more," Ariel said mildly. "Humans are a minority in the galaxy." She changed the subject to answer her sister's question. "The restaurant owners are probably just trying to make us comfortable. They hope we'll tip better if we see a friendly face. There's still a lot of anti-human prejudice in the universe."

"Go figure," Raena said dryly. She reached for her fork and snagged a bite of fish for breakfast. Ariel was amused that Raena didn't comment on the cuteness of the boy. Had it even registered?

They ate in companionable silence until Raena prompted, "Tell me about Gavin."

Ariel gulped down a chewy piece of tentacle and reached for her xyshin. She said, "When it came down to the wire—and I always knew it was going to, when I worked with Gavin; the man had the most incredibly bad luck—I always knew I could count on him. He was as good in a scrape as anyone I'd ever hung around. He always had our backs. I guess that's because he spent so much time watching his own."

"What happened between the two of you?"

"I started him on the Dart."

Raena shook her head slightly.

"It's a Templar drug. By coincidence, it mimics natural chemicals in the human brain. It helps you focus. You set your attention on something before you take it, and as long as the drug stays in your system, your whole life centers around the goal you've set. You're aware of other things; you find yourself doing whatever you have to do to get them out of your way so you can get back to your project. The Templars used it to focus on their trade objectives."

"I'm surprised we're similar enough to them that it works on human chemistry."

"That's the odd thing," Ariel said. "Turns out our chemistries were very similar inside their carapaces."

Raena slurped one runny sea creature off a half-shell and licked her lips. "What were you doing with it?"

"My mother introduced me to some sculptors from Devonine. She'd commissioned a piece for the villa. She liked this couple and decided one or the other of them would make me a good husband. They, on the other hand, were so focused on their art, they saw making nice with a moneyed girl as a business proposition. So they gave me the Dart and let me weld sculptural pieces and we had a great time. Our relationship was pretty much mutual. I hooked them up to some art collectors, friends of my dad's. I kept the Dart connections and went back to running arms. They went on to bigger sculptures and bigger sales. Everybody got what they wanted out of the deal, except my mother."

"And Gavin?"

Ariel cracked open a shell and fished out a succulent green piece of flesh. "We'd been together on and off for a couple of years, doing business or just…having sex." Ariel smiled at the memory. "When we weren't together, I spent a lot of time thinking about asking him to marry me."

Raena laughed. "What stopped you when you were together?"

"He'd say something stupid." Ariel shrugged. "Or I would. You've seen how he is with me. It's like he can't forgive me for having advantages he wasn't born with. He makes me work for every kind word. I always *believed* he loved me, in his way, but we weren't ever going to have peace. Sooner or later, he'd push and I wouldn't back down…"

"But you love him," Raena observed.

"Yeah." Ariel drained her drink, eyes closed against the truth. "I guess I still do."

"Ari . . ." Raena touched her cheek lightly, just a feather's brush. "Look. He loves you, in his confused, belligerent way."

"But he loves you more." The truth was sharp enough to cut.

"Did I ever have anything I didn't share with you?"

Nothing but Thallian, Ariel thought, but that wasn't true. She shivered so hard she knocked her water glass over. Raena picked up a napkin and helped mop up.

"I've shared everything because I've always loved you." In Raena's voice, it sounded like the most reasonable thing in the whole world. "So if I love Gavin enough to share him, and I love you enough to share you, does it matter who loves whom more?"

"It's breaking my heart."

Raena dropped her hand high on Ariel's thigh and squeezed. "Stop thinking with your heart."

Ariel forced herself to smile. "You think he's missing us yet?"

"I doubt he's awake yet, after the show we put on for him last night. But why should that stop us? Let's wake him up if we want to play."

Ariel turned the conversation serious once more. "I need to ask you one more thing before Gavin joins us."

"You want to know about Thallian."

Ariel shuddered. "Did you love him?"

"I thought so. But it was a survival instinct. I was completely at his mercy. Love was the only bargaining point I had, the only thing

I could give him that he couldn't coerce from anyone else. I think it saved my life, put him at my mercy somehow."

Ariel stared at her, seeing instead Thallian as he'd entered her cell on the *Arbiter*. "Do you still—"

Raena cut Ariel off. "All I have left is the memory of how I used my body to manipulate him."

Ariel wondered again what it must have been like for Raena imprisoned twenty years in darkness and solitude, knowing that Thallian would be waiting outside if she ever got out. Ariel considered whether anyone else would have survived the tomb, or if only Raena—with her ferocity and stubborness—could have pulled it off. Ariel rubbed her arms, chilled by the realization that there was much she didn't understand—or even know—about her little sister.

As if she'd followed Ariel's thoughts, Raena said, "I spent a long time asking what I'd done to deserve Thallian. You and I got into trouble when we were young, but it was never anything serious. Not really. If I killed people, I did it to protect us. I wasn't evil. I wasn't especially unhappy following you around. So why did Thallian find me? Why did he fall in love with me? Why did I deserve to be hunted by him?"

A pause stretched between them. Ariel wondered if Raena was expecting an answer, or if she would confess something. In twenty years of soul-searching, you could pillory yourself for every sin, real or imagined, that you had ever committed. Ariel didn't need that long to punish herself for mistakes she'd made in her life. One long sleepless night served her well enough.

But this wasn't about her. "Did you ever understand it?" Ariel asked gently.

Raena's smile was tight, as if her teeth were gritted behind it. Then she said, "Only recently. Doc helped me see it. The question is not why Thallian was in my life. It's why was I in his? The answer is that I'm the only person who can hunt him down."

"And do what?" Ariel asked.

"End him."

* * *

After lunch, Thallian called a family meeting. The boys stood at attention, all gray eyes downcast. In front of them, Merin and Aten—the last of Jonan's brothers at home—lounged. Aten's chair breathed for him now, a steady sighing that echoed in the briefing room.

Thallian paced. "I need some numbers," he said. "I need to know types and conditions of our stock of weapons."

"As you command," Eilif said.

"I need to know the number of staff we can expect to come to our aid should we be attacked."

Sound rippled around the room as the boys assimilated that request.

"Of course, Jonan," Merin said.

"And I need to know the capabilities of all the working craft at our disposal."

"Give me a crew of boys and that will be done," Aten agreed.

"Choose the ones you want," Jonan conceded. "The rest can aid Merin and their mother."

He was halfway across the room and headed out the door when Jamian called, "Father?"

Thallian spun on the boy, who did not meet his father's eyes.

"Have you had word from Jain?"

"He was injured," Thallian responded, lips curled into a grimace. "He's on the mend. He and Revan have not been recalled yet. They still have work to do."

Emboldened by the answer his brother had received, Jarad asked, "Are we at war, Father?"

"It won't be war," Thallian soothed. "But we need to be ready."

* * *

Sloane let the hot water pound on his head. Gallons of flowing water: such a luxury after a lifetime lived aboard ships or on space stations, where every drop was rationed and recycled. Water

temperature on shipboard was always too icy or practically scald-
ing, never as adjustable as one would like. He tried to remember
the last time he'd taken a vacation. On a planet. With real gravity
and an atmosphere that didn't burn his sinuses with chemicals.

The Dart had been in his system for such a long time, keeping him focused on finding Raena. He remembered jettisoning the
last of the drug before he fired Kavanaugh. Stupid, stupid: fighting
with someone like that who would've been glad to watch his back.
Maybe he could have even invited Kavanaugh along on this vacation. One more gun was never a bad thing. And the kid had always
seemed to have a thing for Ariel, a kind of puppy infatuation that
might have worked out okay here while they were hiding out, leaving more time for Gavin and Raena.

As if in response to that selfish train of thought, the women bustled into the shower room, peeling off their running gear as they
came. For a moment, Gavin considered chasing Ariel away, figuring
she'd already gotten her share of Raena's attention for the morning,
but once the water struck her flawless golden skin, it was too late.

Raena watched his perfectly normal physical reaction to two
naked, wet women with a hooded smile.

Sloane reached out and hauled her over for a kiss, pressing her back
against the wall. Between the tiles and his body, Raena found enough
leverage to climb up and hook her legs together in the small of his
back. As he entered her, she broke the kiss to reach for Ariel.

On fire with jealousy, Sloane pounded into Raena harder, trying
to win a smidgen of her attention back. Raena grinned into Ariel's
kiss and dug her nails into the nape of Sloane's neck. She didn't
open her eyes or make a sound.

It took Ariel's moan for Sloane to realize he had even less of
Raena's attention than he thought. Ariel quivered like she was going
to lose her balance at any moment. The sight, and the memory of

so many like it, triggered something in him. Hating himself, he could do nothing but surrender.

* * *

As Ariel skinned into her underwear, Sloane remarked, "Your family never formally adopted Raena, did they?"

She shrugged. "My mom did."

"After your dad's death?"

Ariel's eyes narrowed. "So?"

"So Raena had been missing for how long by then?" Sloane didn't give her time to answer. "What was the point of a posthumous adoption, Ariel? Why rewrite history?"

"We were raised as sisters. It should've been—"

He cut her off. "Is that really true? Or is that another revision?"

"Look," Ariel said, "anything we wanted, my parents gave us. Me *or* Raena. If we wanted clothes, we went shopping. If we wanted guns, we picked them out of the shop. When I got a jet-bike for my birthday, Raena got one, too."

"So she could keep up with you," Sloane pointed out. "What'd they give her for her birthday?"

"Nobody knows when it is."

"I know when it is," Sloane corrected. "I looked up her birth record. Your parents didn't bother."

Speechless, Ariel fastened her bra. Then she recovered enough to say, "We always just celebrated it with mine."

"I shouldn't have to explain this to you, Ariel. Your dad was a businessman. You understand what that means. He knew the value of an investment. If you buy a bodyguard, you see that person is well-fed, well-trained, and generally kept happy. Because when it all comes down, you want to know that bodyguard is going to take a bolt that's meant for you. An unhappy bodyguard is going to choose the wrong moment to duck."

She wriggled into a fresh pair of slacks and tied the sash before asking, "What are you getting at, Gavin?"

He pulled on his own pants. Let her wait.

Finally, unwilling to drop it, he continued, "I'm saying that Raena was bought and paid for. Healthy human children, especially girls, they never came cheap. I'll bet your dad didn't forget that. I'll bet he never let Raena forget it either."

"Suppose you're right," she snapped, not really conceding. "What's the point of bringing that up now?"

"It's just that I've been thinking. When you said you were sisters, that formed an image in my mind. And then I watch you together."

"The point?"

"I was wondering, back when you were kids, how all this got started. I wonder if Raena crawled into your bed, a slave doing what she could to please her mistress, or if you climbed into her bed—did she even have a bed of her own?—and she didn't dare say no to you."

Ariel didn't answer while she tied her sandal straps. Then she asked, "Why are you being cruel?"

Sloane pulled his shirt on and began to button it. "It's just that I lie awake thinking sometimes. And I wonder what the difference was between the relationship she had with you … and the one she had with Thallian."

Ariel snatched up her blouse and thrust her arms into it on her way out the door. Sloane watched the door slam behind her. Was that what he'd wanted all along, to chase her away?

Lounging in the shower room doorway, Raena asked, "Was it something she did? Or are you just feeling mean?"

Sloane stalked over to pour himself a drink. "How much did you hear?"

"All of it." Raena waited until he'd gulped the warm green, then took the glass from him and swallowed some herself.

"Why didn't you say something sooner?"

She gazed at him placidly. "It was all true, once."

"And it isn't anymore?"

She passed the drink back to him and watched him drain it. "It's changed for Ariel. Couldn't it have changed for me, too?"

"Has it?" he demanded.

"Yes." She took the empty glass from him and filled it from the bottle of water. "I love her, Gavin. I barely remember a time when I didn't."

She took the glass over to the bed and stretched out. Sloane grabbed the bottle of green and flung himself down in the armchair nearby.

Sipping her water, Raena asked, "Do you want her to give me up, Gavin? Go away and leave us alone?"

"I don't know. Not yet. I just want her to think about how she sees you."

"Have you thought about how she sees *us*? She will."

Raena watched him suck the green straight from the bottle. Sloane couldn't stand the scrutiny. "How does she see us?"

"You pulled me out of that tomb. I owe you my life, just like I depended on Thallian to protect me from the Empire. Just like keeping Ariel happy made my life as a slave bearable. You rescued me because you've obsessed over me for decades. What would you do if I didn't pay you back the way you expect me to?"

He thumped the bottle down on the table. It tipped over, spilling expensive liquor onto the carpet. Sloane ignored it, shoving his feet into his boots. "I don't have to listen to this," he growled.

"Neither did Ariel."

He stopped at the doorway, glaring back to where she sprawled on the bed, still naked. "You don't owe me a thing."

"Am I free to go?" Raena asked, not moving.

Rather than answer, Sloane slammed his fist down on the door lock and stormed out into the hallway.

Raena turned over onto her stomach on the oversized bed. She set her water glass on the alien-height nightstand. She reached the long way down to the floor to right the bottle of green. Then she got up and unrolled the computer screen.

*   *   *

The girl seemed too good to be real. Even through his excitement, Jimi realized that. But she was apparently an expert in antique single-person craft and wrote knowledgably about equipping them for short-range interplanetary trips. Jimi devoured her advice eagerly.

There weren't any pictures of her up on her site, which he recognized as a warning sign. Jimi had crawled the net enough to know that she might be a troll or an older woman, maybe a mom herself and not the girl she pretended to be at all. She might not even be human. Then again, he understood how girls had to be careful sometimes, particularly pretty girls. He'd heard on the newsfeed about human girls targeted by slavers after they'd uploaded pictures of themselves. All it took was a buyer and then no one was safe.

Her page played the catchiest of modern jingles, though. She participated in all the latest memes. Her answers intrigued him, especially the quiz about her alignment. She fancied herself a bad girl.

When the IM pinged on his computer, Jimi jumped. "You're creeping me out," it read.

"Who's that?" he sent back. His heart fluttered in his chest.

"You keep coming back to my node," she answered. "Least you could say hi."

Jimi sat back from the screen. How could she have traced him?

The silence stretched out. Jimi worried that she'd gone away, so he typed, "Hi."

"Hi back," she wrote. "The log has been full of you checking back over and over and reading all my updates. Are you looking for something in particular, a specific kind of craft? I might be able to help, if I knew what you wanted to know."

Jimi ignored the offer. His hands shook as he input, "Can you voice com?"

Another long pause fell. He cursed himself for panicking her. Then his computer speakers said, "Sure. Is this coming through okay?"

The voice made him jump again. She sounded exactly like he'd imagined, all business, her voice low and sweet. He wanted to hear more of it.

She obliged. "So, anyway, why are you lurking on my pages?"

"I want to get off this rock," he said, surprising himself with his honesty.

"How are my little essays on twenty-year-old personal craft gonna help you do that?" she asked.

"I might be able to piece an old hopper together," he hoped. "Everything else is too well-guarded."

"Can't you just shimmy down to the spaceport and pounce on the next cruise ship out?"

He laughed. "If anyone from my family went to the spaceport, it would be galaxy-wide news."

Another delay, then she said, "Sorry. Didn't realize you were anyone important."

Her mocking tone stung him. "Not that important," he said wearily. "That isolated."

She waited, but he didn't know what else to add. Desperate to keep her attention, he blurted, "What's your name? Your real name?"

"What's yours?"

He didn't have anything made up, so he told her, "I'm sending you a picture. I'll put it up on my page where you can find it. It's me, last summer, when I caught a sabershark." He made a couple of clicks and uploaded the picture.

"I'm Fiana," she said in response. "Here's a picture of me." She borrowed space on his site to put the picture up. It showed a slim black-haired girl astride an old-style jet-bike. She had on a black catsuit that hugged every curve, as slight as they were. She wore gargoyle goggles, complete with spikes around the smoked lenses. Below them, her mouth was a delicate warm pink.

"What color are your eyes?" he asked.

But she was gone, signed out of the web. While he lingered over her photo, it evaporated.

Jimi cursed. He hadn't thought to save it or print it or make any sort of copy. He'd just assumed she'd given him the image to keep.

Furious, he slammed out of the web himself.

CHAPTER 8

When Sloane returned to the hotel room, he intended only to collect his things and clear out. He was surprised to find Ariel asleep on the bed, stretched out like old times with nothing on but the sheet. Raena was curled up in the big armchair with the comp spread across her lap. He just about turned around and walked out, rather than face them again. Apologizing never crossed his mind. He'd had too much to drink to go backward.

Raena smiled and some of the fury melted out of him. "Finally," she said. "I'm hungry."

"What are you still doing here?" Sloane asked, not entirely ready to drop the argument. "You are free to go."

"I've known that all along." Raena stretched, gesturing over her head with one hand, then the other, fingers splayed. "I wanted to make it clear to you that I am here solely because I choose to be."

"All right then. Let's not fight."

"Okay." She said it as if it didn't matter to her one way or another.

The comp screen drew him like a magnet. He came over to see what she was looking at. "Shopping?" he asked hopefully.

"Sort of."

On the screen, a two-dimensional scan of a hologram showed a family group, all with black hair and silvery eyes. All, except the sole

117

woman: a slim, strong matriarch with green eyes and prematurely white hair streaming over her shoulders. Her face and body were eerily symmetrical, as if she'd been manufactured rather than born. Something in the shape of her oval face reminded Sloane of Raena.

Except for the obvious differences in maturity, the boys might have been a time-lapse series of the same child over and over, complete duplicates of each other. They all had the same long straight nose, the same strong sharp chin.

In the center of the group sat a man dressed in a black suit of some elaborate brocade. His carefully trimmed black beard was silvered by streaks trailing down from the corners of his mouth.

Sloane groaned. "Thallian has a family?"

"The boys are clones. I'm not certain how many of them there are." The corner of Raena's mouth quirked upward. "Some people grow their bodyguards in vats."

Sloane reached past her to shut the system down. "So he's raising a private army."

"It doesn't matter," Raena said. "I'll kill them all, if I have to."

"Unless they kill you first."

"I'm a ghost," she said, her voice hollow and empty enough to make him consider it. "I'm already dead. They can't do anything to me that hasn't already been done."

"Then leave it be." He grabbed her arm, fingers meeting around her wrist. "You're weak. You've been sick. They don't know you exist. Keep it that way."

He would have shaken her—wanted to, in fact—but she'd set herself and he couldn't budge her. That made her point more effectively than anything she might have said. Still, Sloane didn't want to accept that, didn't want to believe it, and most of all, didn't want to lose her again.

"You know there's nothing you can do to keep me here," she reminded him quietly. "You gave me permission to go. I'll go when I'm ready."

"I could drug you. Lock you up. Put a chip in your neck like a dog and follow you."

"You could," she agreed. "And you'd be no better than him." Her smile was icy. "You are better than Thallian, aren't you, Gavin?"

His fist clenched and he wanted nothing more in the world than to hit her, snap that smug smirk right off her face. She watched his eyes, not his hand, ready to take the blow and turn it against him. Something cold shot down his spine. He knew she would kill him if he stood in her way. He knew it as surely as if she'd planted the thought in his mind. More than he didn't want her to go, he didn't want to die to prevent her.

She watched the fight go out of him and stretched up to kiss his cheek. "I'm disappointed," she whispered. "I thought you were going to test me."

"Get out," Sloane said wearily. "I don't want to fight with you. You're going to do what you're going to do and there's nothing I can do to stop you, so just get out. I'm going to hammer myself into unconsciousness."

He watched her struggle with whether to stay and placate him. It occurred to him that Raena had been a slave or a prisoner for nearly thirty years. Little wonder she didn't know how to act when offered freedom.

"I'm serious," he said, sinking onto the corner of the bed. "Take Ariel, go out and have some fun. Buy yourself a party dress. All I want now is to be alone."

* * *

No one noticed she had come into the room. Eilif stayed near the door, in the shadows, holding as still as possible. Sometimes she just wanted to be near her sons, basking in their camaraderie, without acknowledging the distance that she felt when being called their mother.

The boys were channel surfing, paging one after another through the news feeds. Only Jamian knew what he was looking for, but the others jeered and argued as the channels zipped by. Their interests were so diverse that they seldom agreed on watching one show en masse. Usually, she found them huddled together in the same room, each curled over his individual screen.

"That's it," Jamian said and paged back a few stations.

The room on the screen looked like an abattoir. It had been a little featureless transient single-occupancy sleeper, all hard surfaces that could easily be hosed down. Now, crimson painted it in directional splatters, as if artery after artery had been opened. The newscaster chattered nervously about the smell that lingered in the room. He apologized that the body had been taken away before the news cameras had been allowed inside, but he assured that the station would obtain the autopsy images by 03 Galactic Standard Time.

Jamian paused the playback so the boys could feast their eyes.

"Uncle Revan wouldn't have made such a mess," one of the boys said in an awe-struck voice.

Eilif thought it was Jarad, but then he guessed, "It was Jain, wasn't it?" Jarad's voice held its familiar note of envy.

"It was Jain," Jamian agreed. "His first kill."

And then the room exploded in cheering and laughter, all of them talking at once, voice layering over voice until Eilif's head hurt and she had to slip away before they noticed her there.

* * *

Ariel hadn't smoked in years, but she missed it now. Maybe it was the atmosphere of the casino's game room, thick with various incenses and inhalant vapors. Maybe she just needed something to do with her nervous hands.

The dimly lit room flickered with the lights of gambling machines from dozens of peoples. Like Raena, many of the players wore shaded glasses, fine for facing the bright games but which caused them to bump into each other in the darkness. Although fights were rare, snarling was common. Ariel wasn't sure why Raena had chosen this place, except that its owners had left the cavernous Templar architecture more or less unchanged. There wasn't anything flat for Ariel to put her back against.

When they were kids, Ariel's friends wouldn't allow Raena to gamble with them. No one trusted her. They couldn't ever catch her cheating, but she could keep angles and numbers in her head well enough that she didn't bet without confidence in her superiority. It made it spooky to play against her.

Raena cruised past the gaming tables, but chose not to play against anyone directly. Like old times, she ended up at a pachinko machine, feeding in balls with mechanical precision. Somehow she had figured out the sound these particular machines made when nearing a payout. Twice she took chairs recently vacated by losers only to win in ten rounds or less.

Any time now, casino security would catch onto her and 86 them both.

"Relax," Raena counseled. "This is supposed to be fun."

"Gambling's only fun when there's a risk," Ariel argued.

"There is a risk. We could be booted out."

The current machine sang a happy song, then spat out streams of shiny metal bearings. These were the same color as the catsuit Raena had picked out earlier in the evening. She looked dipped in mercury, flashing with the reflected lights from the games. She might as well have been naked for all that the suit concealed, but the reflected glare made Ariel's eyes hurt when she stared at Raena's figure. With Gavin hogging their hotel room, Ariel wondered where they might go to be alone. Her racer wasn't really large enough for company. Maybe a room in a different hotel?

"I'm past this," Raena said, gathering up six plastic cups dangerously full of little silver balls. "Let's cash out and find something else to play."

They wandered a little, trying to locate the cashier's window. Ariel noticed the three apparently simian bruisers trailing them.

"Do they work for the casino?" she whispered to Raena.

Her sister didn't turn around. "Maybe. If so, they're there to make sure I don't get mugged on the way to cash out. They've got nothing on me."

She put the cups into the window and turned the permaglass so that it faced the cashier. A moment later, the window turned back toward her. On its shelf lay a gold chit.

"Are you looking for another game?" This morning's waiter— the boy with the topiary facial hair—cut smoothly between the security men and Raena, so that Ariel blocked him from their view.

"Yes," Raena said, plucking the flyer from his fingers without breaking her stride.

He kept moving on his original trajectory, so fluid that the security guards didn't even know there had been a conversation.

Glancing over the flyer, Raena asked Ariel, "Want a drink? It's on me."

She led the way to an alcove in the wall. Folded inside was an even more shadowy bar. Six video screens showed different views of a race taking place overhead in the Kai City towers. Pilots in jetpacks zoomed between the skyscrapers on some kind of treasure hunt. Raena slipped her chit into the robot waitress and requested two glasses of xyshin. "Just can't get enough of this stuff," she confided. "I was drinking it the night Gavin contacted me. He ever tell you about that?"

"Not in much detail."

"I thought he was another bounty hunter. Instead, I was only one of the errands he was running that night. The other stop we made was to visit a dealer called Outrider."

"No!" Ariel gasped. "The Messiah dealer?"

"Think about it," Raena encouraged. "It was probably galactic news. Government destabilization on Nizarrh, right about the time I was arrested?"

Ariel shook her head apologetically. "It's too far back. I'd have to research it."

Raena shrugged. It was hard for Ariel to decide if her sister actually cared. Raena continued her story, regardless. "One of the reasons Gavin was so hot to find me on the *Arbiter* afterward was that the soldiers who pistol-whipped him left him for dead in a broken bag of Messiah. They assumed that the drug was powdery and would float, that he'd inhale it and die. Instead, the gummy drug practically glued Gavin to the floor, but he didn't ingest any of it. So he had a score to settle, when he came after me."

Ariel laughed. "Here he got all high and mighty on me when I brought up the Dart. He didn't do drugs, never had any traffic with them, he said. Now to find out he'd been running Messiah…"

"Ask him about it," Raena urged. "I bet he thinks I don't remember."

A commotion drew their attention out toward the game room. The boy with the exuberant facial hair suddenly sailed across the casino floor. His feet touched a gaming table and launched him upward. He pegged a stone pillar, bounced off a bank of slot machines, caught a chandelier, and swung above the gaming floor. Behind him trailed a motley assortment of creatures, also bouncing from any surface that didn't move out of their way.

Raena tossed back her drink. "Here's my game," she said. She tucked her winning chit into an internal pocket in her catsuit and hurled herself after the leader. Ariel could only gape at the chaos unfolding in the wake of the passing game of tag. Gamblers sprawled on the floor, tripping up the security force. Drinks spilled on gaming machines, causing sparks and short-circuits and spewing acrid smoke into the cloudy air. Everyone was shouting or laughing or calling for help.

Ariel could have taken all the tag-players down with one little gun, but of course, even the security on Kai went unarmed. She wondered if that was what Raena had wanted to find out.

* * *

The comm chimed repeatedly, a trilling sequence of notes that hauled Sloane out of his determinedly sought oblivion. Rubbing the knife-point twinge in his forehead, he flailed at the connection to acknowledge the call. He expected he was being summoned to bail Ariel and Raena out of some kind of trouble, probably for inappropriate public affection.

Instead, Kavanaugh's craggy face filled the screen.

Sloane growled, "How did you find...?"

"Shut up, Gavin, and listen," Kavanaugh said sharply enough to make Sloane's hangover throb. "Lim was tortured to death."

Sloane rubbed his head, trying to force the hangover back into hiding. "Lim who?"

"He was my engineer when we worked for you," Kavanaugh snapped. "His death was nasty. All sorts of bits of him cut off or burned away. Somebody mean is looking for her."

Sloane sank to the edge of the mussed bed. Choking his heart back down into place, he said more calmly than he felt, "I know. I rigged up some of the old scanners on the planet. We checked the feed one night and saw a human crew searching the tombs for her. But before she left the planet, she set a booby trap. Killed some of them a week ago or so. After that, she scrambled feed. She was afraid they'd trace it back to us."

"Well, they've found another way to link you to the operation. Now they're hunting down the rest of us that worked for you."

He should have killed them himself, Sloane thought wearily. It would have been a mercy; at least he would have made it quick. From the beginning, his plan had been to gas the whole archeological crew in their sleep, then nuke the site from orbit. That was the sort of thinking the Dart encouraged in him. But once Raena appeared and he cleaned himself up, his plans got all scrambled. Instead of wiping out all traces of the operation, he left Kavanaugh to bribe the grave-robbing crew to keep their mouths shut, thinking: *This is what Ariel would have done.* Too bad money wouldn't comfort them under torture. Someone would talk, struggling unsuccessfully to save what was left of his own life. They wouldn't know what Sloane did, that there was no bargaining with Thallian.

Luckily, none of the crew knew where he'd gone, or so he'd thought. "How did you know where to reach me, Tarik?"

Wrinkles folded in around Kavanaugh's brown eyes, but his smile wasn't amused by Sloane's tone. "I'm on Ariel's payroll this week. I was expecting to find her now, 'cause I don't know what name you're traveling under. Turns out you're just the messenger boy."

"Great." Sloane looked around the trashed hotel room—bits of lingerie draped over everything. More importantly, he saw that the bottle of green was empty. "She's not here."

"I'd guessed that."

Sloane found one of Raena's bottles of water tucked between the bed and the chair. He flicked it open and took a long pull.

"Drinkin' water, Gavin?"

He shook the question off. "Are you hidden?"

"For the moment. And Doc is safe, too. She thanks you for asking."

Sloane chuckled, surprising himself. "Wish she was here to prescribe me something to kill this hangover."

"She'd just tell you to have another drink," Kavanaugh pointed out.

"Have to get dressed for that," Sloane groused. "Everything not water in the room is drained dry."

"If you're going out anyway, get yourself some of that Clear stuff we used to take back in the day. It works as well as anything. According to Doc's research, that is."

There was no way to dig his way out of all the bad history between them, so Sloane simply asked, "How'd you find out about Lim?"

"I'm not on vacation, Gavin. I been watching the galactic news, like everybody else."

"This made the news?"

"It was vicious, like stuff no one's seen since the War."

Sloane reached for the comm, then thought the better of it. Kavanaugh could have simply left a message for Ariel and refused to speak to Sloane at all. Sloane had sobered enough to appreciate the younger man's decency. "Thanks for the warning, Tarik."

Kavanaugh looked pleased. At heart, he was still the boy Sloane had rescued more than once. "Don't mention it," Kavanaugh said, but that wasn't what he meant at all.

* * *

Thallian had the boys scanning the galactic news hour by hour, watching the story of Jain's first kill unfold. Of course Revan was as cautious as Jain was reckless, so the murder scene had been stripped of anything that might identify the family before the body began to cool. Still, Thallian was shocked by how quickly the grave-robber's death had swelled to galactic news. Didn't people have more important things to think about?

Raena had surely seen the story by now. It would flush her out and make her run, just as bad news had done in the old days. Raena had never been one to cower in place, accepting her fate. Even at the end, she'd kept running, aiming for death if not for freedom.

He wondered how she liked her freedom now. It pained him physically that he hadn't glimpsed her since she'd left the tomb. The engineer's description of her had been garbled by pain or fear. He'd said she disabled his whole crew, killing none of them. That was so unlike the girl Thallian had trained that it had to be a lie. Or else Raena was so debilitated by her captivity that she was no longer a threat or much of a challenge. Thallian prayed that wasn't true.

The man Lim had said that her hair was still black, still long. He remembered her high-heeled boots. In the darkness of the tomb and with the speed of her attack, he claimed not to have gotten a very good look at the rest of her. Still, he swore he recognized her wanted poster. Of course, a man would agree to just about anything as a slow-burn laser removed his fingers.

Thallian ached to have something to do. All he needed was a direction and he'd be off after her. Failing that, he'd be happy to administer a good, well-deserved beating to someone. Unfortunately, all of the family was faithfully occupied with tasks he'd assigned. The servants toiled invisibly behind the family's ranks, out of Thallian's reach. In a room full of boys hunched over galactic news feeds, he felt cut off, alone.

Thallian found himself staring at his own reflection in a sleeping screen. What would she see when he found her again? Would she be disappointed by the silver in his beard, the crow's-feet around his eyes? He was still in fighting trim. He yearned to prove it to her.

* * *

Mykah was amazed by how well the human girl kept up. The lap through the casino to pick up players was the easy part, merely a matter of staying out of the grasp of the casino security goons. The next challenge was to gain some height by scrambling up the outside of the crumbling Templar edifices, then leaping across to the balconies of the newer chromed glass monstrosities that had sprouted like fungi on the corpse of the old city.

Since the new girl didn't know the game's destination, she couldn't pass Mykah up and get ahead. Instead, she shadowed him silently, never even seeming to breathe hard, which her reflective catsuit surely would have betrayed. Every time he glanced over his shoulder, she was there. Grinning.

Mykah wriggled through the open transom window on the thirty-second floor of the Vierdlak Tower. The girl jumped in after him, feet first. She landed in a crouch and glanced efficiently around the office before she stood. He realized that the heels on her boots were so high that she had been effectively doing everything on tiptoe.

"What are we here for?" she asked.

"They're playing a scavenger hunt out there with the jetpacks. We're going to collect some of the prizes they're after."

"And disrupt the game?"

"And fuck its corporate sponsors," he answered. "The game itself means nothing."

Mykah smiled as Coni, his blue-furred Haru girlfriend, crawled through the transom and dropped to the floor.

"What's your name?" Mykah asked the girl, distracting her as Coni opened the safe.

"Raena," she said. "What's yours?"

He told her.

"Are you really an evil genius who poses as a waiter?" Raena asked. Coni laughed behind him.

Flustered, Mykah said, "What about you? Looked like you were flirting with your mom this morning over breakfast."

Raena laughed, too. "That's my girlfriend."

"Got it," Coni warbled, handing over a packet wrapped in garish red liquid crystal paper. Mykah tucked it into the rucksack on his back.

"What's next?" Raena asked.

"Can you fly?" Coni chirped. She led the way through the office door, vaulted across the tops of a warren of cubicles, and leaped into a vacant conference room with a view of the desert beyond the city. She and Mykah pulled down the curtains and quickly attached them to struts leaning in the corner of the room.

"Zel dropped out when we made the last jump between the casinos. There's a pair of wings for her," Coni observed, nodding toward Raena, "but she doesn't have a harness."

Mykah said, "She's little enough. We can double up on my wings."

"That's okay," Raena promised, which Mykah thought was sweet. No one used the old-time slang any more. "I can hold the struts myself."

"That wind is going to rip them right out of your hands."

She grinned. "Wouldn't be any fun if it wasn't any challenge."

Mykah nodded, going for the silent, serious type. He could always catch her when she started to fall. Once he had his own wings sorted out, he helped Coni open the window. Coni paused on the ledge, then jumped, and flipped out her wings to slow her descent. Raena watched how she did it and stepped to the edge, looking out rather than down. She raised the wings, braced the ends of the struts crosswise against her chest where the wind would force them back into her rather that bending them out behind her back. She'd have a bruise in the morning for real.

She looked back over her shoulder. "See you in hell."

Then she was gone. Mykah hopped onto the edge, flung his wings out, and prepared to dive after her. Instead, she'd caught an updraft and soared past him. The wind ripped the laughter from her lips but not from her eyes.

* * *

Raena had left the game flyer behind on the little round bar table. The diffraction-printed flyer didn't give any details about the game itself, just posed a series of questions: Would you like to fly? Are you able keep up? Who can climb the highest and fall the fastest?

The whole concept sounded utterly terrifying to Ariel. She wondered if the darkness in her tomb had burned Raena's fears away. Maybe the solitude honed her somehow, too. She seemed fixated on getting herself strong enough and fast enough to take Thallian down.

Ariel had no doubt that Thallian would come after Raena. Ariel had always known men like him, petty aristos who counted their lovers as possessions and couldn't countenance rejection. Thallian would never, ever admit Raena did not belong to him. He'd keep coming after her until one of them killed the other.

Ariel remembered her only encounter with her sister's former commander. Ariel had been smuggling for Coalition Supply, delivering guns to Sune as the human population prepared to secede from the Empire. She didn't know the Coalition base had fallen, brought down by Thallian's "diplomacy," until she and the supply convoy arrived there.

Thallian's warship made short work of the unprepared convoy. The shockwave as the cargo ship exploded pitched Ariel against her controls. Fighting for consciousness, she magnetized her onboard computers as the *Arbiter* reeled her in. She never had a chance to escape. In the tractor beam, she couldn't even eject.

After their escape, Raena said Ariel could have popped the fighter's canopy and sucked vacuum. Race traitors had escaped Thallian that way before. To be honest, suicide hadn't occurred to Ariel.

Now that she understood what went on in Thallian's detention, she wouldn't make that mistake again.

She sipped her drink and remembered every second of her stint in the holding cell on Thallian's ship. The *Arbiter* it had been called, the bastard's sick joke. Thallian's idea of arbitration was to take everyone hostage, then torture them until they broke and told him what he expected to hear. If they died in custody? Unfortunate collateral damage.

When he strode into her cell, it felt like sand filled her lungs. She couldn't get any air.

"You are a race traitor and therefore sentenced to death," Thallian told her. "Since the eradication of the Sune base, you have no one useful left to betray. I am here to discover if you have any other uses."

Gasping for her life, Ariel toppled off the cell's bench and fell to the floor, fingers clawing uselessly at her throat.

Thallian kicked her hard in the ribs, knocking her onto her back. Coronas rayed around the too-bright lights as her consciousness flickered.

Thallian knelt beside her to unbutton her blouse. He stabbed a needle as long as his hand into her chest.

The respite was instantaneous. Ariel coughed and sputtered, choking on the air that rushed to fill her shriveled lungs. Thallian caressed her breast as the drug paralyzed her limbs. All the while, his gray eyes locked on Ariel's. When he smiled, he seemed to have too many teeth.

He lifted back her onto the cell's utilitarian bench. Ariel was so confused by being rescued from the brink of death that she didn't immediately register that he had continued to undress her until nothing impeded his pleasure. Ariel couldn't even close her eyes to the shame.

When he'd finished—and he used every trick he could to prolong her degradation—Ariel realized that Raena had come into her cell at some point. Thallian watched as recognition passed between them.

Expressionless again, Raena took Ariel's limp arm, turned it over, and gave her a second shot. Despite the hypersensitivity of her abraded flesh, Ariel didn't feel the needle go in. Then tears flooded Ariel's eyes, blurring her vision and spilling heedlessly into her hair.

"That will be all," Thallian said.

Ariel's hopes raised a fraction, but Raena simply left the cell. Her sister had been dismissed. She'd left Ariel on her own with the madman.

"Now," Thallian purred, "tell me how you know my aide." And Ariel, scared and aching, ashamed and desperate that he'd leave her alone, furious to have been abandoned by Raena, told him everything. More than Gavin would ever know.

Shaking the memories away, Ariel took a trembling sip of her xyshin. The liqueur was too sweet for her taste, the sort of thing teenaged Raena had adored. So many contradictions in her little sister twenty years later, like the joy she took in the mirrored catsuit, reflecting the world back upon itself and making herself invisible while burning like magnesium. Ariel couldn't reconcile that with the little teenager who always dressed in black, trying to erase herself, sink into the shadows, and never be seen again. If it hadn't been for Ariel, twenty years ago, Raena might have succeeded. The Empire would have worked the trick that Raena could not.

That Raena had forgiven her after the depths of Ariel's betrayal meant more than life itself. That Raena would arrange another prisoner's death, doctoring the records to make it appear that Ariel died in custody: that would have been harder to stomach if Ariel hadn't been so relieved to be rescued. Raena stole her a ship, got her the clearance codes, and then refused to come along. She intended to stay behind to cover Ariel's escape, as if anything could be hidden from Thallian. So Ariel bashed her sister on the head with a scanner case and took her hostage.

As soon as he knew they were gone, Thallian charged Raena with treason and put a bounty on her. He wanted her back, no expense spared.

That such a beast still breathed was blasphemous. Never in a million years would Ariel have asked Raena to face him again. And yet, what choice did she have?

Raena left the flyer behind as a warning. The time was coming. She would leave them soon.

If only, Ariel prayed, I could die before then. I cannot watch this happen. I cannot wait to hear if she survives him a third time. I cannot stand the suspense.

A reptilian figure slipped into the video lounge, his back to her, and quickly transacted some business. Ariel caught a whiff of something familiar. Before he could dodge away, she asked in a low voice, "Can I buy you a drink, friend? You have something there that interests me."

CHAPTER 9

Revan thought Jain would never settle down and go to sleep. The initial execution had worn him out, but now that its details dominated the galactic news, the boy was too excited to wind down.

Revan remembered back when Jonan had become galactic news. That had been the start of the bad times, before the Thallians lost nearly everything. Once they'd had a beautiful palazzo on the shores of the Shining Lake. The family had filled the rooms with music and science. There had been seventy of them, brothers and cousins and uncles. Then Jonan's part in the dissemination of the Templar plague came out, followed by the revelation of the family's part in replicating the disease: in well-rewarded service to the Empire, of course. The family had been reviled.

Disgraced, hunted, and eventually betrayed from within, only Jonan, Revan, Aten, and Merin remained. Four left of seventy, nine boys, and Dr. Poe working alone to make more.

Revan sat on his bunk, listening to Jain working out on the other side of the thin bulkhead.

In another world, Jain might have been Revan's own son. Or if Revan had been born into another family, on another world … which of course never could have happened. Revan was a product of cloning, just as Jain was. On another world, neither of them would ever have been cloned. They never would have been born.

He rubbed his eyes, aching for things that were gone, things he could never have. He wished he could sleep.

Eilif was a blessing, a spot of brightness in their exile. Of all the things he'd never possess, Revan coveted her the most. He knew he would never have the nerve to tell her of his feelings. He knew too well what Jonan would do to both of them—Eilif first—if he found out.

Still, it wasn't fair that Jonan would cast aside such a wife for this aide of his, crazy and dangerous though she might be. If it ever came within his power, Revan would help Eilif find her way to a better life.

The thought itself was so painful that Revan fastened the alligator clip to his other nipple and flipped the switch to the generator's timer.

* * *

Kai City turned out to be larger than Sloane realized, full of too many dark nooks that a pair of amorous "sisters" might crawl off into after they'd been expelled from their bed. Sloane forced himself to stay focused and avoid the temptations of this planet's version of Patpong Road, even though the touts promised shows that would grow hair on his palms or turn him orange.

As he searched, he decided not to pass along Kavanaugh's message. If the girls didn't know Thallian was looking for them, Sloane would have more room to maneuver. Besides, Ariel's choice of Kai was inspired. Thallian wanted Raena alive and as unharmed as possible. Without access to energy or projectile weapons, Thallian's people would have to come after her in person. It would be a whole lot easier for Sloane and the girls to fight off what they could see.

Nearing the end of his patience for the search, he wished they'd all decided to wear communicators when they'd been together in the hotel room. Just before dawn, he finally found Ariel in the video lounge of the Shiapan casino. She was rolling her own herbs, a dish of crushed-out butts before her. Raena was probably off powdering her nose.

Before he slid into the chair opposite, he cornered the waitress and ordered another round. Best to come bearing gifts.

"New dress?" he asked.

Ariel looked up at him blearily as she accepted the drink. "Are we back on civil terms?"

He nodded. "Would another apology do anything but annoy you?"

She sparked the spliff, considered his question, and shrugged, blowing smoke away from him. "I can't remember ever hearing an apology. So if you want me to leave, I'm just about done with this planet."

"*I* don't want you to go," Sloane said quickly. He was relieved to discover he couldn't send her off alone to face the kind of death that took Lim.

His words warmed the Ice Queen façade and won him a smile. "Yeah, it's a new dress," Ariel answered finally. "I like the way it feels when I walk. The slit would look better with a P368 on a thigh holster though."

"What wouldn't?" Sloane agreed amiably. He looked around the video lounge, trying to calculate the direction of the restroom. How long would Raena be?

Ariel was sobering up now that she had the spliff mostly burned down. "She's not here," she said, hurt in a way that choked her. "She took off with a kid about half my age hours ago. I've seen them on the video disrupting the jetpack race, but even that's been a while."

"She's what?"

"She's gone. She's training. She's finding the physical challenges that we haven't been giving her and she's testing her strength." Ariel crushed out the butt and began rolling another smoke.

"And you just let her go?" Sloane asked, trying to make sense of it.

"Raena's not going to leave you tonight," Ariel said, like he was being stupid. "This thing tonight is just a game to her. She wants to see if she's ready."

Sloane shook his head, rejecting the idea. It was time to enlist Ariel in the plan he'd formulated as he'd searched for them. "I need your help," he confided. "I want to hear Raena moan."

Ariel gazed at him, eyebrows raised.

Sloane decided to clarify. "I want to drive her wild. I want her to lose all control. Apparently, I can't do it without your help."

Ariel laughed at him, then laughed harder at his expression. When she finally caught her breath, she pointed out, "Raena could very easily kill us, if she loses control. She's stronger than both of us put together."

Sloane crossed his arms on his chest. "Aren't you willing to dare it?"

"It's never bothered me," she said. "Raena's always been like that."

The words slipped out before Sloane thought to censor them. "Bet she wasn't with Thallian."

Ariel scowled. "You're an idiot, Gavin. I bet she was exactly as silent with him. I bet it drove him just as crazy as it does you. I'd bet that's why she's so badly scarred. I think he couldn't stand that she could exhaust him and not make a sound, so he beat her bloody hoping to get a response. If you want to go that far, don't ask for my help."

"I'm not talking about hurting her!" Sloane snarled.

"No," Ariel said, her voice low as a threat, "you're talking about making her do something she doesn't want to do. If Thallian couldn't make her lose her self-control... But that's what it's all about, isn't it? You think if you love her long enough and hard enough, if you break her down, she'll stay."

Sloane glared back at her. "How can you possibly be jealous of *Raena?*"

"How can *you* possibly be jealous of Thallian?" Ariel shot back. "Raena cannot love you any differently than she does. Isn't it enough?"

"No," Sloane said coldly. "It's not enough to stop her from leaving."

"She's leaving because of us, you sparkwit."

Sloane's thoughts leapt to all sorts of conclusions. Eventually he just asked, "What do you mean?"

"It's the same reason she kept running from him before. He will kill whoever is in his path to her. You may be jealous, Gavin, but Thallian has murdered hundreds of humans, maybe thousands, as well as the whole species of Templars. He doesn't care about anything other than himself. And Raena. When he finds her, he'll find us. She will die to protect us, but she's afraid that won't be enough."

"I thought…"

Ariel nodded. "She's not going back because she loves him. She's going because she hates him."

"We can't let her go."

Ariel laughed again, the same brittle sound as before. "I don't know how we can stop her. But I don't see why we can't give her a night to remember us by before she goes."

"You know her so well, how do you recommend we do that?"

"With Raena, if you find something she likes, don't stop. Especially if you think you're hurting her. Don't stop."

* * *

Jimi found Fiana's instructions clear and easy to follow. The little hopper he'd chosen for his escape was built for short-distance jaunts—say, from planetside to a moon and back—which meant it should handle space and atmospheric re-entry without a fuss. Working from Fiana's specs and Uncle Aten's stash of spare parts, Jimi was able to reconfigure the fuel lines and upgrade the engine.

It would be cramped inside the hopper's little cockpit for a longer trip: no amenities, for sure. But thanks to a stranger he met on the interweb, he had a chance to escape his home and his family.

Except that security was tighter than Jimi had ever known it. Their father had tensed to the breaking point, seeking only a reason to snap. Jimi recognized he'd be killed as a traitor if anyone discovered what he was doing. He definitely didn't trust any of them to cover his tracks. Desperate, he hoped that someone else would screw up in some way and provide a distraction, so he could fly.

Until then, he kept his flight bag packed in preparation. He didn't have much he wanted to remember from this place, but there were games and some music that he treasured and would hate to have to replace. Mostly, he took things that he hoped could easily be translated into money, even if they were antiques.

He hid the bag separately from the hopper, so it wouldn't arouse suspicion. For that same reason, he didn't allow himself to check on his stuff once it was hidden. He'd just have to trust that he'd hear about it if someone found the bag before he fled. He was fairly certain nothing inside it could identify him. It belonged to a boy. Which one would be a matter of speculation.

Jimi wished again that he had a print of that picture of Fiana. It would have been nice to have a token of his guardian angel. And some way to thank her.

* * *

Gavin was toweling his shower-wet hair when he returned to the bedroom. The large lump moving under the covers giggled. The unexpected sound knocked the wind from him. He'd been so focused on Raena—how to distract her and how to control her—that he'd missed the obvious. Maybe keeping her was as simple as making her life fun.

He wondered how much fun she'd had in her years before Thallian took her in hand. Ariel definitely recognized fun and surely could have afforded it, but had Raena been allowed to choose their diversions? Or had she tagged along faithfully because that was her job and would keep her owners happy?

He sat in the chair by the bed and listened to the girls whispering and laughing under the blanket. It made him sad that they were so oblivious, even though keeping the news from them had been his choice. Somewhere in the galaxy, Thallian's family was hunting down and torturing anyone who might have had a connection through Sloane to Raena. He wondered how long he could keep her hidden on Kai, how long he could keep her safe.

Today, he vowed, they would get out of the hotel room and have fun. When they'd sucked up all the fun that Kai had to offer, they'd find another pleasure planet and begin again. If Raena had to stay in hiding, Sloane vowed that she wouldn't ever again sink to the depths she'd struggled through on Nizarrh. There had to be a way to keep her hidden in style.

* * *

Fun was good in theory, but of course Sloane hadn't gone so far as to outline the particulars. Raena wasn't content to be a spectator. She wanted to try the indoor five-diamond slope, the desert rafting, the ocean surfing, the high-rise climbing. She wanted to go everywhere, see everything, and do anything. She devoured Kai like a ripe fruit, letting the juice drain down her chin. Her exuberance pushed Gavin and Ariel, with bodies twenty years her senior, to their limits.

It was only a matter of time until one of them hurt themselves. Afterward, Ariel wondered if maybe Raena had been testing them, trying to send them a message. They were old now. They couldn't keep up. They would be liabilities when she faced Thallian. It was necessary she leave them behind.

Or maybe Ariel gave her sister too much credit for empathy.

Dark tag seemed to be the most innocuous of the potential diversions. They strapped themselves into flimsy plastic armor that covered their torsos. Fishbowl helmets provided 360-degree night vision, as well as minimal protection for their heads. Once they were garbed, they were released into a dark, cavernous room inside an enormous mirrored maze.

The goal was to avoid the "monsters" already in the maze and other teams of players armed with light pistols. The light-sensitive armor would hold an image any time a beam of light struck it. Depending on the color the armor turned, blows were either glancing or "mortal."

Raena crept ahead, putting her back against the wall at each corner before she peeled around. Her caution seemed exaggerated, until someone popped around a corner they'd already passed and shot Sloane in the back. Five minutes into the game, he was disqualified. It had taken longer to put his armor on.

After that, Ariel paid more attention. She took point and let Raena watch their backs. The farther they wound into the maze, the more creatures leapt at them. Ariel quickly ran down the charge in her light pistol.

"Now what do we do?" she muttered.

"Cheat," Raena suggested. She pointed up at the top of the maze walls. "Help me up."

Ariel cupped her hands together into a stirrup and boosted Raena. The little woman chinned herself up on the edge of the wall, swung her legs over, and stretched down to haul Ariel after her. Her arms felt like cabled steel.

Ariel struggled to get a seat on the slim edge of the wall. Her life had been relatively active and she considered herself in good shape, but when faced with the paper-thin walls ahead of them, she wasn't sure she could do this.

Raena stood up and offered her hand. Ariel took it and crept gingerly to her feet. The wall felt like a knife's edge under her shoes, but of course Raena stood poised on a pair of outlandishly high heels.

To take her mind off of the potential for gravity to assert itself in the least convenient way, Ariel said, "Lead on. You've got the functional gun."

Rather than slide along the top of the wall, Raena turned a silent cartwheel and then started off at a jog.

Ariel followed more slowly, desperate to keep Raena in sight in the huge, dark room. That meant she was watching her sister and not her feet when the wall turned. Ariel didn't.

The fall was only two meters, but the narrow hallway didn't allow Ariel to get her feet down first to take the shock. She landed hard on her right arm, aggravating the old injury from her first gun-running trip with Gavin during the War. She heard the bone break again. Familiar molten pain gushed down into her fingers and raced up toward her heart. Battle training won out, though. Ariel didn't make a sound.

When Raena didn't come back for her, Ariel got into a crouch with her back against the wall and pushed herself to her feet. Cradling the broken arm against her chest, she limped back in the direction of the entrance.

✳ ✳ ✳

"Wow. Have you seen this?" The message rose on Jaden's computer followed by a pointer. He trailed its lead to a video of the most amazing aerial stunts. A tiny woman in a shimmering mirrored jumpsuit turned lazy rolls and dropped into heart-stopping suicide dives between the towers of some anonymous Templar skyscrapers. They looked like the spires of a termite mound.

Jaden watched the loop three times in succession before he passed it on to Jarad, seated next to him. Eventually, from the rapt curl of shoulders bending toward screens, Jaden was sure all his brothers were watching the little acrobat do her tricks. She looked as if she had been born to fly. He wondered if she was a teacher, if she could be induced to come to them and give them the sky.

It was only a matter of time before Jamian passed the link on to Jain, stationed far away with their Uncle Revan. Jain, more than any of them, probably needed a momentary escape from duty.

Not one of the boys stopped to wonder where the link had come from in the first place.

*   *   *

While Raena continued the game of dark tag, the maze employees insisted on sending Ariel to the hospital. Gavin came along to keep her company as the doctors worked. He didn't voice his impatience, but his constant jittering made it clear that he felt like *one* of them should be keeping an eye on Raena.

To their surprise, she lay sprawled across the hotel bed when they returned, fiddling around with the computer.

"I'm glad you're back," Raena said, getting up to give Sloane a hug. "I'm out of water," she said, pouting playfully.

"I'm on it," Gavin said happily, obviously relieved to find her still around. He kissed her good and hard, then went off on his errand.

Raena returned to sit in front of the screen. "Feeling better?" she asked.

Ariel nodded, flexing her fingers. "Good as new, at least until the next time I drop onto this arm. How'd you do in the game?"

"I took them all out." Her sister shrugged. "It wasn't any fun once you guys were gone."

Ariel crossed the room to plant a kiss on the fuzzy top of Raena's head. "That's the nicest thing anyone's said to me all day."

"That's because you've been hanging around with Gavin all day," Raena teased.

Ariel couldn't respond. Raena's screen displayed a scatter of images of Thallian and his sons.

"Sit down," Raena ordered, taking Ariel by her good elbow and guiding her back to the chair by the bed.

Ariel's whole body trembled so much that she was grateful for Raena's steady hand on her arm. "You've found him?" Ariel gasped.

"Not yet," Raena said, very calmly. "I'm narrowing my search."

"What are all those pictures?"

"For kids who all look alike, his sons have quite an album on their family channel." Raena popped up from the arm of the chair to pour some of Gavin's whiskey into a pair of glasses.

Ariel took hers, but held it without raising it to her lips. "How did you get through their security so easily?"

"I spent a lot of time with him. I know how he thinks. Unsurprisingly, he's trained his clones to think in just the same ways. The rest of the galaxy may have forgotten the keywords, but I knew exactly what to look for. I've had nothing else to think about for twenty years."

Ariel was so shocked that the words burst out before she'd really thought them through. "You're not using Thallian's kids against him?"

Raena gazed at her, giving her time.

"They're children," Ariel pleaded.

"So was I," Raena reminded. "I was eleven when your dad bought me, fourteen when Thallian took me away. Tender years never protected me from the galaxy."

Ariel stared at Raena, trying to absorb the justification. Words entirely failed her. She'd known Raena longer than anyone had, but this inability to make her point even considered felt like she confronted a stranger. Ariel didn't want to believe her sister could be so cold.

"Thallian will have trained his sons to die for him," Raena predicted, "just like he trained me. He won't spare them out of some gauzy idea of the value of childhood."

"You're not him," Ariel pointed out.

"Yet," Raena agreed. And smiled.

"No. I don't accept that."

Raena went back to the screen and began closing things down.

"Don't do your scary bullshit to me," Ariel said more harshly.

Raena nodded and turned back around to face her sister. "All right, Ari. You don't deserve it. But you know me much better than Gavin. Do you think that there is anything in the galaxy you can say to stop what we both know is going to happen?"

"No," Ariel admitted.

"Then let's hope I find Jonan before he finds me. Let's hope his kids have the sense to keep out of our way."

Ariel gulped the whiskey until the glass was empty.

* * *

"Uncle Revan," Jain said hesitantly into the hall comm outside Revan's door. The old man had been in his cabin an uncharacteristically long while. Probably Revan had doped himself to sleep, which seemed to be the only way he could unwind. Jain was familiar enough with his father's moods to think twice before rousing another of the Thallian old guard, but he was even more certain he'd face a beating if he didn't pass on the information as soon as he could.

"What is it, Jain?" Revan asked, deep voice as steady as ever.

"There's a video the boys sent me," Jain reported. "A news loop of a sporting event that got disrupted by pranksters. I think you should see it."

Revan's silence was not encouraging.

"I'm pretty sure it's the girl we're looking for."

Just when Jain was going to offer to send the link in, Revan's cabin door opened. "Where did it come from?"

Guessing at the video's provenance, Jain said, "Father has the boys scanning the news."

"No. Where was it shot?"

Jain realized he didn't know. "Come see it," he asked, covering his tracks. There were times when he could hide behind his sheltered upbringing. "I was hoping you could identify it."

Revan stepped backward out of the doorway, allowing the boy into his cabin. The generator leads and alligator clips still lay out on the desk. Jain recognized them, but kept his face impassive. He leaned over the monitor, typed in the string, and brought up the video of the girl in flight.

"She's young," he said apologetically, "but the engineer Lim said the Templar stone kept everything sealed inside it incorrupt."

When the short video ran its course, Revan said, "Again."

Jain reached forward and made it play once more. He'd already watched the loop a dozen times, each time growing in certainty that this was their quarry. Now he watched his uncle's face rather than the monitor. Revan's attention was riveted.

Revan said, "That Templar architecture in the background is fairly distinctive. We're looking for a pleasure planet somewhere that's populous enough that she could travel there anonymously. The city lies between a desert and the ocean. Start looking for vacation resorts that fit those criteria. If you can identify one with a recent jetpack race, that will lead us to her."

Jain nodded sharply and went to do as he was told. As he left the cabin, he heard Revan reach out and start the video again. He wondered if his uncle took any joy in the girl's aerobatics or, for that matter, any joy in her sleek, muscular form. All his life, Jain had known Revan as an ascetic, forbidden by family doctrine to mate. Would the old man take some pleasure from the girl once she was their prisoner? Would he at least turn his back and allow Jain to? What was the point of hunting down girls who would wear garments like the mirrored jumpsuit if you didn't put them to use afterward?

Jain hoped his uncle would forgive him a momentary detour, just long enough to get his mind back on business. Surely Revan had been young once, too. Jain ducked into his own cabin but didn't turn on the light.

* * *

Sloane got the girls dressed up and out to dinner. Seeing as it was the only meal they would eat in this stretch of daylight, he didn't see why they shouldn't splurge. He took them to Fire.

Despite the pyrotechnics put on by the tableside chefs, Ariel seemed preoccupied. Sloane wondered if she'd checked in with Kavanaugh or flicked on the news, but Raena was in high spirits to the point of silliness. She was totally taken with having her food set aflame before her eyes.

Sloane decided to just relish Raena's enjoyment and let Ariel join in when she felt up to the task. When she didn't bring up the slaughter, Sloane wondered if maybe it was just the hours or the drinking catching up to Ariel. She wasn't as young as she used to be. He'd probably read too much into Ariel's funk.

When Raena suggested a sunset walk on the beach, that seemed like the perfect way to pass the time until they could all go back to bed.

* * *

On the comm, Revan looked haggard, his gray pallor emphasizing the redness of his eyes. "We're closing in on her," he reported.

The boys burst into cheers, which elicited a smile from their uncle on the screen.

"How close?" Jonan demanded.

Revan sent over the video of the girl in the mercury-colored jumpsuit, soaring between the Templar skyscrapers on cobbled-together wings. "Jain recognized her from the video Jamian sent him," Revan said over the pictures. "We've identified the buildings as Kai City."

"How long ago was she there?" Jonan insisted, leaning toward the screen as if to shake the answer out of his brother.

"Yesterday. She and some other pranksters disrupted a sky race in Kai City." Revan's voice held notes of pride and relief.

"Was she bound by law?" Jonan asked.

"Not yet. In fact, several sports organizations are trying to contact her to offer her contracts."

Eilif watched her husband study the video as it looped again on the screen. She knew he'd always loved the other woman and that he'd only married Eilif as a poor substitute. She knew him well enough to see the longing vibrate through his body. Soon he'd have his true love back in his grasp.

Eilif shied from following the thought to its logical conclusion. She'd always known her days at Jonan's side were numbered. Still, she had nowhere else to go. So she would welcome her replacement with a smile, then find somewhere quiet to hide until they forgot all about her.

One of the boys shifted at the edge of her vision. Eilif looked from Jonan to her oldest son. For the person who'd discovered the evidence his father sought so single-mindedly, Jamian didn't look proud of himself. In fact, his mouth had tightened to a grim line as he turned to the other boys. His question repeated several times, whispered from one boy to the next, before Eilif could make it out: *Where had the video come from?*

* * *

Sloane watched Raena walking ahead of them, a silhouette against the deepening burgundy of the sunset. Ariel understood something of the pain he was feeling to have found Raena after so long and know he couldn't hold her. Nothing could stand between Raena and her fate.

This was the moment to change the subject, Ariel decided. "I missed you," she said.

Sloane's head jerked toward her. "You did?"

She thought his surprise was genuine. She smiled a little sadly. "Didn't you know I was crazy about you?"

"You could've said so."

"I did say so," she reminded.

"Not lately."

Tired of the tone of complaint in his voice, Ariel's temper flared. "Gavin, you shot me. Or don't you remember? You hijacked my cargo. You killed Ximena and Harat. I knew it was the Dart. I knew it was my fault you were on it. But I couldn't forgive that kind of betrayal in a friend, let alone from the man I loved."

His stride faltered. "I hear that right?"

Ariel kept moving. It was easier than meeting his eyes. "What'd you think you heard, old man?"

"Something about love." Sloane matched her stride again.

Ariel found she couldn't answer. To speak was to have her heart broken. Again. How could she tell him that she'd never loved anyone as much as she loved him? So much time had passed. They were no longer young. Anyone could see he preferred Raena.

But Sloane wasn't a man to let it go, now or in the past. "If you loved me, why did you leave me alone my whole life?"

"You weren't alone. How many times were you married, Gavin? You've got kids somewhere, your corporation, and your Dart connections. Looked to me that you had no room in your life for an arms dealer with a heart of gold. And anyway, you shot me. How could I ever turn my back on you again?"

"But here you are," he pointed out.

Too quickly, she said, "Because of Raena."

Sloane caught Ariel's arm and drew her toward him. Their lips met, then their bodies. She fought her desperation, kept her arms from clinging to him. When Sloane finally stepped away, he left her breathless and aroused.

"That wasn't for Raena," he said.

"No," she agreed, "that was for you."

The last of the light drained from the sky. From this angle, the palisade of cliffs hid the lights of the casinos. The beach was very dark suddenly. The sea sounded very close.

Sloane pulled a hand lamp from his pocket and shone it around them. Faint light reflected up into his face. The worry there was painful for Ariel to see.

She spared him from calling out by doing it herself. "Raena?"

"Here," her sister answered.

Sloane flashed the torch beam in that direction. Raena was closer than she had been before darkness fell. She perched on a large rock, knees drawn up to her chest. Ariel wondered if she'd been listening to them, or if she'd been staring off into the future.

Sloane hurried over to the rock and began to climb it. He'd thought Raena was gone, Ariel realized, vanished with the light. And the panic he felt was only a fraction of what he'd feel when Raena really disappeared.

Despite the steamy breath of the night on her skin, Ariel shivered. As Sloane left her standing in the darkness to take the light to Raena—who probably could see better in the dark without it—Ariel had another realization.

Raena wouldn't say goodbye to either of them. She'd just vanish, gone to confront Thallian. She intended to leave Ariel behind to console Sloane. Raena knew everything Thallian had done in Ariel's cell. She knew Ariel could barely face the memory, let alone the man himself. Ariel was meant to prevent Sloane from rushing after Raena and plunging headlong to torture and death.

Ariel watched Sloane scramble up the rock face. He slammed his knee against an outcropping, but paused only momentarily. He had to reach Raena, had to touch her to reassure himself.

There wasn't anything Ariel could do to stop Gavin from confronting Thallian. She could only go along to watch Sloane's back.

She imagined how badly the gun would shake in her hand.

"Come up," Sloane invited, gesturing with the lamp.

Ariel shook her head. "I think I'll go back to the room. I'm a little chilled, all of a sudden."

Raena said, "Let me warm you."

Ariel tossed her head back as she laughed. "Wake me when you come in."

"Promise," Sloane answered.

Ariel turned away before the first tear spilled down her cheek.

CHAPTER 10

Sloane waited until Ariel passed beyond the edge of his light. He saw the orange flare of her igniter as she lit another spliff. "Is she okay?" he asked.

"No." Raena hugged her knees tighter to her chest. "You're breaking her heart."

"I can't help if I love you," Sloane said defensively.

"Ariel can't help loving you," Raena answered softly. "Life is cruel."

"Do you want to go after her?"

"It wouldn't help," Raena said. "She's deciding whether she will die for you if she needs to."

Sloane stared at the motionless girl beside him. Raena seemed faintly luminous in the diffuse light of his lamp. She gazed inscrutably back at him. Exasperated, Sloane asked, "What are you talking about?"

"Ariel is deciding if she'll come with you when you go to your death at Thallian's hands."

Rather than ask if that was something she foresaw for sure, Sloane demanded, "Will she die?"

"If that matters to you," Raena answered, "you ought to consider waiting for me here."

"Have you seen her die?" Sloane insisted.

"No," she admitted. Before Sloane could relax, Raena continued, "She will wish she was dead. She barely survived him the last time."

"Then don't you go." Sloane grabbed Raena's wrist and yanked her off-balance against him, so he'd know he had her full attention. "If you don't leave me, I won't have to come after you. And Thallian won't hurt Ariel. It's all up to you."

That bittersweet half-smile slipped onto Raena's face as she deftly twisted her wrist free from his grasp. The motion was so quick he wasn't sure how she'd done it. Then she laid her cheek against his shoulder. "Thallian is already looking for me. I'd rather go meet him on my own terms."

She moved her fingers over Sloane's lips. "Don't tell me to run," she said. "I've wasted enough of my life running from that man. If you'd let me die on Brunzell, I might have averted some of what will happen. The longer I wait to go, the more dangerous Thallian will be."

"If we're all going to die," Sloane snarled, "what difference does it make?"

"No one said we're all going to die," Raena corrected. "And we're alive tonight. Why not enjoy it?" She hugged him abruptly, then went slithering over the edge of the rock, somehow finding handholds in the darkness.

"Where are you going?" Sloane asked, shining the light around until he found her down on the sand, peeling her shirt up over her head.

"Swimming!"

"Is it safe?"

"Is anything?" She unwound the skirt from around her legs and dropped it on the sand. Sloane saw she was wearing a knife sheath on her thigh and nothing else. Raena gazed up at him, black eyes shining and fists on her bare hips. "Come on," she said. "I bet the sea is warm."

He clipped the hand lamp back onto his belt and crept down the rock after her. Finding toeholds in the darkness was a matter of faith, of putting his foot down and hoping to touch something that would support his weight. Sweat slicked his body, clammy under his shirt, when he felt the sand under his boots again.

When he turned to look for her, Raena swarmed up over him, pushing him back against the rock face as she climbed his body. She caught his lower lip between her teeth. Sloane ran his hands down her back, marveling again over the ridges of her scars.

"You can swim, can't you?" she breathed into his ear.

"Yes."

"Good." She unwrapped her legs from around his waist and slid down the length of his body until her feet found the ground. Her fingers raced his to the closures on his shirt. She gave up, letting him undress himself as she covered his chest with small nips, never enough to be painful but enough to remind him she had teeth. As if he could ever forget that.

She helped him slide his trousers down and knelt at his feet to pull off his boots. She placed them precisely one beside the other on a rock ledge, then sat back on her heels, hands caught together behind her so that her back arched and her breasts pushed forward. Tipping her head up to meet his eyes, she grinned and asked, "What is your bidding?"

"Don't play with me," he growled, teasing her back.

"Can't help it. Everyone is so serious these days."

A gentle swell of water materialized around her as the tide came in. The foam clung to her legs and hips, bubbling in the scattered light from the hand torch. She broke the pose to do a walkover backward into the froth. "Come on, Gavin. I can't remember the last time I swam in an ocean."

He waded out after her, wondering what lived in Kai's ocean. Was it nocturnal? Was it hungry? Ahead of him, Raena was waist-deep and moving away. She leaned forward into the water and pulled hard with her arms. The torchlight caught a glint of something in her hand. Sloane fought to stand still against the nudge of the surf, waiting to see it again. There it was: she'd drawn her knife and was carrying it in her hand.

He could go back to the hotel room, he realized. Ariel would be grateful if he did. Even as he thought it, he bent into the water and kicked off. This was undoubtedly another test. If he wouldn't follow Raena here, she'd know he wouldn't follow her to meet Thallian. Swimming in an unfamiliar pitch-black ocean was probably the safer of the two options. He just wished she'd brought him a knife, too.

He kept his eyes on her small black head, which bobbed a surprisingly far distance out, and stroked through the water toward her. On his lips, the water had a metallic tang like iced steel. Around him the temperature was pleasant, maybe even a little too warm for comfort.

Something large and white appeared on the water ahead of him. Sloane thought it was a reflection of the moon, but when he paused to tread water and look up, nothing glowed in the sky. A second glow rose up from below, followed by another, and another. They floated up from a frighteningly long way down.

Raena startled him when she suddenly burst up out of the water at his side. Sloane lost his rhythm, then panicked as he started to sink. The glowing creatures were all around them now, undulating menacingly. If Raena hadn't sunk her fingertips into his biceps and held him at the water's surface, he might have given in to fear. Even now, he wanted to clutch her.

She rotated him back toward shore. The still-burning torch stared unblinking in the darkness.

"What are we going to do?" Sloane didn't like the shiver in his voice.

"Once they come to the surface, they seem to stay," Raena observed. "They must be feeding on something. If we swim down, we can slip past underneath them."

"Down?" Sloane echoed.

"Well, seeing as I can't fly without a building to leap from, our only other choice is to stay here and wait to see if they develop a taste for humans."

"How did I let you talk me into this?" he groaned.

"Was there talking involved?" she asked. "I thought you just followed the first naked woman you saw."

He gaped at her, wondering how much she meant to hurt him with that. Raena gazed back, seemingly just as relaxed as if they were bantering in some surfside bar.

He'd put his life in her hands, expecting nothing more than a quick swim in the ocean, then a roll on the beach. A little gratitude for everything he'd done for her, everything he'd given up for her, his whole life thrown away hunting her, and for what? So she could go back to the monster she'd served before the War ended, the one who taught her to kill without remorse, to take pleasure in causing pain and fear.

She handed him a fabric strap with a silver buckle. "We're going to have to stick together," she said. "If you swim too deep or jog left when I go right, you'll be on your own. I don't have anyway to find you down there."

Numbly, he took the buckle in his hand. She had the strap's other end wrapped around her fist. He realized it was her knife's sheath. He thought about asking her for the knife as well, but decided just as quickly that he'd feel safer if she kept it. If anything attacked them, the one with the knife would have to fight it off while the other one fled. Ashamed of himself, he held his tongue.

She continued to calmly give him orders. "I don't want to tire myself out with pulling you," she said, "so I'll let you set the pace.

Let me steer. I'm much more used to darkness than you are. Those animals give off enough light that I can see."

Gavin nodded, still too close to panic to speak.

"Deep breath," she encouraged. "We won't go far on the first dive."

She watched until he was ready, then turned a fluid arc and plunged into the water. It was tricky to find a rhythm that didn't pull the holster strap out of her hand. They floundered a little before Raena set out strongly, pulling him along despite what she'd said. They hadn't gone too far when they found their pace. Gavin realized she needed to swim two strokes for every one he took. Still, she kept going, not straining. Just as he began to worry about running out of air, she touched the heel of his palm with her forefinger and tapped him to indicate "up."

They might survive this, he thought hopefully. And hopefully he'd have the strength left when they reached the shore to demand the mercy fuck she had better be saving for him.

* * *

Eilif confronted Jamian in the corridor as he headed to bed. "You have to tell him," she said.

Jamian stared at her, guilty as only a teenaged boy could be. Then he regained control of himself. He was a Thallian, after all. In a cold voice he asked, "Tell him what, Mother?"

"I heard you questioning the other boys."

Merin had stopped just beyond the dim security light behind Jamian's back. He wasn't the brother Eilif would have chosen to talk to first. Jonan sometimes let his affection for the boys color his judgment, but Merin never allowed anything to distract him.

"The video is a trap," Eilif said before Jamian could argue.

"How do you know?" Merin asked.

Jamian spun, obviously frightened. He managed to reassert his control again, but Eilif was sure Merin hadn't missed the lapse either.

"The boys didn't find the video on the news," Eilif said. She was guessing now, but it was more important to protect her sons than herself, since she would shortly be irrelevant. "Someone sent them the link."

"You were coming to tell me this?" Merin asked the boy.

"Yes, sir." He hadn't been, but he made the lie sound enthusiastic.

"Which boy got it first?"

"They're going over the logs, but we think it was Jaden. He and Jarad are trying to trace it back now."

"Let's go tell Jonan," Merin commanded. "Not that he will recall Revan and Jain, but we can at least make certain they know they are expected."

* * *

The mercy fuck on the beach wasn't all that Sloane hoped. Raena wasn't feeling mean any longer. She was simply compliant and silent, busy thinking about something that didn't include Sloane.

He dragged things out, hoping to get her attention. Sloane wondered if she was thinking about Thallian, but didn't dare ask because he feared the answer he might get.

Eventually, she came back to him enough to get him off. Then she got up, businesslike, brushed the sand off and retrieved her clothing from the rock. If she'd taken any pleasure in their coupling, he couldn't tell. That the whole transaction meant so little to her broke Sloane's heart.

He followed her back to the hotel room because he didn't know what else to do. Ariel was already pretending to be asleep, so when Raena quietly crept into bed beside her, Sloane lay down on the edge, as far away from them as he could get.

* * *

The room was cavernous, so enormous that Sloane found it difficult to believe it was enclosed, except that the blackness was absolute. He stamped his foot to check the echoes. The dead air around him swallowed the sound made by his bare foot. Where were his boots? Where was he?

Raena's tomb. The realization poured ice through him. He'd never stepped inside, never even returned to the planet once she'd been found. But this utter isolation was just as she described it. It felt like being trapped in the void of space after the stars had burned out.

As he puzzled over the whys and wherefores of his imprisonment, the grinding of stone on stone shattered the silence. His hand dropped to the top of his thigh only to find it naked as well. His gun, his clothes: everything was gone.

In the complete darkness, he didn't know if he was hidden behind something—if there was anything to hide behind—or if he stood in the middle of the room entirely exposed.

Measured footsteps crossed the stone floor toward him. He was tempted to drop to the floor, curl up into the smallest possible ball, and make himself invisible. But part of him knew who belonged to those boots and Sloane would be damned if he'd cower in front of him.

Something slammed into his stomach. Excruciating pain followed, radiating out from the blow. It crawled over his flesh like a thousand insects, gnawing into him. He groaned, staggered, but kept his feet.

Another punch landed against his back. Either Thallian had moved around him or there were two of them. The pain intensified exponentially. Sloane felt his resolve slipping.

The third blow hit him slightly off-center just below the collarbone.

Then Raena was kissing him, strong hands at the back of his neck, directing his mouth to meet her lips. Her naked body pressed hard into his. It didn't take the pain away, but it transformed it. He clutched her waist and began to fuck her as hard and deeply as he could.

"Is he awake?" Ariel asked, horrified. What was she doing in the cave, Sloane wondered. She couldn't be working with Thallian, too.

"Not really," Raena answered, which didn't make sense to him. Was she reading his mind? Answering his thoughts?

"Don't you mind that he…?" Ariel asked, vastly creeped out by the situation.

He felt Raena's shrug. "Gavin," she said with exaggerated sweetness, "wake up. It was a nightmare. It's over now."

He grasped the ends of the dream, the fear and anger and pain and shame and lust, but that was leaching away now. His hips moved slower, in consequence. Raena slid against him, almost regretfully, enough to make him open his eyes.

Ariel had turned on the light and was staring at the two of them. Raena smiled at him, amused and not at all offended. Gavin shuddered and dragged himself off of her. "Somebody get me a drink," he begged.

Ariel turned her back on him to take care of it.

"You didn't have to stop," Raena said gently.

"Yes, I did," Gavin replied. He huddled at the edge of the bed, taking the glass gratefully when Ariel delivered it. She wouldn't meet his eyes, for which he was glad. He drank a healthy belt of the whiskey and wished he could wash the memory away.

"It's hours 'til morning," Ariel pointed out.

"Go back to sleep," Gavin said. "I'm sorry. I—"

"It was a nightmare," Raena repeated. Gavin couldn't shake the certainty that she knew he'd been dreaming about Thallian, about being beaten by Thallian. Still, she lay down on the mattress again and snuggled back into Ariel's arms. With the blanket tucked up under her chin, she looked for all the world like a contented cat.

Gavin remembered how hot she'd been as he'd been fucking her. Was that in the dream or had that been real? She was so wet and ready, so receptive and eager… Did she know he was being tortured in the dream, that she was helping Thallian abuse him? Had he moaned in his sleep? Had his arousal woken her?

He sucked down another mouthful of whiskey, then got up to turn off the light. At least the girls should be able to sleep. Anyway, he wanted to be closer to the bottle.

*   *   *

A planet with no weapons: what a perfect place for a killer to hide. Revan stood at the hatch of his transport, staring out into the morning bustle of the passageways at the spaceport. Somewhere in this city of millions, Raena Zacari was hiding. Or perhaps she was not even trying to hide. Maybe she was busy enjoying herself. Flying playfully with makeshift wings and disrupting games that others were betting on, filming, beaming across the galaxy on news feeds. She was here, taking full advantage of the pleasure planet, safe within a society that would not allow her hunters to bring their tools.

Revan turned away from the busy port to watch the men racking their sidearms in a locker by the door. "Bring the nets," he told them, "and the sleep canisters. No edged weapons. If we draw blood, planetary security will crash down on us. We don't have time to sort that out." Besides, while it wouldn't have been Revan's preference, Jonan wanted her as undamaged as possible.

Revan strode down the internal corridor to check the cramped cell built into the transport's small cargo hold. Bunk, restraints: what more would Zacari need? The room smelled searingly of disinfectant. Revan debated with himself, then switched on the air exchangers. While he might prefer to punish her for all the trouble they'd gone to, all the time they'd spent away from home searching for her, he couldn't afford to have her complain to Jonan about the treatment she'd received.

"Uncle Revan," Jain called from the exterior hatch, "we're ready."

Revan nodded. Let this go well, he prayed, and be done quickly. He ached for home.

*   *   *

Raena insisted on a large breakfast. She led Ariel and Gavin back to the restaurant at the top of the cliff, overlooking the ocean. Her friend, the boy with the excessive facial hair, was working again this morning. Ariel watched them exchange nothing more than nods. Had they slept together the night they'd spent chasing around the city? Raena would surely tell her if she asked. Ariel wondered why she wanted to know. Was she looking for evidence that Raena had cheated on them? What difference would it make?

"Heard anything from your kids?" Gavin asked, in what felt to Ariel like the galaxy's most awkward segue. Like she wanted now to be reminded that Raena's boyfriend was young enough to be one of her brood.

Seeing no way to dodge the question, Ariel answered, "No. They know to contact me only if there's an emergency. They're hidden, at least as well as they can be."

"How many children do you have?" Raena asked, tearing off a hunk of injera and wrapping it around a handful of meat.

It felt odd that they hadn't had this conversation sooner. "Fifteen," Ariel said. "The oldest is 27…28 this year."

"I haven't been gone that long," Raena scoffed. "You've been busy."

"They were orphans," Ariel corrected. "War orphans. I found them after the purges were done and took them in. Bought them out of slavery when I needed to. My family could afford it, certainly owed it to the galaxy. I figured there was no sense in having a lot of infuriated children growing up, hating everything that wasn't human in the galaxy, and looking to take revenge. I did what I could to give them other futures."

Raena didn't respond, preoccupied with some thought that Ariel couldn't guess. Ariel turned the question around to Gavin and asked, "Heard from any of your kids?"

He snorted, but didn't look up from the mound of food on the communal plate. "If any of them knew where I was, they'd turn me in. Who can blame them? None of them have spoken to me in years."

"I've never gonna breed," Raena vowed. "Can you imagine an army of little me's?"

Ariel knew what she was thinking of and choked on a mushroom.

* * *

After breakfast, Ariel proposed a walk through the old market quarter. Sloane should have known that eventually he would get dragged along on a shopping excursion.

He trailed along after the girls. He half-expected Raena to shoplift, just to prove to herself she could still get away with it, but she kept her hands clasped demurely behind her back.

* * *

Revan launched the attack while the trio shopped in the souk. High walls lined the narrow streets of the market, making the area like a canyon. He stationed men on both outlets with Jain in the middle. It should have been textbook.

One minute Sloane and the two women were eyeing exotic fruits stacked under silver-shot canopies. The next, a soldier dressed in nondescript black livery had grasped the blond's arm and tried dragging her away. She lost a precious moment fumbling for the gun that no longer hung at her thigh.

Sloane turned after her, right into another assailant's fist. Sloane staggered into a wall and slid to the dirt.

Raena Zacari spun into her own attacker's grip on her arm and brought the heel of her free hand up hard under his chin. Still turning, she pulled him off balance and used his body to take the blow aimed at her by his accomplice.

Revan would have bet money she would run as soon as the first assault failed. Instead, she dropped the man with the busted jaw and leapt onto the next man. In a movement as economical as poetry, she had broken his arm and several of his ribs, then vaulted over him as he dropped so she could come to the aid of the grave-robber Sloane.

Sloane's attacker didn't even know the girl was coming. Jumping onto his back like a fury, she twisted his head sharply enough to snap his spine, then turned to deal with the man dragging the blond woman away. Less than a minute had passed, and already three of his soldiers were down. Only one was dead, which was a problem. Revan could leave no one behind who might identify the family. He returned his macroscope to its pocket and began climbing down the ladder to the street.

* * *

Jain lurked in the shadows of the market with the net, waiting for their quarry to be alone long enough that he could fling it onto her.

Instead, she was too fast. She moved from one man to the next efficiently, dropping one with a scorpion kick and the next with a roundhouse punch. Her small stature made her tricky for the larger men to grab. The high-heeled boots she wore proved lethal. Most unnerving of all, she laughed through the whole attack, as if it was the most fun she'd had in years.

Time stopped. Her gaze found Jain in the shadows. Her insectile black sunglasses locked on him. And she smiled.

"He's just a boy!" the blond woman screamed. Raena Zacari stalked toward Jain, sleek as a big cat in her ridiculous parrot blue beach dress. Clearly, she hoped to spook Jain into running, just so she could give chase.

"Come on," Jain told her or meant to. His voice made no sound that he heard.

Then a smoking canister dropped at her feet. Others rained down around her. Jain remembered to reach down and pull his mask up from under his chin.

The girl leaned into a sprint. Uncle Revan bulled after her. They came at Jain so fast he couldn't do anything more than raise the net. His back wedged painfully into the corner of the wall.

Zacari wound her fists in the sparking net and yanked hard. She hauled it out of Jain's surprised fingers and whirled, catching Revan upside the head with it. One of her hands snapped out backwards, slapping Jain back against the wall. Then her attention focused on Revan, tangled in the arcing net, as the boy blinked away stars.

She tugged on the edge of the net and sent Revan to the dirt. Then she turned a cartwheel after him and brought the toe of her boot down hard on his throat. Revan didn't get up. She snatched the mask off his face and held it over her own nose. For the first time in the fight, Jain thought she seemed to be breathing hard.

Bending down, she scooped up one of the sleep canisters with her spare hand. Then her head came up, sunglasses fixed again on Jain. This time he did run.

They'd left the jet-bikes parked on a rooftop in the next street. If he could just get there, he could get back to the ship and retrieve the weapons. This could be salvaged. He could still capture her.

Sirens blared through the souk. A mechanical voice boomed, "This is Kai City Security. We have noted an altercation. All parties, stand down. All parties, stand down."

People, frozen in place to watch the fight, now panicked and began to flee. Jain ran with them. He didn't look over his shoulder to see Zacari taking down the first of the security drones with a well-aimed sleep grenade.

* * *

Hunched over the jet-bike's handlebars, Jain wove between the buildings. Even at speeds that tore tears from his eyes, he had too much time to think. Over and over he remembered how the girl had stomped down on Uncle Revan's throat. Jain had no doubt his uncle was dead, but he couldn't understand how that happened. *Just one little woman against eight of his father's handpicked men.*

He recognized some of her movements as she'd worked through the soldiers. His father had clearly trained her. That should have made her easier to defeat—especially for Revan—because they should have known what she was going to do. They'd simply been unprepared to see her do it so fast.

Jain couldn't believe his uncle was dead. It made no sense. Revan had been around Jain's whole life, a calm implacable presence when his father was volatile and dangerous. Jain had respected Revan with an affection he'd never voiced. He felt hollowed by the loss.

A flicker of movement in his rearview mirror caught his attention. He glanced over his shoulder to see Zacari on a jet-bike behind him. This time she wasn't smiling. She'd stretched out over the bike, urging more speed from it. They were too far apart for Jain to hear her voice, but her lips said, "Watch out!"

He glanced ahead just in time to see a Templar spire coming up fast. He wrenched his bike left. He nearly lost control of it, going into a spiral that almost sent him into another spire. He eased off the throttle a little, aglow with adrenaline, and fought the bike for control.

He had to get back to the *Raptor*. If he got there first and slipped through the security in record time, he could get a stun rifle. He could take her off the bike. As long as she didn't break her neck in the fall, he'd be okay. Once she was stunned, he could carry her onto the *Raptor*, get her off of the planet, and go home. If he killed her…

The thought chilled him. He decided that he had to believe that his father would want him back more than he wanted this psychopath in custody. His father would want to know what had happened to Uncle Revan. He would understand that Jain did what he could, but in the end, he'd had no choice. It was kill or die.

* * *

From above, the spaceport looked like a maze, but Jain finally spotted the dock where they'd left Uncle Revan's *Raptor*. Jain zoomed down toward the dock, decelerating rapidly as he dropped, and locked up the brakes just before he hit the dirt. He vaulted off the bike and rolled to his feet. The pursuing bike's engine whined louder as she closed in on him.

Struggling to unbutton his gloves, Jain ran up the ramp to the *Raptor*'s door. Finally he got his hand bared. He slapped his palm down on the security screen and stared into the camera, impatient for it to identify him.

The other bike slammed into the roof of the dock next door. The jet-bike's fuel tank exploded in a fireball. Debris rained down around Jain. Claxons roared as the fire suppression robots rushed to work.

Good. Maybe she was dead through no fault of Jain's. The sense of relief that flooded through him nearly unstrung his knees.

"Jain Thallian," the security computer said in recognition.

As the hatch irised open, Zacari swung down from the transport's roof. She jabbed Jain hard with a stun stick that she must have taken from a Security drone.

The stun stick's charge knocked him into the ship. She followed him in. Fighting the stun, every nerve firing out of order, Jain scrabbled weakly, trying to get his feet under him.

Standing over him, the woman touched the communicator bracelet on her left wrist. "I'm in," she said. "There's a fire in the next bay over, so dodge the fire suppression crew. I'll leave the door open for you."

Jain didn't hear any response.

"What are you going to do?" he whispered.

She smiled as she reached down to haul him to his feet. "Take you home, little boy."

CHAPTER 11

Kavanaugh tuned into the fight kind of late. Raena had been with Ariel and Sloane all morning, so he'd stopped monitoring them and gone off to poke through the news feeds, checking to see how Thallian's goons had been occupying themselves. While Kavanaugh didn't want to find out any more of his men had been slaughtered, it made him nervous to have lost track of the killers. They'd been quiet since Lim's death.

While he was distracted, the local news went wild. Kavanaugh hurried to switch channels. There had been a fight down in the tourist market. All planetary security had been mobilized. At least four humans were dead.

Kavanaugh's hands flew over the computer as he flipped through the local news sites. He wanted one with video.

What he found was nothing compared to what he'd seen in the War. Seven bodies in black uniforms lay strewn across a cramped market street, with barely a splash of blood visible. It was hardly horrifying for Kavanaugh, but for Kai, which had known little violence since the War, this could well have been the worst incident in decades.

Details about the participants remained sketchy. Seven men and a boy had attacked a small party of tourists. A grainy security cam meant for catching shoplifters provided low-res footage of Ariel getting grabbed as Sloane was decked. Fascinated, Kavanaugh watched Raena wipe out her kidnappers. She didn't waste a single step. Never hesitated. Just as she'd done inside the tomb on the Templar tombworld, she worked from one man to the next, removing their threats to her. In this case, she wasn't as gentle as she'd been with the grave robbers.

The tape ended with a rain of sleep grenades. Pale blue smoke shrouded the scene.

The news site reported that several people had been taken into custody. Others were hospitalized. No one was being identified as of yet.

With shaking hands, Kavanaugh signed into the tracking program. He found Raena already inside the port complex, coming his way at something faster than a run. They must have hired or stolen some sort of transportation.

He tried to reach Ariel, but the call went unanswered. Kavanaugh set the engines to warm up, then rushed to pick up the possessions he'd scattered around the cockpit. Once the images of Raena hit the galactic news, she'd need to be elsewhere. The party on Kai was over.

Reasonably satisfied that he'd cleaned up enough to return the racer to its rightful owner, Kavanaugh went back to stand by the hatch. He checked the charge on his gun and made certain that it sat easy in its holster. Who knew what would be following them?

He didn't have to wait long to find out. A battered lone jet-bike hummed into the dock. Raena swung her leg off of the bike and strode toward the ship, definitely unhurried.

The wind from her ride had pinked her cheeks. Her cropped hair stuck out like it held a static charge. She wore an electric blue sheath, slit high enough to leave her legs bare above the ever-present high-heeled boots. She looked like she weighed all of 40 kilos. She'd just fought off eight of Thallian's killers. The two things were still hard for Kavanaugh to get his head around.

Unsurprised to find Kavanaugh, she nodded politely. "Nice to see you again."

"Where's Ariel and Gavin?" he asked.

"Planetary Security's got them." Raena kept coming at him, so Kavanaugh stepped backward out of the way and let her onto Ariel's ship.

"Are we leaving?" he asked uncertainly.

"Before long." She stopped inside the passageway to lift a necklace over her head. She held it out to him. The medallion was some kind of cheap silver metal, tarnished and faintly scratched. It had an engraving of two swords crossed at the blades.

Kavanaugh's heart sank. Putting the tracking device into Raena's medallion had been Ariel's idea. *That* had been one long tense night when they hurried to get the work done before Raena woke in the morning and realized her medallion was gone. "How long have you known?"

"Pretty much since Ariel got here. It's the sort of thing she'd do and expect me not to notice. Still, I figured it couldn't hurt to have you and Ariel keeping an eye on me here, in case Thallian's brother figured it out early and got here before I was ready." She pushed the medallion toward Kavanaugh. "Take it. I want Ariel to have it now. Gavin carried it for long enough."

"Why don't you wait and give it to her yourself?" Kavanaugh reached toward his gun with incremental slowness. He'd need to draw it and switch it to stun before Raena decked him, but he'd prefer to go down with his gun in his hand rather than to even attempt to go hand-to-hand with her.

"Come on, Tarik, don't be stupid. I'm out of here. I don't want to be followed: by Gavin, by Ariel, or by you. You'd all get yourselves killed, and then who would there be to remember me?"

She let him clear the holster at least. Then she took him down with her left fist to his temple. One blow and he didn't remember anything else.

* * *

When the sleep grenade wore off, Ariel woke with a pounding headache. She cautiously peeled one eye open, then winced as light struck her pupil.

She lay in a cell. The walls were rough black rock, the kind of stone excreted by the Templars. Her heart rate kicked back a notch. She was still on Kai, not taken prisoner by the Thallians. That was good. As long as she was in Kai Security's custody, she should be safe.

But what about Raena? The last thing Ariel remembered was Raena advancing on the frightened boy with the electric net. He must have been fourteen? Fifteen? About the age Raena had been when Thallian swept her up, anyway. What had it been like for that boy to grow up with that monster? Clearly, it had given him reserves of courage beyond his years.

Ariel knew with a cold, hard certainty that Raena would kill the boy, all his brothers, and anyone else that stood between her and Thallian. She drew her arms in around her, huddling for warmth that she could not find, and cried because her sister was so broken.

The tears didn't make her feel any better. Instead, they made her feel more dehydrated and the headache that much worse. Ariel wiped her face with her hands, dried them on her tunic, and pushed her hair back toward its braid.

Where was Raena now? Had there been more of Thallian's men, hidden in the fog of sleep gas? Was Raena even now captive on her way to her fate? Best-case scenario was that Raena was also gassed and lying in a Kai Security cell. She'd probably face murder charges for however many of the Thallian thugs she'd killed, but Ariel and Gavin could pool their resources and bribe the court. Every legal system had a price.

Unfortunately, Raena in Security custody was probably safest for everyone. The Thallians couldn't take her away. She couldn't run away. Gavin wouldn't drive himself mad searching the galaxy for her again. And Ariel wouldn't have to waste every waking moment worried what that monster had done to her sister this time.

Still, Ariel hated to think of Raena imprisoned again, even temporarily. Was her sister pacing her cell, tearing herself apart?

Ariel closed her eyes. She knew the only way to pass the time in a cell sanely was to sleep. And if she couldn't sleep, at least to daydream.

But the past was too much of a presence here. She felt physically ill, remembering her last stay in Imperial detention. Ariel had been huddled naked on her bench when a new prisoner was flung into her cell. She'd assumed the man was an Imperial agent until Raena arrived with an interrogation robot. Before Ariel's horrified eyes, Raena snapped the man's neck with her bare hands. Then she ordered the robot to cremate his body and label the ashes as Ariel's. She'd already signed into the Imperial network and posted Ariel as dead in custody: Raena's idea of a rescue.

Ariel shook that memory away, reaching farther back, to the first time she'd met Raena. It had been her birthday. Ariel was turning twelve, an important, auspicious year. Daddy promised her a special present. He'd told her that she'd never guess what it was, so of course she'd been up all night imagining what it could be.

The black-haired girl who followed him into her room in the morning was the last thing Ariel expected to see. "This is Rainy," Daddy said. "She'll be your companion from now on."

Ariel looked from her father to the elfin girl, who stared steadfastly at the ground. *This* was her birthday present? Ariel unfolded herself from her bed and walked around the girl. She looked perfectly human, but Ariel suspected she was just an excellent copy.

It took weeks for Ariel to recognize the truth. By then she understood that Raena would have preferred to have been an android, as if that would have made the sting of belonging to someone else less painful. Ariel worked hard at befriending her slave once Raena's humanity had been established. Still, the guilt of her earliest mistakes cut deep.

* * *

Sloane probed the swollen part of his head, replaying the fight in his mind. Where had they come from? How had they gotten him surrounded? He couldn't believe he'd actually let his guard down, actually relaxed and bought into the tourist role. He was embarrassed that he'd spent so much of the fight sitting in the dirt, gaping as Raena annihilated Thallian's men.

She had looked like some kind of exterminating angel, practically dancing as she took the killers down. He remembered the way the crazy blue sheath dress clung to her torso, the way her thighs were alternately hidden and revealed. Killing those men, Raena had finally come alive. Her feral beauty blazed in a way that made Sloane love her more than ever. The adoration hurt in his chest. He wanted to hold her in his arms again, gaze into her eyes, and ride the remnants of the energy she was undoubtedly still burning off. He wanted her. He wanted to be with her. He wanted to be certain of her loyalty, to own her. He was certain that possessing her was the only thing in the galaxy that would make him feel so alive.

* * *

Ariel had no way of knowing how much time had passed before the Security drones came to escort her from her cell. They marched her down to the Security Commander's office. He was a gray-feathered Shtrrel like her friend Ximena had been. His harsh voice grated her ears as he said, "Come in, Miss Lex. Please sit down."

Ariel stepped away from the security drones and slipped into the chair across the desk from the Shtrrel commander. He remained standing a moment longer, looking her over carefully.

Ariel examined him just as closely. He seemed to be a young Shtrrel, who was much concerned with appearances. His uniform and feathers were impeccable.

She noticed he didn't dismiss her guard.

It was hard to wait for him to open the conversation. She could see her file open on his screen, so he knew who she claimed to be. This identity was well established, almost legal.

"Miss Lex," he said finally, "my staff contacted the board of directors of your foundation. They are willing to pay the fine you've incurred by being a party to violence on Kai."

So her bail would be paid. Ariel fought to keep her smile small and hopeful. She could imagine how furious her mother had been to get the ransom demand, after all of Ariel's promises to keep out of legal trouble. Selling the arms business had been supposed to put an end to all of this.

"Thank you, sir. Did that extend to my friends Den Rebuad and Fiana Ryle as well?" She hoped they'd been aware enough to remember the pseudonyms they'd chosen.

"Was Miss Ryle the third person in your party?"

Ariel's mouth went dry, so she only nodded. She knew that whatever he said next would be bad news.

"Miss Ryle was not taken into custody. My staff is still seeking her in connection to the death of the four unidentified assailants. Do you have any idea who they were? Why they came to Kai to attack you?"

She shook her head, not fighting the flood of tears filling her eyes. "No, sir. We've been here nearly five local days and not been aware of any trouble."

He clicked his beak in a way that Ariel had always interpreted with Ximena to mean a smile. "You and Mr. Rebuad are free to go. We trust you have enjoyed your stay on Kai, but that you won't extend it."

"Yes, sir." Ariel stood. She hoped that he, or someone on his staff, had been the one to deliver the news of Raena's disappearance to Gavin. It would have been easier for Ariel if she'd had to tell Gavin that Raena was dead.

* * *

Jonan stalked through the cloning lab with his hands clasped behind his back. The equipment was antique now; the chemicals difficult to come by. Once every basin had been full of Thallians growing to full-size. Now he had only a handful of new sons maturing and nearly ready to join the others. They weren't the children he'd come to visit today.

Dr. Poe stood over a tub toward the back of the lab adjusting something with his delicate antenna-like arms.

Thallian stopped behind him. "Report."

The old medical robot rotated toward him. "The strand of hair found by Revan Thallian in the Templar tomb contained sufficient DNA for successful cloning." Dr. Poe waved over the basin behind him at the knots of cells multiplying within. "I have ten clones in process. It is too soon to tell how many can be brought to term."

Thallian felt the tension lift from his shoulders. What a gift he was giving Raena. When she arrived, her children would already be growing, waiting to be born.

* * *

"He alive?"

When Tarik pried his eyes open, they felt gummy. He blinked a couple times, trying to focus on the pretty blond squatting beside him with her feet bound in sandals with too many complicated straps. The sea-green dress she had on was remarkably short. He frowned, not in any way in the mood.

"Are you with us, Tarik?" the blond asked.

The sound of Ariel's familiar voice brought him back. He realized he was lying on the floor of her ship. He raised one hand to his head and groaned just to see if it would help. It didn't. She helped him sit up, which made the corridor seem to slosh from side to side. Kavanaugh blinked again, trying to focus.

"Looks like she didn't hit you more than once," Sloane said from somewhere over Ariel's shoulder.

"You ever been hit by her?" Ariel demanded. "Once is enough." To Kavanaugh she said, "You'll need something for that eye."

"I can handle that level of first aid," Kavanaugh assured her. "If you can get me onto my feet..."

Ariel took his arm and tugged him upward.

He leaned back against the bulkhead, feeling gingerly around his face for the edges of the bruise. "How long was I out?"

"Couple of hours," Ariel said. "We just got out of detention. You watch the attack on the news?"

"Just before Raena dropped by. I thought we were on our way out, finally." He stopped to listen. "I was powering up to take off."

"Raena must've shut everything off once she kicked your ass," Sloane said. "The engines are cold. How long is it gonna take us to warm this boat up and get after her?"

"Go do it," Ariel said, not bothering to hide the exhaustion in her voice. "I'll get Tarik squared away."

Sloane headed forward, needing no other urging. Kavanaugh met Ariel's eyes, trying to project sympathy. "Do you have any idea where she's headed?"

"No." Ariel returned the gun Kavanaugh dropped during Raena's attack. "She kidnapped one of Thallian's sons. She's probably stolen his ship. We don't have any idea where she's taking him."

Kavanaugh looked down the corridor after Sloane. "Do we have any idea where *we're* headed?"

"It doesn't matter now. We're being thrown off Kai, thanks to Thallian's botched attempt at kidnapping. Planetary Security is waiting outside, ready to escort us into space."

Kavanaugh inclined his head toward the cockpit. "Gavin's coming with us?"

"Yeah. He's right in thinking my racer is faster than his yacht, even if it's not as comfortable for the three of us."

"What's he gonna do about his yacht? It'll be impounded if he abandons it here."

Ariel glanced toward the cockpit and shrugged.

Kavanaugh couldn't begin to imagine walking away from the amount of money the yacht represented.

Ariel led Kavanaugh back to the tiny galley, where she pulled the medical kit from its cupboard. He took the box from her and set about taking care of his black eye. Ariel dry-swallowed some pain capsules, then sat down to sort out the acceleration straps.

"The last thing I remember," she said, "before the sleep gas took me out, is Raena closing in on this boy. He was maybe fourteen. He held a shock net like he was going to capture her singlehandedly, after she'd disabled everyone he'd been traveling with." Ariel closed her eyes, shivered. "Thallian cloned himself some children. He—"

Kavanaugh interrupted, "That is seriously screwed up."

"Raena showed me their pictures on the web." Ariel rubbed her bare arms. It was cool on her ship, now the atmosphere was kicking in. "Originally, I tried to make her see reason. I mean, I thought they were just kids. Except now, having seen one… They're *him*, in miniature. And having him to parent them? How can they not be as evil as he is?"

Kavanaugh grimaced. "You think maybe she's doing the right thing?"

"Raena told me we were just kids when we went away to war."

"I was," Kavanaugh admitted. "I was thirteen when I stowed away with Doc."

"You got an early start," Ariel said. "I was sixteen. And I was ready to die for what I believed in."

"Me, too." Kavanaugh felt the ship powering up through the soles of his boots. He sat down next to Ariel on the couch and strapped himself in, too. "What's the plan?"

"Not a clue," Ariel said hopelessly. "Raena was poking around on the screen in our hotel room, but you can bet she covered her traces there. She didn't want us to follow her."

"Where's Gavin think he's headed then?"

"Later, if the authorities identify the bodies Raena left behind, we might have a chance of figuring out what rock they crawled out from under. Other than that, it's a big galaxy and we're flying blind."

✳ ✳ ✳

They'd cleared the atmosphere when Kavanaugh reached into his jacket pocket. As he'd expected, Raena had tucked her medallion inside. He fished it out and handed it over to Ariel. "She wanted you to have this."

"Thanks." Ariel turned it over, wedged her thumbnail inside, and cracked the case open along its seam. She pulled the tracer out. The tiny recorder remained in place. "I wonder…"

She triggered the recorder. Raena appeared in miniature, gazing at her with those black, black eyes.

"This is going to have to be my goodbye, Ari. If you're watching this, we've been attacked by Jonan's brother Revan. Either I'm dead or they gave me an opening and I'm gone. Either way, I wanted you to know I really did love you. Have a nice life, Ari. Thanks for all you've done for me."

Kavanaugh looked away from Ariel, uncomfortable at seeing her at such a vulnerable moment. He wished he wasn't strapped down, so he could give her some privacy, but the little ship was pretty much a one-person craft. There wasn't far he could go. If he unsnapped himself now, it would look like he was abandoning her.

"Charming," Sloane snarled from the corridor. "Raena leave me anything?"

"No," Kavanaugh said. He wondered if Gavin was armed, then just as quickly hated himself for the suspicion. Gavin hadn't yet had time to figure out where Ariel hid her gun locker.

Kavanaugh unstrapped himself and slid off the couch, going forward, anything to get away from the confrontation about to explode behind him.

Gavin glared at him as he passed but let him go.

* * *

While Tarik had Gavin distracted, Ariel unsnapped herself. She didn't trust Gavin, didn't like having him standing over her. She fussed with the straps, appreciating the option Kavanaugh left her.

Once she was settled, she asked, "Did Raena ever tell you she loved you? In so many words?"

Sloane had to think about it. "Yes," he said nastily. "More than air, she said. More than life."

"Did she mean it, Gavin? Or was she teasing you?"

He thought back to that day on the archaeological base when he gave her the bubble bath in the rocket casing. Raena had clearly been playing, but he knew what she meant. Or believed he did.

"Why do you care?" he asked. "Jealous?"

"Of course." She said it like it was the most obvious thing in the universe, but it still stung to admit it. Her face burned.

"You think she meant it more when she said it to you?" To press his point, Gavin stepped too close. "She's managing you, Ms. Shaad. She knows just what you want to hear. She's giving you an out to keep you out of her way. Because you're weak."

Ariel blinked, stunned. The worst of it was that he'd probably read Raena right. Gavin knew she'd hear the truth in his words and be hurt by them. And he didn't care.

Anger made her shaky. Ariel argued, "What does love even mean to Raena? She's never seen another person as an equal. Either she had to take their orders, or she held their lives in her hands. She had our lives in her hands, Gavin. She let us go."

"What are you talking about, Ariel? I thought you were *sisters*." He made the final word a curse. "That's pretty much a gig for life."

She wanted to step back but was afraid to bump into the lockers behind her. He was too close. When he lost it, she was going to get hurt. As much as she wanted to argue, wanted to make him see reason, she didn't want him to kill her. She knew he was capable of it. Trying to defuse him, she asked, "What am I to you, Gavin? We both know I'm not your rival for her."

He stared at her, unwilling to back down.

She saw it in his face and nodded. Anything they'd had before was over. "Thank you for being honest with me. I'll have Tarik drop you at Mallech. You can negotiate with Kai, get your ship out of hock, do whatever you need to do."

"We can't let her go alone," he protested.

"I know," she said. "You can't let her go."

Her compassion infuriated him. "I can't believe you're going to let him have her, Ariel. You know what that means."

"She didn't want me to die for her," Ariel reminded, finally figuring out how to turn enough to step back. "Only you want me to die for her. And getting killed by Thallian isn't going to bring her back to you. She's gone, Gavin. She *left* you."

He swung at her, but she was ready. He hadn't seen her pick up Kavanaugh's gun from the acceleration couch, but she couldn't miss at this range. She only had to take the first slap before she shot him.

* * *

Horrified, Jaden watched the news clip again. The footage was grainy and difficult to make out, but he watched in growing certainty as the little woman Uncle Revan and Jain had been hunting demolished the family's soldiers. She worked from one to the next, fast and assured, and took down everyone in her path. Including Uncle Revan.

Jaden checked the time-stamp on the footage. It had been recorded earlier in the evening: morning on Kai. Odds were that no one else in the family had seen it yet.

He didn't know what to do. It was his watch now. He sat alone in the monitoring room. He could call someone, report...but whom could he confide in? If he told another of the boys, he might take credit for the find and then Jaden would get in trouble for not stumbling on it on his own watch. If he told Uncle Merin, he would remember that Jaden had been the first one to see the video of the girl, the one who had drawn Revan and Jain into her trap. If he told his father that the girl had escaped...

Jaden trembled, wracked with indecision. There was no one to whom he could unburden himself, no one he could give this terrible news. No matter what happened, he would be punished for being the messenger.

He could ignore the video. Pretend he didn't see it and leave it for someone else to discover in the morning.

That wouldn't protect him though, and he knew it. He'd be in trouble for missing such an important development. They would think he had slept at his post again or wasted the hours playing games. He couldn't dodge this.

So he did the only other thing he could think of. In order to buy himself some time, he wrote a quick little program to filter the news. He didn't want to block all the news coming from Kai. That would be suspicious. Still, he could make certain that word of the fight—with its anonymous assailants and unclaimed bodies—never reached the people who wanted the news most.

* * *

Ariel looked up from Sloane's body to find Kavanaugh in the passageway, one of her guns in hand.

"He dead?" Tarik asked.

"He wishes." Ariel returned Kavanaugh's pistol hilt first. "Thanks for your help."

"I'm sorry it came to that."

"Me, too." She knelt at Gavin's side, turning his head gently to take his pulse. "I wish this ship had a hold."

"What are you gonna do with him?"

"I guess we can lock him in my cabin." She wasn't happy about the possibility of him trashing her stuff, but what else were they going to do? Lash him to the galley couch? Then they'd have to deal with his insanity every time they left the cockpit.

"I'll get him," Tarik offered. He bent down and slung the older man up onto his back. "Lead the way."

* * *

Sloane's muscles ached as the stun wore off. He sprawled across Ariel's bunk, remembering that she liked a mattress that cradled her and sheets so smooth they felt like water. In the last week, he'd taken pleasure in following her with his eyes. She'd been obliging as he sated himself on her body. He had to admit though, he was over her. He had loved her, in his way, back when she was young and full of fire. Now she was cautious and old. She had kids and her mother to care for. She had a life where she could accommodate him, but he didn't want to be settled.

He knew he was lucky she hadn't pitched him out the airlock. He was warm, safe for the moment, and up until he'd slapped Ariel, he'd had options. But Raena was gone and nothing else mattered.

All those years he'd thrown money away on the Dart, believing it kept him focused on finding Raena, and now the obsession wouldn't leave him, even though he'd been clean for weeks. Was it possible that he'd become addicted to her?

The memory of their first meeting overwhelmed him. He closed his eyes tight against it, but that was no defense. She'd looked so young and so lost, drinking alone in a dive on Nizarrh. Coalition Command had offered him good money to bring her in. He wasn't in a position to ask why, figuring simply that any-one wanted by the Empire was looking for asylum.

Money was tight those days, so Sloane took what jobs he could. If that meant running Messiah from time to time, he didn't have to like it, but he did have to eat. It wouldn't have been his preference to take Raena along with him on that particular jaunt, but Imperial soldiers crawled all over Nizarrh. Odds were she'd be caught before he could get back to her.

Gavin was smitten from the first by Raena's attitude. She'd descended low enough that she honestly didn't care what happened to her, so long as Thallian never touched her again. That level of nihilism found an echo in Sloane.

Then their incipient romance went to hell. Thallian's men boarded Sloane's ship. He'd stowed Raena, the tiny little thing, inside one of the cargo lockers he'd hidden in the walls. It had been shielded—she should have been safe—but the commander dragged his robot arm along the wall and forced Sloane to open any panel that sounded unusual.

Sloane watched Raena shot down just before Thallian's soldiers left him to die in a broken bag of Messiah.

The unconscious girl dragged away by the circle of soldiers was a hell of an image to wake up with. Sloane really didn't have much choice about going after her. He needed the money she'd bring from the Coalition to pay off Outrider for the wasted Messiah, as well as the stuff the soldiers stole on their way out the door.

The med tech ID was easy to come by. He'd spent enough time in detentions of one form or another that he figured he could bluff his way into this one. It wasn't a grand plan, but it had the elegance of simplicity. And when he saw what Thallian had done to her in the cell, he knew he'd made the right choice.

But he couldn't get her off the ship. They could have avoided the soldiers, but Raena didn't really want to escape. Escape meant more running. She was tired. She wanted out.

With the clarity of hindsight, he realized that the kindest thing he could have done for her was to put a bolt in her eye.

He remembered his last glimpse of her then: a goddess in black, killing with such relish that he smiled to watch her. Apparently, Thallian's troops were less afraid of death than they were of their commander. They were willing to risk death to capture Raena alive.

He should have run after her then. He should have died at her side. He could have saved them both decades of torment.

Now she had vanished once more and he didn't even have the Imperial recording of her trial as a starting point.

If Ariel kept her word—when had she not?—she'd drop him off on Mallech. He could scrape together a new identity, return to Kai City heading an "official" investigation, get himself back into their former hotel room, and pray that Raena left him something to trace on the room computer. If that didn't work, he'd have to interrogate Thallian's surviving henchmen. They'd pretty much abdicated their humanity when they tortured Lim to death. Sloane saw no reason he shouldn't sink to their level.

He didn't have anything left that meant anything to him beyond the search for Raena. He wondered if he had ever told her he loved her.

CHAPTER 12

Since she'd nominated herself the evil mastermind of this adventure, Raena chose the biggest cabin on the stolen transport. Evil had its perks; she'd seen plenty of evidence of that.

She had traveled on a similar diplomatic transport while she served on the *Arbiter*. This one was slightly different, less posh. She wondered if Thallian ever let anyone else take his private transport out for a spin. Maybe it simply hadn't survived the War.

Beyond the door, her crew settled into the rest of the ship. She heard laughter and voices, but didn't hurry out to meet them. Mykah vouched for them, which was good enough for now. Pranksters would suit this excursion fine. Anyway, she didn't want to get attached.

Mykah commed her when it was time to strap herself down. Once the transport left Kai and got under way, Raena searched her new cabin thoroughly, looking for some revelations about Thallian's older brother. Who had Revan Thallian been? Why had he served Jonan instead of vice versa? Did he enjoy hunting down his brother's ex-girlfriends? Was she the first or only the most recent?

His cabin was unsurprisingly spartan. The only personal objects she found lying around were the generator leads ending in alligator clips, from which she deduced that Revan Thallian felt the need to torture himself. She found a certain kinship in the idea. She liked that he was comfortable enough with the predilection that he didn't hide the evidence in a locker. Instead, it was right out on the desk for anyone to see.

When she opened his closet, she found it filled with black clothing. No surprise there, either. Black clothing didn't show the blood; Jonan taught her that. When she worked for him, she wore only black, too.

As she poked through the black shirts, the black jackets, the black trousers—all carefully sorted and hung so as to avoid wrinkles—a flash of indigo caught her eye. She nibbled her bottom lip, amused, as she pulled the dress Gavin had given her to the front of the closet.

This damn dress was going to follow her everywhere. She intentionally left it behind in Gavin's hideaway on Brunzell, but one of the Thallians must have retrieved it from the closet. It wasn't that she objected to the cut or even its particular color. The dress just felt like one more piece of evidence that she had been owned, that she owed a debt that she could only pay off with her body. She wanted to be done with all that.

In point of fact, she never wanted to wear anything again that she didn't choose for herself. She considered pitching the stupid thing into the incinerator, but something stopped her. She wondered if perhaps she might still have a use for the dress, if she could use it to send a message to Jonan, maybe turn it against him somehow. She'd have to consider how to make it a weapon.

Raena went to sit on the precisely made bunk and rested the generator leads in her hand. She was extremely tempted to go back to the hold and torture Thallian's son. The force of the craving caught her off-guard. For the first time in decades, she had someone entirely in her power. The boy existed at her whim. By tormenting him, her thoughts whispered, she could get back some of what Thallian had stolen from her. She could begin punishing Thallian for everything he'd made her do. Since he'd taught her how to torture—and how to drink pleasure from it—didn't it make sense to apply the lesson to the victim he'd offered up to her?

She imagined the things she might do. Jain Thallian was just a boy, fourteen or fifteen at most, who had grown up sheltered from the galaxy. Cloistered, one could say. She wondered if he'd ever seen a live girl before. Ever touched one.

Her hands ached with the desire to disassemble him.

The downside, she realized, was that she'd have to deal with Mykah and his crew afterward. At this point, the voyage was still a game to Mykah. He had become a space pirate, hijacking a ship from a band of killers and ransoming a hostage to his family. In his mind, his friends were the good guys. Raena found that innocence a pleasant change from Ariel's worry and Gavin's ennui. She should let the pranksters remain innocent as long as they could with a bad influence like herself around.

Raena suspected that, in reality, there was nothing useful she could learn from the boy anyway. When the transport eventually reached Thallian's hidey-hole, she'd need security codes to sneak past the family's defenses. But judging from how easily the family had given up every other secret for which she'd probed, it was only a matter of time before Coni teased the passwords out of the ship's computer or one of the boys told her all that he knew.

Thallian never encouraged Raena to be conservative with prisoners, but this might be a good opportunity to experiment. Sparing Jain might ultimately be more beneficial than killing him.

* * *

When Raena came out of the cabin, Mykah was eager to introduce her to the rest of the crew he'd brought along. He led her into the cockpit. In the driver's seat hunched Haoun, a big bipedal reptilian creature armored with green hexagonal scales. He'd driven tourist shuttles on Kai and would pilot the transport. He nodded hello.

"What do you think?" Raena asked in her newly learned Galactic Standard. "Is this old tub drivable?"

"The old Earther drives aren't fast, but they've kept this one in perfect shape. It should get us there, as long as we're not racing anyone." His translator made him sound very urbane, while the actual sound of his sibilant voice raised the hairs on the back of Raena's neck, some kind of vestigial reaction.

"No one else knows where we're headed."

Under the console lay Vezali, who had tentacles rather than legs. They shifted so constantly that Raena wasn't certain if she'd counted them right. Vezali had worked for one of the casinos, rebuilding the gambling machines to keep them winning in the House's favor.

"You know the pachinko machines at the Shiapan casino plinked in a certain sequence as they were getting ready to pay out?" Raena asked.

Vezali blinked her single eye. "I'm surprised you could hear that on the gambling floor." Her metal-inflected voice came through a translator around her waist. "It's not just the pachinko machines. Almost every machine had a tell, so the casino staff could move in and take over the soon-to-be winners."

"I should've stuck around longer," Raena said.

"Nah. Their security is trained to watch for people who pick up the tells. They would have encouraged you to play somewhere else."

Raena remembered the apes who'd trailed her and smiled. Not subtle. Even Ariel had noticed them. Good thing she'd quit while ahead.

Getting back to business, Raena said, "I need to have one of the escape pods shielded. I want it to read like there's only one occupant as we go down to the planet, only the boy."

"Let me look it over," Vezali said. "I'm sure I can rig something. It will depend on what kind of supplies they've left me to pillage."

"Thank you."

In the glare of the copilot's panel, where she'd wedged herself to leave room for the others, Mykah's blue-furred girlfriend protested, "Keeping the boy awake is dangerous."

"Keeping him alive is dangerous," Raena countered. "Sleep gas could solve your problem, but I don't advocate it. People react differently to the gas. It might just give him a screaming headache. It could put him into a coma. That won't help us." She held her gaze until the blue girl backed down, then assured, "He's not coming out of the hold. He won't ever see any of you. You won't have to deal with him at all."

Coni subsided into the copilot's chair, arms crossed, clearly unhappy.

"Any luck finding the clearance codes?" Raena persisted.

"I'm still trying to decrypt the log," Coni said. "I'll concentrate on this current journey of theirs. The last time they used this transport was almost five years ago, on some kind of a supply run."

"If it isn't any trouble," Raena said, "send the translated logs back to my cabin when you get them figured out. I'm curious to know what they had to say about this little excursion."

Coni nodded, so Raena ducked back out. No need to make nice, if her mere presence was going to creep the blue girl out. She wondered if it was simple jealousy. Had Coni come along merely to keep an eye on her boyfriend? Mykah said she was good at cryptography. Raena hoped Coni was on board for the adventure.

* * *

Eilif was forbidden access to the computers, so she couldn't search the news herself. She hung around the computer room, hoping to hear the boys find something about Revan and Jain. She wondered that they hadn't heard anything unusual from the pleasure planet where Revan had been headed. Maybe one woman's disappearance wasn't a big enough story to make the galactic news. Maybe tourists vanished from Kai every day.

Still, it seemed strange that Revan's men could swoop in, capture their objective, and escape without anyone reporting her gone. After the news debacle of Jain's first kill, Eilif was impressed that Revan had managed this kidnapping so quietly. She was glad he hadn't put her son or himself at any more risk.

If she were honest, she preferred Revan of all the brothers. He'd always been gentle with her. He'd even remembered to thank her from time to time. She knew she was unworthy of anything more, but the few pleasantries they'd shared made her heart soar.

She hoped he would be home soon.

* * *

Thallian's son was asleep when Raena spied on him through the window into his cell. Even though he could hardly be comfortable stretched out on his back and pinned in place by the lockdown cuffs, he slumped on the bench, mouth open and snoring. Raena thought it kind of charming. When she was a kid, she had been able to sleep anywhere, too.

Raena opened the hatch. The boy snapped awake, tense as a wire. The scent of the air changed when his eyes caught her. Raena inhaled deeply, licked her lips, and stepped inside. "I've brought you some dinner," she said. "Nothing fancy, just ship's rations. I never had time to learn to cook."

She set the tray on the floor, dragged the chair over nearer the bunk, and sat down. She felt the chair's magnetic feet seal to the deck.

"Let me up," the boy growled.

"Oh, no, Jain. If I stun you too many times, there's a chance of permanent nerve damage. Your father showed me what that looks like on a prisoner. It's not pretty. So we're going to deliver you back to him fully functional, if that's okay with you." She set the tray on his chest. "I'll feed you."

He thrashed as much as he could, tipping the tray to the floor. Raena smiled, but didn't bend down to pick it up.

"The smell of that food is really going to bother you in a couple of hours," she predicted. "You'll be sorry you wasted it and sorry you can't get down there and lap it up."

He glared at her and demanded, "What do you want from me?"

"Nothing. Can you believe it?" She sat back in the chair and propped her heels up on the edge of the bunk near his head. He spat on her boot soles. She left her feet where they were. "I can't imagine that you know anything of interest to me," she told him.

He chose not to argue. "Where are you taking me?"

"Home."

"My home?"

"I've never had one, myself," she said. "Well, I lived in that tomb for twenty years. I suppose that counts as home, sort of. You wouldn't last long in there. Did you ever go inside? It wasn't the blackness or the cold or the hunger so much as the solitude."

He ignored her, so Raena continued. "I watched the video where you set off my landslide. Nice piece of work, didn't you think? Been a long time since I'd rigged a demolition—might have overdone it just a little. I didn't mean to take down the whole mountainside. It looked like I killed two of your guards."

"And blew out my hearing," the boy said. "Luckily, Uncle Revan was able to patch me up."

"I'm glad. Otherwise, we wouldn't be enjoying our conversation now."

He had to twist his neck to hold his head up enough to see her. Judging from his expression, he thought she was crazy. He let his head relax back onto the bench.

"Did you find my message?"

"One of the men did. They found the hair you left, too. We sent it home to my father with the wounded."

Goosebumps rippled over her. Great. One of her hairs was now in the hands of a man who'd cloned human shields. Something else she would have to deal with when she reached Thallian.

"Yes, Jain," she answered, "we're going to your home."

This time he flinched. "You know where it is?"

"Of course. One of your brothers betrayed it. When I leave you alone, you'll have time to work out which one it was. Maybe, if you're polite, I'll tell you when you guess correctly."

"You can leave me alone now."

"I could," Raena agreed. "But I thought we might chat a little longer."

"I have nothing to say to you."

"Then you can listen," she said. "I want to tell you a story about my relationship with your father."

*　*　*

At fourteen she'd been a slave for three years. She wasn't particularly unhappy. At least, she couldn't put her finger on one thing where she could say, "Yes, my life would be less hellish if this were different."

Of course, she couldn't go wherever she wanted, or take a day off, or be alone. She couldn't leave the compound without a specific errand. She had to play nice with Ariel's spoiled rich friends and the kids they slummed with. Still, slavery meant that Raena wasn't living in the street or whoring for some filthy junkie pimp to keep herself in chemicals. Ariel's connections provided all the chemicals they needed, clean and uncut, straight out of a laboratory, in exchange for guns Ariel stole from her father's factory. Raena's job was to see that Ariel didn't get killed by one of those same guns.

So the work, as she understood it, wasn't all that different when she took Thallian's offer of employment. She knew from the beginning that he was an agent of the Empire, but she begged him to take her along anyway. This slave was running away.

She hadn't thought farther ahead than that. It surprised her when Thallian put his aide out of his cabin and installed Raena there. She'd never had a room of her own, so she didn't question her good fortune.

The beatings began as soon as Thallian required her to fence with him. No matter that she'd never held a sword before. He wanted to underline how unworthy she was to carry one.

As he handed her the wooden practice sword, he snatched the medallion from her throat. Her hands were full of the wooden sword hilt, but she managed to catch the chain.

Thallian cracked her wrist with his own practice sword. Clumsily, she yanked her hand back and forced her throbbing fingers to support her own sword. Thallian attacked her at full speed.

She did what she could to protect her head from the rain of blows. By necessity, that left her body open to Thallian's attack. He chose a point on her right thigh where he hit her repeatedly, returning again and again to it after each combination of blows. Eventually, despite her determination, the leg refused to support her weight any longer. It dropped her to the mat.

The point of Thallian's sword followed her down. He nudged her chin up just a bit with the blunt sword point. He added enough pressure on her throat that she understood he could kill her if he chose to, even with a blunt wooden sword.

"You don't deserve to guard me," he said. "Your size is a dare that many beings will not be able to refuse. You look like an easy target. A joke. So until you can prove differently to me, I will keep your weapons for your own safety."

Thallian withdrew his sword point, only to strike her sharply on her forearm. Her nerveless fingers dropped her sword.

As hard as it was to hear, Raena understood his reasoning. Tears of pain and frustration rose to her eyes, but she blinked them back. She crawled up onto all fours and touched her head to the mat.

"You have something to say?" Thallian asked.

"When is my next lesson?"

* * *

"Why did you tell me that?" Jain wondered.

"Because we have something in common," the woman told him. "We were both trained by your father to withstand pain."

Was that a threat? Jain closed his eyes. An image of the man Lim flashed through his mind: drooling, begging incoherently, only fear keeping him from blacking out.

Zacari had arranged her chair so that Jain could only see her by straining. He wanted to watch her, to see what she would do next, to dodge the blow when it came, but she'd made it uncomfortable and awkward to do so.

Finally, he could stand the tension no longer. He opened his eyes and twisted around to look at her.

She hadn't moved. Her boots were still propped up near his head. There was something eerily lighthearted in her expression, despite the scar between her eyebrows and the blackness of her eyes. Her crazy, staticky hair made her look fun, youthful. He knew she was really a freak as old as his mom, preserved by her twenty years in prison. It didn't matter. She smelled wonderful. Exotic. Enticing. Dangerous.

"Ready for me to go?" she asked.

"Yes," he hissed at her.

"All right."

She got up from her chair and strode across the cell on her ludicrous high heels. The black leggings she wore left very little to his imagination. Even so, the smoke-gray bomber jacket she wore as a top could conceal any number of threatening implements in its many pockets.

She didn't turn back as she left the cell.

Once the air had settled, Jain discovered she was right. The smell of the food he'd spilled across the floor made his stomach grumble. He hadn't eaten since they'd landed on Kai, and then only a quick carb bar because he'd been so eager for the hunt.

He tried not to imagine himself eating dinner off the floor, but any thought of food only made his mouth water now.

He forced his thoughts to his father and shivered. What would Jain ever tell him?

* * *

Mykah was in the common area as Raena passed through. Since everyone else had something to do, he'd made it his mission to track down all the weapons cached on the transport. Now he had an impressive array spread out on every flat surface and grouped roughly by type.

"They were armed for bear," he told Raena.

She smiled. "What's that mean?"

One corner of his mouth quirked up. "It's something my grandfather used to say. It meant they were armed to hunt something big and dangerous."

"That would be me," she said casually, picking up one of the little pistols to check its charge. Fully loaded.

"Thought so." Mykah lounged back against the wall. "So what's your deal? Were you government-engineered?"

"Maybe. I don't know. My mom was crazy, part of this radical militant cult back in the Imperial days. I grew up being trained to fight for humanity."

He nodded, as if he expected her to continue. She chose not to. No point in freaking him out or in telling truths no sane person would believe.

He surprised her by saying, "You're older than you look. That girl in the Imperial wanted poster, that's you."

Raena looked up from the weapons to give him her full attention. "Where'd you see that?"

"Coni's finding it easier to break the encryption on stuff they imported into the log—the old Imperial files—than the stuff they recorded firsthand."

"That makes sense. So you know I was charged with Imperial treason by the guy I'm going to meet, the kid's father."

"There's a recording of your trial in there, too," Mykah said. He didn't seem especially excited by this or threatened by it, nothing more than massively intrigued. It was still all a game to him, she realized. A live-action puzzle.

"Were the charges true?" he asked. "The mining prison, the ships, the soldiers…"

She nodded.

"Then why didn't they execute you? Wasn't that what the Empire did back in the day?"

"It was complicated," she admitted. "I wanted them to kill me. I expected it. But they decided to use me as a way to punish Thallian. I was imprisoned as a way to threaten him, to keep him in line."

"They imprisoned you in stasis? Is that why you haven't aged?"

"I wish it had been stasis. That would have been kinder." The grin that split her face felt like a skull's grimace. She shook her head, shook it away. "It was a long sentence. It gave me a lot of time to think."

"And you decided to go after this crazy fucker, right?"

"Right. He created me. So I'm the only one who can take him down."

Mykah glanced away from her at the piles of weapons. Raena let him change the subject. "You want a lesson on all this stuff?"

He beamed like he'd just hit the jackpot.

* * *

"I need to use the commode," the boy told Raena when she eventually checked on him again. His tone told her that he was used to issuing orders, to having them obeyed. Several of his brothers in the family portraits were older, but Jain was clearly the alpha. Raena wondered if he was his father's favorite, if that's why he'd been singled out for this little adventure.

"Did you hear me?" he repeated. Anxiety made his voice strident.

Raena drew the Stinger pistol from the holster on her thigh. It was a sporting weapon meant for precision target shooting, but it could drop a man with minimal damage to the body. She changed the settings with an audible click. Then she placed the barrel against his temple.

"I heard you, Jain. Now I want you to listen to me. Think about your dead Uncle Revan. Think about how fast I am. Think about whether you want to see your family or your home again. You have a full bladder and you haven't eaten in at least ten hours. Do you want to try me?"

"No."

"Then I'm going to unlock the restraints." She stepped back a couple of paces and pressed a button on the remote in her pocket.

"And leave me some privacy?" he asked hopefully, rubbing his wrists.

"No."

Once he'd gotten up, she sat on the foot of the bench, pistol steady in her hand. "These are nice weapons," she said conversationally. "Antique, though, like the transport. I'd say the family's fortune is running out, isn't it? No money for new toys."

Raena gave the boy time to answer, but he didn't rise to it. She hadn't really intended him to, but she wanted the conversation to feel the way he expected—cat and mouse—so he could feel superior to it. She wanted to feed his sense of entitlement, his self-worth, because that would be an easy way to dismantle him later.

"Unfortunately, galactic memories are long. No one's forgotten that the Thallian family engineered the plague that wiped out the Templars. No one's forgotten that your father was the 'diplomat' who disseminated the plague."

He still didn't argue, but she could see the tension gathering across his back as he hunched against the truth.

"As long as you have to protect your dad, all of you have to hide together in silence, watching your treasures fall apart around you.

Without Jonan, you could change your names, leave your home, lead your own lives. It must be very frustrating for you."

The boy smiled at her, revealing sharpened teeth. Raena forced herself not to flinch. Jain was younger now than she'd ever known Jonan, but she could see the old man in his son. Their eyes were the same shade of silver. They shared the same cheekbones, the same jawline. Raena wondered if the boy would grow a beard like his father's when he was old enough.

"It's worse for us," Jain said. "We all have his face. His DNA. Even if he died, we couldn't go out into the galaxy. Any ID check anywhere would recognize us for the mass murderer our father was."

"Trapped like rats," Raena summarized.

Jain bristled, but didn't argue.

He flushed the commode and reassembled his black clothing.

As he crossed back toward her, she waved the pistol toward the bucket she'd set down inside the door. "Wash the floor."

"What?" He stared at her, so shocked by the order that he couldn't parse it.

"You heard me. There's a brush in there, too. Get down and scrub up your mess."

The boy dragged the bucket over to the spilled food and slopped some water onto the floor. Grudgingly, he knelt down and began to scrub. Then he said, "My father will kill you."

Raena laughed. "I'm sure Jonan has a lot of things in mind for me, but killing me is the last thing I can look forward to from him."

She settled back onto the bench and said, "Let me tell you another story."

* * *

She didn't like the situation very much, but it wasn't for her to like or dislike. Thallian invited the delegation of nobles on board the *Arbiter*, seemingly with the intention of offering them Imperial hospitality. He arranged an ambassadorial reception in the main conference room.

The Chief Minister was as conciliatory as one could desire. He did not deny there was terrorist activity in his system. He offered to work with Imperial authorities to ferret out the terrorists. After the bombardment of his capital city, which Thallian's arrival had ended, he agreed to the establishment of an Imperial base in the ruins of the former Ministry building.

Raena didn't trust him and neither did Thallian. She stood at attention behind her commander's chair and kept her face impassive as the negotiations spun out. Everyone had stepped through an energy scanner on their way into the room. Her dress sword and Thallian's sidearm were the only weapons she could see. She expected the attack to come from some form of edged weapon, which meant the assailant had to be within arm's reach of Thallian. She watched the men closest to him intently.

She felt the change when the weapon was drawn, saw the ambassador shrink away from Thallian and the new Imperial governor he had installed. She eased her sword from its sheath, but did not strike yet. She knew better than to create martyrs.

The Imperial governor's head exploded, showering Thallian's cape and the floor. The smells of death and surprise clouded the air. Raena pulled Thallian behind the Chief Minister—standard Imperial procedure. Using Thallian's shoulder for leverage, she vaulted onto the tabletop.

One of the men at the far end of the room had some sort of primitive projectile weapon, something that had escaped the energy scans. He was momentarily paralyzed by the enormity of what he had done: taken a life and dragged his homeworld into the War.

Even as Raena neared him, she saw the shock wearing off to be replaced by resolve. The bore of the weapon swung toward Thallian. Raena dodged between him and the gun.

As she raised her sword blade for a quick kill, the gun went off.

The sharp impact spun her away. She turned on legs that were still steady and brought the sword slashing diagonally through the assassin's body. The stroke decapitated him and removed his weapon arm.

Security officers clattered into the room, stun staves ready. The native party stepped away from the bargaining table, hands meekly raised.

Raena meant to leap down from the tabletop to secure the weapon, but somehow she misjudged her footing. Pain was a fire consuming her strength. Still clutching her sword, she dragged herself across the floor toward the severed arm.

One of the security officers' armored boots entered her field of vision. He bent down to pluck the handgun from the dead man's grip.

He reported, "Your aide has been wounded, Lord Thallian."

"Are we secure here, Commander?" Thallian asked.

Another security officer, one Raena couldn't see, said, "Yes, my lord."

"Escort the Chief Minister's party to a holding cell until we can sort out responsibility for what's happened here."

"Ambassador Thallian, I—"

"Your protest is noted, Chief Minister," Thallian said. "Commander, you have your orders."

As the security guards herded the prisoners together, Raena tried to pull her limbs in around her body. The floor was cold. She suspected that she would be warmer if only she could stand.

Thallian's shiny black boots stepped into the spreading pool of her blood. Raena winced. It wouldn't be the first time she'd cleaned her own blood from his leathers, but now there was so much blood...

Thallian squatted down beside her. He traced her face with one velvet-gloved hand. "You sacrificed yourself for me."

"My duty, my lord." She tried again to get up, but her limbs might as well have belonged to someone else.

"It's a clean wound," Thallian noted. "Looks as if the projectile passed straight through." He pulled his glove off.

Raena closed her eyes, expecting to feel his feverishly warm hand on her face. Instead, a pain yet more excruciating chased away the rapidly expanding numbness.

She opened her eyes to watch Thallian withdraw his finger from the entry wound. Blood slicked his finger and ran down the back of his hand. He held her gaze as he lifted his forefinger to his lips. His tongue darted out. Then, like a child, he inserted his finger between his lips and sucked the blood away.

Anger flooded Raena's system, a heat to replace the chill. "Will you let me die, my lord?"

"Never," Thallian promised. "Never."

CHAPTER 13

The stolen ship was silent as Raena prowled its corridors. Mykah and Coni had retreated to the boy's cabin to share its narrow bunk. Vezali tinkered in the cockpit, familiarizing herself with the old-fashioned human-designed controls. Haoun sprawled on cushions on the floor of the lounge, the only space large enough for him until they dismantled the bunks in the soldiers' quarters. His breath made an eerie whistle as he slept.

Raena peeked in on Jain, snoring on his bench. She clicked the remote in her pocket and unlocked the restraints, but he didn't wake. Poor kid.

At last she returned to her own cabin. She crossed the darkened room to switch on the computer screen. Her fingers found the control to dial down the brightness as she perched on the corner of the bunk.

She had a message from Jimi asking last-minute questions about water and rations. He thanked her for her directions on aiming himself toward the shipping lanes. She wondered if Jain could guess which of his brothers had betrayed the family's hiding place. She wondered if Jimi had done it intentionally.

She wished the boys would be more forthcoming about their childhood, if it could be called that. She was curious if they had been beaten in the name of training. Had their innocence been enough to sate their father's appetite, or had he needed to break their bodies as well? How much had he used them, created them in her image?

Knowing wouldn't change the outcome, she told herself. Weapons needed to be disabled, no matter how they'd been forged.

On the Shaad family channel, she found a message from Ariel. Raena sat back, considering if there was anything her "sister" could tell her that hadn't already been said. She reached out to delete it unread, but then hesitated. Maybe later she'd want to read it. Maybe she'd want some assurance that someone in the galaxy still loved her, still understood her, no matter what she did. For now, Raena backed out of the channel, covering the traces that she'd been there at all.

Powering down the computer, she stretched out on Revan's bunk, head at the foot, and wondered if she could sleep. It would be easier if she had some company. She'd spent too many years sleeping alone.

* * *

Mykah snuggled close to Coni, breathing in the spicy scent of her fur. She always made him think of the bright scent of cinnamon.

He was tired in a way he hadn't been in a long time, wrung out by the excitement of finally doing something grand. He'd searched the stolen ship from fore to aft, collecting up a surprising array of weaponry and inventorying everything else the Thallians had stocked on board. Then Raena had given him a lesson in what the various weapons did, how they had been modified, and what they could be used for now. His head felt very full.

"I don't like it," Coni muttered low in her throat. The frequency raised the hair on the back of Mykah's neck. He shivered sleepily.

"Don't like what?" he whispered.

"Don't like locking that boy in a cell."

"We're taking him home unharmed," Mykah said.

"That's what she told you."

Mykah nodded. "That's what Raena said. You don't believe her?"

"If we're just taking him home, why does he have to be locked down all the time? Even humans have rights."

Mykah laughed at that. It was a joke older than he was, dating back to the War. Did humans have rights after they wiped out the Templars? Well, he couldn't remember all the permutations of the joke now, but eventually when you got to the punch line, it was supposed to be funny when you said, "Even humans have rights."

"Maybe he's dangerous," Mykah suggested.

"Dangerous to us, maybe. Dangerous to her?"

"I see what you mean." Mykah propped his head up on his fist so he could see Coni in the half-light coming from the computer screen. Her eyes took on a sheen in the darkness when the pupils opened up and amethyst reflected back. The first time he'd seen her eyes glow, Mykah found it eerie. Now they'd spent enough nights together that he found it enchanting.

Coni wouldn't give up yet. "She may not be torturing him, but she's tormenting him. And I don't like it."

"Let's talk to her in the morning."

"*You* talk to her in the morning," Coni insisted.

"Promise." He leaned down to kiss her cold lips, breathing her in once more.

* * *

It had been too quiet. The last word they'd had from Revan had been his assurance that they'd located Raena. He'd said it was only a matter of time until they had her safely stowed in their hold. Revan showed embarrassing enthusiasm for returning home.

Then nothing.

It wasn't like Revan to keep a secret or withhold a surprise. After too many hours had passed, Thallian knew that his brother's plan had failed. Raena had escaped. And Revan, damn him, was too ashamed to admit it.

Jonan had been in a fine rage since that realization. No one but Eilif had dared speak to him. In fact, Jaden had cringed out of his father's path, for which Jonan repaid him with a pair of broken ribs. Jonan found himself surrounded by fools, idiots, and incompetent children. He wished he had been able to go after Raena himself.

The sense of failure crushed him and made it hard to keep drawing breath. Jonan knew that he had to have Raena back or everything he had left was worthless. He stood in the darkness in front of the wall screen, watching her fly again and again, a sparrow with the agility of an eagle, looping and diving amongst the skyscrapers. Playing! That she could feel such joy speared him. He hated her for it. He swore that he would make her suffer in proportion to the pleasure she'd taken in her freedom.

And he would make her like it.

* * *

When Raena gave up on the pretense of sleep, she found Mykah bustling in the galley. "Breakfast?" he asked.

"Just some fruit," she said, picking an apple out of the crisper.

"There are eggs. I'm not sure what kind of eggs, but they taste good. I think Haoun brought them onboard."

Raena surprised herself by saying, "None for me, thanks. But if you wouldn't mind, fix my share for the kid? I'm going to see if he's hungry enough to behave himself this morning."

Mykah nodded and leaned over the stovetop. She was glad he approved.

She took Gavin's knife from the top of her boot and proceeded to section the fruit. She'd thought it was an apple, but the flesh inside the thin crimson skin was bright yellow. It tasted like fresh air and sunshine. She wasn't entirely sure she liked it.

Mykah glanced over his shoulder at her. His attention caught on the knife.

"Got a question?" she asked.

"I noticed you're not strapping the boy down any more."

"No need to." She ate another slice of the fruit, puzzling over it. It was kind of appealing, but so different from what she had expected that she wasn't sure she could finish it. "His name is Jain."

"I wondered. He gonna be coming out to join us later?"

"I doubt it." She weighed whether to tell Mykah the whole story. As much as she enjoyed his naiveté, she didn't want any ill-considered rescue attempts on the boy. Not that she was worried for herself, but someone else might get hurt. She needed the whole crew to make this run successfully. "Did you see the news about that man who was tortured to death, like the old days?"

Mykah nodded.

"Lim—the dead man—was one of the crew that busted me out of prison. And our guest Jain was the one who killed him, while the Thallians were in the process of hunting me."

Mykah turned the heat off, scraped the eggs together onto a plate, and fussed a little with the garnish. Raena smiled, amused. She'd forgotten he'd been a waiter before becoming a pirate. He handed her the plate. She added the rest of her fruit to it, adjusting the slices to make them more aesthetic.

Mykah smiled back at her before growing serious. "Is that true about the boy?"

"Coni will confirm it when she decrypts the logs."

Raena started to take the plate to Jain when Mykah added one more thing. "We've been watching the news from Kai. The Business Council is trying to hush the story up—violence on a weapon-free world is bad for tourism—but they still haven't identified the men you killed. There's been a lot of commentary about how weapon bans don't protect people, how everyone has a right to protect themselves, and yet more discussion of humans as inherently violent and dangerous. Do you think the Thallians will have seen the news and figure out we're coming?"

"It's possible," she conceded. "We'll just have to send them a message that contradicts the news. I need Coni to break those logs as soon as she can."

* * *

Jain didn't ask her any questions about the food. He set the tray on his lap and hunkered over it, shoveling in bites as though she might snatch it away from him. Raena straddled the chair, facing him. She was pleased with herself for thinking to let him sate one hunger while she told him about another.

Even though she had been a slave, she wasn't used to beatings outside the training arena. She was, however, used to paying attention to the arousal of her masters. Thallian's arousal would have been obvious even if she hadn't been watching for it.

Once she discovered that, it had been easy enough to redirect him from beating her. There were other ways that he preferred to hurt her. She used that to keep herself alive.

"My father would never fuck a slave," Jain snarled at her.

"I wasn't *his* slave," Raena corrected. "He didn't own me, although I'm sure that later he regretted stealing me away from my mistress. If your father had purchased me legally, the Empire wouldn't have allowed me as much freedom as it did. Instead, Jonan had me enlisted as his aide, a free woman in service to the Empire. So when I escaped, Jonan couldn't simply drag me back and have me collared. The Empire had a greater claim on me than your father, and they weren't certain of his loyalty. So I was the pawn they used to control the prince."

Jain protested, "How do I know that anything you say is true?"

"You can ask your father when you get home. If you dare. Ask him about this."

* * *

Looking back on it, Raena realized she'd called Thallian to her quarters to give him something to remember her by. She didn't expect to survive the escape she'd arranged for Ariel from the *Arbiter*.

Raena knew only too well how "interrogating" prisoners excited Thallian. He had been promoted to his diplomatic position after he'd plucked her off of Nyx, so she'd had the dubious honor of watching him grow to love his work. At first Thallian had been content to use robots against prisoners. Then he discovered how much more satisfying it was to have a hand in the physical torture. The latest refinement included sexual abuse. As he was going to kill his prisoners anyway, he saw no reason not to make full use of them.

Raena wanted to spare Ariel as much as she could. It wouldn't matter to Thallian if the blond girl was unconscious. He would make certain that state was no haven for Ariel either. She would remember for the rest of her life, with the clarity of a nightmare, whatever he did to her in that cell. Raena stepped between them as soon as she could.

She lay under the bedclothes in her quarters, hands folded loosely over her bare midriff, waiting for him to answer her message. What could she use to distract him? Perhaps if Thallian thought she was jealous of the attention he paid to her former mistress. If Raena could make him believe that she'd called him away out of envy . . . but her jealousy had to be powerful and convincing. Thallian would sense dishonesty. That was what he did.

She thought over all the advantages Ariel had: wealth, privilege, parents who adored her, state-of-the-art toys. Ariel owned everything Raena had always coveted. Effortlessly. Raena could not allow her to have Thallian as well.

Raena heard him outside the door. Envy was exactly the correct ploy to distract Thallian. Eclipsed in the Emperor's favor, Thallian understood the emotion very well.

He stepped into the darkened room and locked the door behind him. "Come here," he commanded.

She moved through the darkness to stand before him, hands clasped behind her, gaze downcast.

He took her throat in his gloved hand and nudged her chin upward. "You never told me you were a slave."

She waited a breath, uncertain whether he expected an answer. When the pause continued, she said, "My lord, I told you I'd been a bodyguard."

"A slave," he repeated, fingers twitching tighter around her throat. When she didn't answer, he thrust her away. Raena staggered. She wanted to rub her throat, but didn't dare move her hands from behind her back. This had to be played very carefully. She had to survive to get Ariel out of that cell.

"I am a prince," he reminded. "You are a runaway slave."

"That's true, my lord."

Thallian turned on the lights. The brightness made her wince.

"Your mistress is beautiful," Thallian purred. "Unfortunately, she has no value to the Empire now that the Sune hive has been destroyed."

He wanted her to plead for Ariel's life. Raena looked up at him, to see Thallian's sharkish grin. He stripped off his gloves, one finger at a time. Blood dripped from his shirt cuff.

"Her fate is in your hands, my lord." That held a satisfactory amount of bitterness. She added, "I am in your hands now."

"Stand against the door," he said.

Without hesitation, she laid a hand flat against each side of the doorframe. She heard Thallian undressing behind her but did not turn her head. She tried to keep her imagination focused on her bed, on what she would do to atone for interrupting his 'interrogation.' She imagined her blood staining the sheets and streaking Thallian's body.

With an unhurried motion, he coiled her long straight hair into a rope and wound it around her throat. Then he stepped back, leaving her time to wonder what he had in mind tonight. Something wet fell across her back, striping her diagonally from shoulder to hip. She reset her stance and forced the tension from her muscles.

He touched an igniter to her hip. Flames raced up along the accelerant. In a moment, her skin would burn.

Raena breathed out softly. Thallian would torture her until he was satisfied. Crying about it would not help her. She preferred that the rest of the ship not hear her scream.

She thought about his weight atop her, pinning her to the mattress. She thought about his breath panting into her ear. The nape of her neck was still tender where he had bitten her yesterday, grinding her flesh between his sharp teeth. She knew that in his way, he loved her like nothing else in the galaxy. She knew he'd never met a woman like her before and never would again.

* * *

Eilif huddled into an uneasy sleep. Only in sleep could her body forget the insults Jonan had done her. Only in sleep could Dr. Poe's medicine heal her to face another day.

She saw herself standing on a windowsill among unfamiliar skyscrapers. She held a metal strut in each hand. Spotless white fabric snapped in the wind that tore the moisture from her eyes and whipped her white hair into her face.

Raena Zacari leaned against Eilif's shoulder, grinning, black eyes alight. "Jump," Raena encouraged, her hand firm on Eilif's spine. "I'm right behind you."

Eilif let herself be pushed off the windowsill. As she plummeted toward the crowded street below, she debated whether she wanted to fly or if it would be better to let gravity call her home.

Raena dove past her laughing, then flung her wings open and soared upward again. "Come on, Eilif," she shouted. "Join me!"

Eilif opened her wings and felt the air bear her upward. The joy that surged through her jolted her out of the dream.

* * *

Raena stopped by the bay where Vezali was running diagnostics on the escape pod. The pod itself was less than a meter square inside, not room enough for the boy to stand up. One of Vezali's tentacles waved hello when Raena poked her head in.

Raena asked, "There'd be a lot more room in the pod if you got rid of some of the padding, right?"

"You'll want the padding when you hit the planet," Vezali argued.

"Can we shave it down? I've been thinking about Mykah's confiscated arsenal. I'd like to take some of that with me, but I'd prefer the boy not know about it."

Vezali's eyestalk bobbed in the imitation of a nod. "I've disabled the comm and stripped out everything but the cabinetry, as you suggested. *You*'ll have a big enough space to ride in, but there won't be room for much else. You definitely don't want anything as hard as a gun bouncing around in there with you. As it is, inside the console won't be comfortable or very safe, but I've shielded it, made it look like the circuitry had magnetized. It should fool their sensors enough that they won't know you're in there."

"Perfect. Thank you. I'll try to find myself a helmet for the ride. And any space you can clear for weaponry..."

"I won't be able to shield very much space, or they'll get suspicious," Vezali warned.

"Do what you can and I'll pack it tight."

* * *

Coni called to Raena as she passed through the common room. She made her way forward, trying to present as reassuring a façade as possible when she entered the cockpit.

"The logs are done," the blue-furred girl reported. "We have a set of command codes, passwords for the security satellites, and a route through the minefield, presuming of course that everything wasn't scrambled after the transport left to get you."

"Thank you. That makes all this much easier." Then she added, "Any of you had combat training?"

"Mykah's played a lot of simulator games."

Hunched into the pilot's chair, Haoun made a snort that might have been a laugh.

"What about you?" Raena asked him.

"Since the War, there wasn't been much of anywhere to get combat training, unless you're somebody's bodyguard or part of some security force. There aren't any standing military forces any more."

Raena supposed that what Haoun said should have been obvious to anyone not buried in a hole for the last twenty years. "Point taken. I'll train Mykah and Vezali on the exterior guns. You just fly like your lives depend on it and we'll be okay."

There was an awkward pause as they digested that advice. Then Coni reported, "I've sent the decoded logs back to your cabin, like you asked." Raena got the distinct feeling she was dismissed.

"Thank you," she said again and left them alone. She wondered how Mykah, human to all outward appearances, had hooked himself up with these three. Not that it mattered, really. In her former line of work, Raena had had very little interaction with nonhumans—outside interrogation rooms anyway. She found it very odd to have her curiosity about other people coming back so strongly after spending so much time with Gavin and Ariel. Funnily enough, she hadn't been curious about them at all.

* * *

At first Raena found it a shock to watch Revan's log. She knew Thallian's sons were clones; she hadn't realized his brothers were as well.

She remembered Jonan as a man in his forties, old enough to have been her father. He could very well have aged to look like Revan, clean shaven, heavier in the jowls, black hair going silver, forehead etched with a worried frown. And yet Revan's voice was different, slightly higher in pitch and not as resonant. Less commanding.

Seeing Jonan's clone stirred up complicated feelings. The fear she dealt with easily enough. On Kai, she'd proven equal to Thallian's handpicked kidnappers. But she remembered how it felt to have Thallian's attention, the amount of pleasure she'd taken from him while he'd thought he was abusing her, the delight she felt in frustrating and subverting his dominance. Raena had spent enough time alone that she no longer hated herself for anything she had done, or thought, or felt. Still, she was surprised to be overwhelmed, however momentarily, by the past.

She set the log to play again and paid more attention to its subject matter.

If his log was any indication, Revan Thallian had been a man of few words. He had recorded only the barest facts of their journey: the trip to the Templar cemetery world, the avalanche and Jain's injury, Jain's intellectual leap that connected Raena to Sloane, and the disappointing interrogation of the engineer Lim. Raena suspected Sloane had known about Lim's murder. She wondered how he had managed to hold his silence. No wonder he'd acted so squirrelly their last few days on Kai.

Apparently, the Thallians hadn't had any real breakthrough on the hunt until they saw the video of Raena in flight. She smiled. She should remember to thank Mykah for passing that along to the boys for her.

In the end, Revan's log wasn't the fascinating catalog for which Raena had hoped. She wanted to learn more about the Thallian family structure, their home, their defenses, and their patriarch. Revan took those secrets with him to his anonymous grave.

* * *

The boy looked up when Raena entered his cell, but didn't stop his calisthenics. She wondered if she was meant to be impressed by the muscles beneath the black clothes he'd worn around the clock since she'd captured him.

"I need your help, Jain," Raena said. "It's time to send a message to your father and let him know we're on our way. I want you to lie back on the bunk and let me strap you down again."

"What makes you think I'll help you with that?"

"I've been aching for some exercise," she said cheerfully. "Let's go."

He looked her up and down, from her black corona of hair to the pointed toes of her high-heeled boots. Clearly, he remembered what those boots had done to his uncle. Without a word, he marched over to the bunk and lay down. Raena was impressed he was clear-headed enough to realize he couldn't beat her head on.

She waited until he'd positioned his arms, then clicked the remote to lock him in. She dialed down the brightness in the room until a single light beamed into Jain's face. "Hey!" he protested.

"Got to make this look real," Raena explained. She placed the Stinger pistol against his temple. Finally, she set the camera to hover at a good height, where his face, bound hands, and the pistol barrel were in the frame.

Raena grabbed Jain's chin and pretended to examine his face. "Maybe I should have beaten you up a little bit."

Jain closed his eyes. "That's not necessary."

"No? I wonder if they'll think you've collaborated with me. If you gave me the command codes for the transport and brought me through the satellite net."

Jain stared at her, the shadow of fear flickering through his silver eyes. "Why would I do that?"

Raena ignored the question. "I know what your father does to collaborators."

"Stop it. Shut up. They know me. They've known me all my life. They know I won't betray them."

She noted that Jain said "them," not "him." Interesting.

Picking up the conversation again, she said, "I hope they do trust you, Jain. For your sake. I hope you don't find yourself wishing I'd broken a few bones or removed an eye. Given you a couple 'war wounds' you could wear as badges of pride."

She gave him a moment to consider. She had no doubt that he'd seen Thallian punish some suspected traitor, whether or not the victim had been guilty of betrayal.

"What do you want me to say?" Jain growled.

"Tell them you are the only survivor, but you are unharmed. Tell them we demand a ransom of one million standard credits."

"One million!" Jain shouted.

"Can your dad afford more?" Raena teased. When Jain said nothing, she continued, "To be paid to the Fund for Orphans of the Great War. Payment must be made within one standard Earth day, or you'll be coming home in pieces."

Raena watched the boy's face. Expressions flickered over it so quickly that she'd need to watch the video later to catch them all, but he was alarmed by the amount she had named. As she watched him break, she felt sorry for him. He would have to live with that sense of failure for the rest of his life.

How would it be for Jain—the chosen son, the alpha amidst the clones—to be captured by someone as small as Raena and dragged home in restraints, only to be ransomed as a prank? Although his faith in himself had been shaken when he ran from her in the market, his self-regard had been obvious from their first encounter in his cell. She knew firsthand that solitude could make a person question everything he knew about himself. She wondered if he'd ever in his life been alone as long as he'd spent in the holding cell: two days with no brothers to bully, no father to fear. The craving washed over her again: to take him apart, make him share his secrets, and bare himself to her as she had been doing to him. It was easier to resist this time. What purpose would it serve to own him? Her fate was sealed. She had to face Thallian, no matter what. There was no running for her. His supply of sons—and, for all she knew, brothers—wasn't unlimited, but Jonan wouldn't hesitate to expend them all chasing her. Even if she made Jain hers, she had no way to keep him.

"He won't do it," Jain said morosely. "He'll never ransom me. He won't take me back without a fight. You might as well kill me now."

Raena turned the lights back up and reached up to deactivate the camera. "Thank you, Jain. That will be perfect."

"What? I didn't say what you wanted."

"You said exactly what I wanted." She weighed whether to continue, but decided to be honest with him. "He'll know I've broken you."

She had wondered if the boy would cry when confronted with her opinion of him, but he didn't. He was one of those who went entirely internal, leaving his outside cold and seemingly controlled. "It was Jarad who betrayed us, wasn't it?"

She'd nearly forgotten that she'd dared him to guess which brother had identified their homeworld. "No," she said, letting him hear the honesty in her voice. "It wasn't Jarad."

She tucked the camera under her arm and turned to leave the cell. At the doorway, she clicked the remote and unlocked his cuffs. The boy threw himself at the door as it closed.

✳ ✳ ✳

Raena leaned over the computer, watching the recording she'd made of the boy. She watched him say, "He'll never ransom me. He won't take me back without a fight. You might as well kill me now."

Despite herself, she had developed affection for Jain. What would happen if she let him go? She tried to imagine the Thallian scion turned loose in the galaxy. Fourteen years old, no experience talking with anyone outside his family, no understanding of money, and no skills to survive where one had to find one's own shelter and food. In all probability, he'd end up enslaved or, if he was lucky, serving as someone's bodyguard. While she saw a certain poetry in that, she wouldn't wish it on anyone else. He might not be fortunate enough to find a mistress like Ariel.

Raena wondered if her sister might adopt the boy and make him one of her gaggle of war orphans. Ariel had spoken up for protecting Thallian's children. Was she serious enough about it to want to take one into her home?

Raena laughed at herself. That offered no real protection for the boy. He'd want to contact his brothers, if not his father, himself. Either way, Thallian would come for Jain. Jonan had never been one to share his playthings; he wouldn't be able to stand the thought that his favored son might find a better life outside his control. Ariel would never be safe and could certainly never trust the boy not to betray her when the first opportunity arose. She probably didn't have the strength to look into the face of her rapist every day, either.

Anyway, Raena needed the child. If one believed in fate, Jain was fated to return home. Whether he survived or succumbed, he'd have to make his own way. Any more of her interference would be unwelcome. Besides, he might enjoy having another opportunity to capture her. She wondered if he'd freeze in place the second time.

She turned off the recording and switched to the second log, Jain's personal diary. Perhaps she could find what she needed in there. Either way, time grew short. She needed to finish this up, send the message off, and set the wheels in motion. They were only a day away from destiny.

CHAPTER 14

Aten brought the news that there had finally been some contact with the *Raptor*. Of course, it would be crippled Aten who came, the one with so little left to lose and therefore nothing to fear. In his pity, Jonan listened to his wheezing brother speak and then sent him away unharmed.

The message they'd received was brief. They got no response when they acknowledged its receipt. They believed the transport was not much more than a day away. That much Jonan knew before he spooled the message to play.

Jain filled the wall so recently vacated by Raena and her wings. The video jumped and skipped so that the sound didn't exactly sync with the picture. "Uncle Revan is dead," the boy said simply. "So are most of the men. An explosion at the spaceport on Kai damaged the transport, but we are limping home. I have her. Unharmed."

The message dissolved into static. Jonan set it to play again.

He had her. Jain had her. The elation that coursed through Jonan sparkled effervescent. He'd known it was the best decision to send his favorite son along to capture Raena. Of course Jain hadn't let him down. Some kind of reward was in order. Some sort of ceremony acknowledging his superiority…

* * *

Eilif huddled at the back of the shadowed conference room unmoving, watching Jonan replay Jain's message over and over. Jonan hadn't seemed to hear the news that Revan was dead. Instead, he trembled with euphoria.

Her skin felt as if she'd been dowsed with icy water. There were so few of the brothers left now. Revan had told her stories of the palace when it had been full of activity, bustling with warrior-scientists experimenting and sparring and driving each other onward. Now only three brothers survived.

And one was mad.

* * *

The uncertainty was killing Jaden. He'd watched Jain's message with the rest of the boys. Unlike the others, he knew that Revan had been murdered in the fight capturing Zacari. He also knew from watching the news surreptitiously that some of the soldiers had survived the fight, but languished in prison on Kai. So far they hadn't been recognized, but what if they identified the family or betrayed their homeworld? Would the galaxy come raining down to punish the last of the genocidal Thallian clan?

Jaden prayed the soldiers' conditioning would hold and no names would be named. He couldn't figure out how to warn everyone without incriminating himself. If Uncle Revan had been home, Jaden would have unburdened himself to the one uncle he trusted. But Revan was dead. Jaden could only hope that Jain would take responsibility for the mess he'd left behind on Kai.

* * *

Getting back onto Kai was easier than Sloane expected. The Planetary Business Council expected *someone* to come and investigate what had happened there. What they didn't realize was that although the botched kidnapping attempt was hugely significant to them and their bottom line—it wasn't a priority to the galaxy-at-large. Perhaps if someone could connect the men in planetary custody to

Lim's brutal execution, but no one, it seemed, knew about that relationship other than Sloane and Kavanaugh.

Sloane spread around a story that he and Raena—or Fiana Ryle, the name she'd been traveling under—had been agents charged with guarding Miss Lex, charitable do-gooder and all-round nice gal. The cover story got him back into their former hotel room, but of course, Raena had scoured away anything traceable there. She was tricky enough to track Thallian without his gang of teenaged sons noticing, and Sloane, though he'd acquired many questionably legal skills over the decades, was no match for her when it came to computer security. He'd hired someone and still hit a dead end.

While that washout was in progress, Sloane checked into the Thallians' ship. It was a matter of researching all the craft that had landed in Kai City the night before or the morning of the fight, comparing that list to the ships that had blasted off soon after Raena whupped Kavanaugh. When Sloane narrowed the list down, he found an antique Imperial diplomatic transport.

The fact that the old-fashioned transport had been near a jet-bike explosion in the docks threw Sloane off momentarily. If Raena crashed her bike, what had she been doing in the interim before the transport took off?

Gathering her crew, he realized. Raena could do a lot of things, but as far as he knew, she couldn't fly a ship as big as a transport alone. She'd hired someone to go with her.

That infuriated him almost past the point of endurance. She knew *he* was a good pilot. For that matter, so were Ariel or Kavanaugh. Why had she gotten strangers involved?

And where had she gotten the money to pay them? Sloane promised himself that if he found out that Ariel had bankrolled the trip, he would execute her.

That was a project for later. Other problems were more pressing. The transport's registration was in order, though minimal prodding proved it false. Tracing the transport's ownership led him into recurring loops of sales and changes of ownership, false identities and unlikely coincidences. It did not bring him any closer to the transport's actual port of origin.

Time was growing short. Every hour that Raena was gone was an hour closer to her showdown with Thallian. If Sloane didn't find her destination soon, he'd miss the party. There was little point in showing up for the aftermath.

Still, because the transport used outdated Imperial technology, it wouldn't be all that fast. Sloane figured he could catch up, if he stole a modern racer. He put some feelers out, trying to locate one in the Kai City docks.

*　*　*

"You've played video games, right?" Raena asked Mykah and Vezali. "Shoot the spaceships out from between the stars?"

They nodded.

"This is just like that." Raena charged up the guns and flipped on their displays, toggles she'd helpfully labeled #1 and #2. "We don't have anything out there for you to target, but climb into the guns and fire off a few shots. Get the feel of it."

Mykah jumped in, practically aquiver. Every inch a space pirate, Raena wanted to assure him, but she held her tongue, aware that Coni was probably monitoring them. It was in everyone's best interest if she didn't flirt with someone else's boyfriend.

Vezali moved more cautiously into her gun, tentacles flowing forward and pulling herself along. Raena was impressed by the way the tentacles could be legs or arms according to Vezali's needs. It would be fun to train the girl to become a killer.

Mykah swiveled his turret, experimenting with how fast he could move without inducing vertigo. Raena leaned back far enough that she wouldn't get cracked by someone's elbow. There wasn't much room inside the bubble.

"Odds are that you won't see another ship. I'll tell Haoun that if he sees anything bigger than a hopper coming off the planet, he should run. But everyone will feel better if someone knows how to protect the ship while you're running."

"We can't do it from the cockpit?" Vezali asked.

"No. The transport's missile magazines were empty," Mykah answered. "The only long-range defense we've got left are these energy cannons."

"Having a live gunner with visual confirmation of targets was the old Imperial fail-safe to identify real targets, as opposed dummies, chaff, and defensive EFF signals." Raena leaned across Vezali and flipped switch #3. "The firing control software will light targets on the LED. You prioritize which quadrants the guns focus on."

"Is there any trick to it?" Vezali asked.

"Yeah. Fighters, even old ones like Thallian is likely to have, fly really fast. Don't be a hotshot. You just lay down covering fire and give Haoun enough time to get away. If you wait to make sure a target is destroyed, you're gonna get shot up bad. And since you're the ones sticking out of the ship in this bubble, you're gonna be the first to die."

"Got it," Mykah assured.

She wasn't sure if the temptation to duel would be too much for Mykah in the heat of an attack, but for now, he sounded level-headed enough that she felt certain he understood her.

* * *

Raena brought Jain another meal, this one the same gluten and vegetables that everyone else onboard was eating. He picked at the unfamiliar food with his fork, before hunger got the better of him and he gulped it down.

Around a mouthful of food, he asked, "No more stories?"

"You've heard all my secrets," she told him. "Your father loved me and beat me. I fucked him every chance I got. I would have stayed and let him kill me, but my former mistress stole me back from him."

"You haven't told me how you ended up in that tomb. How long did Father know you were there?"

"From the beginning. He was afraid to come after me until the grave robbers disabled his scanners." She watched him react to that and knew she'd guessed correctly.

"So what was he afraid of?"

* * *

Raena woke sluggishly. She found wires trailing from her scalp. Cuffs pinned her wrists to a solid steel chair. Through a plastic tube, cold fluid drained into the back of one hand. That, she suspected, was either a sedative or muscle relaxant.

"My aide deserves better accommodations, but I don't trust you not to abuse them."

Fright blackened her vision. Raena forced herself to look up into those familiar silver eyes. Why, of all of them, did she have to be captured by Thallian?

Surprisingly, her voice was steadier than her trembling insides. "Next time, my lord, why don't you just execute me and save yourself the trouble?"

A searing, nuclear-bright flash exploded in her brain, sweeping thoughts and breath out of its path. Raena felt her body jerk uncontrollably. Tears of shame melted down her face.

"No drugs for you, my dear," Thallian whispered as the torture burned itself out. "The Emperor does not want you stupid and senseless when he asks why you betrayed us."

"What's in the IV?"

"Nourishment. Those shocks will drain you, but you're not to have food or sleep until our guests arrive."

"Prisoners of war get better treatment than this," Raena observed. "Whose order was this?"

"I'm disappointed you have to ask. I intend to keep you safe until the Emperor arrives." He brushed her tears away with a velvet-gloved hand.

White light blinded her. Again her thoughts were shattered by the attack. This time Raena allowed no tears to escape. Hatred stronger than any power she'd previously imagined allowed her to hold her head up and spit onto Thallian's cheek.

"Does it amuse you to debase me?" he asked coldly as he wiped his face with the back of his gloved hand. "I may care for you, Raena, but you understand that I serve the Empire."

She shook her head as much as she dared. "You're such a greedy little servant. You hope that if you abuse me enough, the Emperor will take pity and throw you what's left of me. You may own my body some day," she conceded, "but whatever will remains of me will make you regret it. I will kill you. I swear that, Jonan."

"Perhaps." Thallian smiled again, aroused. The hatch slid open behind him. "Perhaps."

Raena stared after him as if her gaze could dissolve the cell door. Around her, the room measured two meters square. That bastard knew she hated small rooms. In fact, he knew too much about her.

A brilliant flash demolished her thoughts. When it subsided, Raena decided the torment must be untimed, so that she couldn't anticipate the next jolt. Such was hideously typical of Thallian's torture devices. She committed her mind to rest until the next blast.

* * *

Sometime later, Thallian returned to gloat. "How have you occupied yourself, my dear?"

Raena stared at his perfect black beard and imagined wrenching it back with one hand as she slit his throat with the other. "There are forty-eight electrodes glued to my skull."

"Very good." He gave her his most charming smile, the one that hid the points of his teeth. "Because I do care for you, Raena, I designed my machine to give you no pain. The jolt merely disrupts your brain waves. It does no physical harm. The discomfort comes from the convulsions. Your body injures itself. There's a lesson in that for you."

"How generous," she mocked. But knowing the pain was imaginary made the next wave easier to bear. The seizure rolled off of her, leaving a residual ache in her muscles.

"In theory, you will never be allowed enough breathing space to plan your escape." He toyed with her restraints, just beyond the reach of her fingers. "I am curious to see if the voltage will indeed prevent you. I hope our visitors do not arrive before you attempt escape."

Thallian bent closer to her. "Do you regret deserting your post?"

"Not at all," she said as bravely as she could. "Enjoy this while you can. The Emperor will not allow you to keep me very long."

Thallian grabbed her jaw. His kiss stank of death, corruption, everything venomous and rotten. She felt his gloved hand slide down onto her windpipe. Raena prayed he would kill her.

He released her before she blacked out. As he stepped back, his smile was smug, pleased with his self-restraint. "If the Emperor decides you deserve a show trial, he will return you to me afterward. I'll have you yet, Raena, and then you won't have this chair to protect you."

Time passed, but Raena had no way to measure it, no meals or sleep periods to break the monotony. Whenever the torture machine allowed her a respite, she imagined the things she might do to Thallian if given a chance. Perhaps she would castrate him, a millimeter at a time, with a slow-burn laser. Or simply destroy his beautiful face with her knives. She hated herself while she hated him, because she thought she *had* loved him once.

Sometimes a medical tech would come to check the needle in her hand or to adjust the flow of nourishment. It occurred to her to beg them to help her escape, but she decided against it. With her thoughts scrambled, Thallian could outguess her every move.

When he finally suggested the techs as an escape route, Raena only laughed at him. Her acceptance of her fate confused, then enraged Thallian. Thankfully, he grew bored with taunting her.

Left alone, her mind played tricks. Sometimes the walls crept inward though she watched to keep them in place. Sometimes she imagined she saw far-off occurrences as though she participated in them. Thus she stood on the deck of the Emperor's flagship as it neared the *Arbiter*. She listened to the Emperor discuss her fate with his advisors. The only mercy that interested her now was death. She hoped someone would insist on that.

✳ ✳ ✳

The trial was a joke. Raena had difficulty restraining her amusement. She wanted to applaud after they read the death toll. She took full responsibility but stopped short of saying she'd do it all again. Execution should have been a foregone conclusion.

The best part of the whole experience was watching Thallian try to defend her. He requested frequent conferences with the judges. She wished she knew what offers he'd made—what promises—bartering for her.

In the end, after the death sentence had been handed down, the Emperor called everyone into the high judge's chambers. Head held high, Raena marched into the opulent room, dwarfed by the armored Imperial guards. She felt eerily calm and triumphant. Death—escape—was close at hand.

Thallian and Marchan, the Emperor's pet and Thallian's chief rival, entered the room and took their places on either side of their master. The Emperor grinned at her like she was his next meal. "What a chase you've led us on, little girl. Now you are returned at last."

She smiled. She waited to be shot down on the carpet so thick that it felt spongy beneath her boots.

"You're too valuable an asset, Zacari, to be executed like a common conspirator."

She didn't understand what he was saying, but felt Thallian's burning anger. Only later did she understand that she was the Emperor's weapon against Thallian. Everyone knew Thallian was jealous of Marchan, that he might resort to anything to advance to his rival's position. Raena hadn't yet grasped that she was the only thing that Thallian wanted more.

At a signal from their master, the Imperial guards turned on her. Their staves arced as they touched her. Plasma swarmed over her like a black cloud, paralyzing her bit by bit.

Her last sight was Thallian's eyes. He knew he was being tested. He made the choice to excel. Raena could look to him for no rescue. Relieved, she surrendered consciousness.

*　*　*

When she woke, she lay on the cold stone floor of a cavernous room. A shaft of light draped her, thinning as the soldiers outside the tomb replaced its slab. She stumbled toward them, knowing her strength could not possibly equal theirs.

The light thinned to a sliver, filtering around the edges of the stone. As she watched, darkness became absolute. She moaned.

She ran at full speed toward where she remembered the slab to be and attacked the rough black rock with her bare hands. The Emperor's words echoed within her. They decreed a punishment more horrible than becoming Thallian's slave, more terrifying than death. They sentenced her to imprisonment in the dark tombs of the Templar cemetery world.

As she sank to the smooth black floor, her knee knocked something over. Raena crawled after it, stubbing her fingers on the hard stone until she found the electric torch they'd left her. She sat in the utter stillness, staring around in the torch's even emerald glow. Its power would drain soon enough. Until then, she would watch the walls to keep them from creeping inward.

*　*　*

Story told at last, Raena got up from the chair in Jain's cell and stretched. It felt good to have finally shared the memories with someone else. She felt like she had been carrying them alone for a long time. Only now that the story was told did she wonder that neither Ariel nor Gavin had asked her for it. They'd watched the record of her trial and they knew where she served her sentence. But neither of them had really wanted to know what it was like.

"What are you going to do to me?" Jain asked.

Raena decided he deserved to know. "We're going to return you to your family."

"In pieces? The ransom won't be paid."

"I never intended it should be."

He eyed her and read something in her honesty that he hadn't expected. "You never even asked for it, did you?"

"No."

"Why the ordeal with the camera then? Did you actually make a recording?"

"Yes. I thought you could give me something I could use. See how the Emperor inspired me? I saw you as a pawn against your father, but I realized that you were right. He *will* kill you if he thinks you've collaborated with me. So I've made a way for you to go home, if that's what you want."

He didn't even ask what other options he might have. "I have to go home."

"Then your survival depends on how well you lie to him. Don't tell him that you ran from me. Don't tell him I held you prisoner. Tell him I died in custody."

"It won't matter." Jain sighed. "He won't rest 'til he screws your corpse."

Raena laughed. "If I didn't know he had his own private cloning lab, I'd offer to cut off a finger. Send you home with a relic he could enshrine in his bedroom. But I shudder to think what he'd do to my clone."

It was Jain's turn for a bitter laugh.

* * *

Sobering, Jain pointed out, "You didn't really answer my question. Why, if he knew where you were, if he wanted you that much, did my father wait to send for you until you'd gotten out of the tomb?"

"Because he was afraid, Jain." Zacari watched him to gauge how he'd take the news. "At first he was afraid to disappoint the Emperor. He knew his loyalty was under scrutiny."

"But after the Emperor was executed?"

"Has Jonan ever left home since he came crawling back? He is afraid of the rest of the galaxy, afraid he'll be punished for all the fun he had torturing and killing back in the day. He is afraid to be mocked. As long as he's holed up, he can play king, respected, feared, and obeyed. If he came out, he'd have to face the truth. The galaxy sees him as a villain."

Jain knew he should speak up and defend his father, but he had the sinking feeling that she was right. He'd never seen his father as ruled by fear. It explained a lot of things.

The realization ached. He'd always studied his father's behavior, but now he felt as though he'd never understood the man. He hadn't ever been as close to his father as Raena had been and never been allowed as much time alone with him.

"Jain," she said gently, "you wouldn't have wanted my place."

"I'm his favorite son," he said softly. It felt like betraying a confidence, but he knew every word he'd listened to had been a betrayal.

"That's never protected you," Zacari reminded him as she left the cell.

Jain tried to hold onto his hatred of Raena Zacari. He'd seen the recording of her trial. He knew she had done terrible things while fleeing his father: killed men, destroyed ships and property.

Jain had seen her kill the soldiers on Kai. He'd watched her squash Uncle Revan like a bug. She was a villain, too.

And hadn't she deserved to be used by his father, since she was merely a runaway slave? It didn't matter that his father hadn't known that; it didn't stop being true.

Jain closed his eyes. He wasn't a slave, but his father had beaten him. He'd suffered broken bones and humiliation in order to please his father.

Zacari had held Jain prisoner for two days, eating ship's rations and able to exercise. She hadn't even struck him. The only real torture she'd inflicted on him had been the isolation, so that he'd come to anticipate and even enjoy her visits.

Jain shuddered. Now that he saw it for what it really was, what she had done to him had been very subtle. She had broken his faith in himself, his faith in his father and his family. She'd done it in the gentlest way possible, but she'd changed him forever. And she'd done it intentionally.

Because she wanted him as an ally.

Because she wanted him to persuade his father to let her go.

Jain could imagine how well that would go over. His father would probably raise the *Arbiter* and mobilize all hands to go after her now. He would never leave her alone. Even Raena knew it.

Jain only hoped that once he got safely home, he could stay behind as everyone else trooped dutifully to his death. He never wanted to leave home again. He most certainly didn't want to get between those two. He wondered if he *should* ask her to mutilate him, so he'd have an excuse to stay behind.

* * *

Of course Mykah let Raena take her pick of the arsenal. He helped her carry a crate of miscellaneous weaponry back to the escape pods. Since there wasn't room for both of them to work inside, Raena crawled in. Mykah handed guns through the hatch to her.

"There are no restraints in the escape pod," he pointed out, "other than the crash web."

"I won't need anything more than that," Raena assured him. "I've got him tamed."

Mykah scowled at her skeptically. "I saw the recording of what he did to that engineer. I'm not saying that the kid can take you, but your attention might wander on the way down to the planet."

She continued to fit weapons into the nooks Vezali had created behind the padding on the escape pod's walls. "I'm more worried that Coni's going to stage a mutiny in my absence and take off with the transport. I don't want to get stranded down there."

Mykah laughed. "Coni throws a lot of attitude, but this crew is a democracy. We'll come back to pick you up. We want to see how this story plays out. And we owe you for giving us this sweet old ship."

She smiled at him. It transformed her face and made her almost pretty. "Thanks, Mykah. But really, if you see any ships in that system that aren't carrying me, wipe the transport down and ditch it the first chance you get. Thallian is a grudge-carrying bastard. You do not want to try to prank him."

"You're doing it," Mykah pointed out.

"Yeah, but I'm also his greatest weakness." She laughed when she said it, but Mykah figured that didn't make it any less true. He and the crew had been watching her tell her story to the kid. The vulnerability with which she confessed her past humanized her more than anything else she'd done on board.

"You don't want to go through the hoops I did to get my position," she summarized.

"No lie," he assured her. He decided to be honest with her. "Look. Coni is kind of freaked by who you are, what you've done."

"Fair enough."

"But we all understand that this Thallian guy is a mass murderer of epic scale. He must have a pretty wicked lair wherever he is. If we just drop the kid off and turn the family over to the authorities, there's gonna be all-out war prying him out to bring him to justice."

Raena didn't dispute any of that. She smoothed the padding back into place. The escape pod looked as good as new.

"We believe you can execute him," Mykah said as she crawled out into the corridor. "We believe you will bring justice to him."

"That's my plan," she said. "He started this, but I mean to stop it."

∗ ∗ ∗

Sloane was asleep when his request to question Thallian's minions was finally approved. He slapped himself awake, trying to think coherently. He needed a plan.

Because of Kai's weapons-free policy, he couldn't bring anything like a weapon into the prison, not a gun and nothing with an edge. He was certain Thallian had trained his soldiers to withstand a simple beat-down. Sloane needed a quick, easy, and reasonably untraceable way to torture the men into revealing their homeworld.

That meant a side trip to the pharmacist.

CHAPTER 15

"**A**ll right, Jain," Raena said as she flicked on the lights. "Time to go."

He woke raggedly, disoriented. "Where are we going?"

"Escape pods."

He pushed himself into sitting up and thrust his feet into his boots, rubbing his face. "What's happened?"

"We're coming to the edge of the satellite field. Time for all the planet-bound members of this crew to disembark."

"I'm not a member of your crew."

"Of course not," she agreed easily.

The attack didn't come when she expected it: in the cell with the chair at hand to use as a weapon. The boy was cool-headed enough to wait until they had almost reached the pod bay, so that he'd have a shorter distance to drag her body, less chance of being seen by her crew. Jain spun just outside the pod bay's doors, where the corridor was narrow and she didn't have much room to dodge.

Not that she tried to dodge. She caught the elbow he'd aimed at her skull. Wrenched it down behind his back. Slammed his head into bulkhead.

Jain tangled his leg in hers and threw them both to the deck. While she scrambled off of him, he yanked the Stinger from her holster.

As he rolled over to take aim, she kicked his wrist hard enough to numb his fingers. The Stinger flipped out of his grasp. Hauling him across the floor with one hand, she coiled the other arm around his throat. He'd seen her break a man's neck. The fight drained out of him.

"That was a good attempt, Jain," she congratulated. "You can be proud of yourself. You got my gun."

Then she judiciously applied pressure until he blacked out.

Once she'd gotten back to her feet, Mykah stepped out of the other escape pod. "How'd that work out for you?" he asked, another Stinger held loosely in his hand.

"I think it went pretty well." Raena hoisted the unconscious boy onto her back and dumped him onto the bench seat of the escape pod Vezali had modified. "Oh, good," she said as she came back out into the hall. "You found him a change of clothes."

"I figured what he was wearing was probably getting a little rank." Mykah offered Raena the Stinger he was holding, hilt first.

She slipped it into her holster, leaving the disabled one on the floor. "Thank you for everything, Mykah."

He nodded, studiously cool. "Thank you again for busting me out of my old life."

"Least I could do." She retrieved the comm bracelet from the locker across from the pods and slipped it back onto her left wrist. Then she strapped on a jet-bike helmet. "You guys know what to do?"

"Spring the pod, set off the explosives, and run and hide. In that order and no other."

She nodded.

"Everyone else is in the cockpit, waiting to hear I've strapped myself down."

"Let's do it, then."

He pulled her into a hug. Raena clung to him, enjoying a moment of pure animal comfort. Mykah gave her strength and courage in the only way he felt allowed, the only way she could accept it. Silently.

Then he stepped back and grinned at her. "Go kill that mother-fucker."

"I'm on it." She crouched back into the pod and locked the door behind her. Mykah gave her a few minutes to strap Jain into the crash web. She noticed the boy's face was developing a nice bruise. That ought to add some verisimilitude to his account. She patted his knee and wedged herself into her hiding place. Then she pulled the panel into place after her and tightened its bolts from the inside. She triggered the comm bracelet on her wrist and said, "I'm set."

Outside the pod on the other side of the airlock, Mykah toggled open the outer hatch, then released the explosive bolts, and ejected the pod. Raena was grateful for her helmet as the impact of the escape pod's rockets shuddered through the minimally padded compartment.

Before long, gravity took over. She and Jain plummeted toward the planet below, toward their fates.

* * *

When he arrived at the prison, Sloane discovered the reason that Kai Planetary Security had delayed in accepting his request to question the prisoners. Of the three in custody, two had attempted suicide. One succeeded. The second had been found only after he'd lapsed into a coma. It was believed that his brain had gone too long without oxygen. If and when he woke, nothing coherent would be learned from him. There was no indication what the thugs had ingested or how they had smuggled it into their cells.

The Gnik in charge of the prison was mortified. Normally, he dealt with professional gamblers, casual shoplifters, con artists who preyed on tourists, and brawlers now and then. Now, when he felt he was under galactic scrutiny, when he was entrusted with truly dangerous criminals, they'd mocked his custody. He lived in terror that the rest of the galaxy would judge him as inept.

Sloane fought the smirk off his face as he swore to tell no one. Then he was escorted to a cell and locked inside with the surviving prisoner.

The middle-aged man had been stripped of his clothing. Face in his hands, he sat on the rough stone bench that served as his bed. Graying curls spiraled across his chest. He was lean, but not dangerously muscled. He hadn't spoken since he'd woken up from the sleep grenade.

Sloane pulled a mask up from his collar and over the lower half of his face. The man didn't look up at him to notice.

Then Sloane struck the canister of RespirAll hard against the stone wall. The can's seam cracked. Icy gas numbed his fingers as it whooshed out. He dropped the can and kicked it over toward the prisoner. In small doses, RespirAll mitigated asthma in humans brought on by breathing alien air. Large doses worked as a kind of truth serum. In fact, it was sometimes difficult to shut people up after they'd inhaled too much.

The sound of the gas got the prisoner's attention. He grimaced at Sloane, not entirely sane.

Sloane crossed the room, standing over the man with an image of the unclaimed bodies in Kai City's morgue in his gloved hand. "Revan Thallian I know." He held up a still of Raena taken from the news footage of the fight. "Raena Zacari I know." He shuffled through the others and held up the picture of Thallian's clone. "Zacari captured the boy and stole the Thallian family's transport. I want to know where you came from."

"We're not allowed to know that," the man rasped, still grimacing. "We're not allowed to know where we live. We might find out how to escape. We might know which direction to run to freedom."

Sloane help up the final image, Thallian's wanted poster.

The prisoner launched himself off the stone slab. He bowled Sloane over backward, clawing after the image.

"Can't see that! Can't show it! The galaxy will find him!"

Sloane's gas mask got knocked askew in the melee. He tried to crawl out from under the madman, but the prisoner had gone into a frenzy that held no thought for his own safety.

Sloane hammered at the prisoner with his fists, hoping to beat some sense back into the man. "Where is Thallian?" he demanded. "Where's he hiding? He'll come after you if you don't tell me. I need to get to him first."

He didn't get any coherent answer before the cavalry, however unwelcome, burst through the door and hit them both with stun sticks. Apparently prison guards on Kai were allowed to carry weapons.

✶ ✶ ✶

When Jain woke, he had been dreaming. In his dream, his mother held him tightly in her arms. He felt safe. He felt loved. He felt unique.

Then he opened his eyes and found himself cradled in a crash web inside one of the *Raptor*'s escape pods. Strapped in beside him was a change of clothing—his dress uniform, in fact—some toiletries, and his rucksack. A holster held a Stinger with two shots fired.

On his other side sprawled the indigo dress he'd found in the closet on Brunzell. As he lifted it to his face to get one last breath of a real girl, a recording sphere rolled out of its folds and onto the floor. Jain scrabbled after it with his foot.

Raena hadn't come with him. She'd left the dress as evidence that he'd had her. It was scarcely better than facing his father empty-handed.

Jain closed his eyes, feeling gentle ocean waves rocking the pod. He must have been out for the whole ride down. He wondered how close Raena had gotten him to home. How much information had his brother given her? Did she know exactly where the city was? What would she do with that knowledge?

Nothing, it seemed, at this moment.

Jain unstrapped himself from the crash web. He crouch-walked across the little pod and tried the comm. Unsurprisingly, it was fried. It didn't really matter. The family would have monitored his descent. Uncle Merin or the boys would be along soon to collect him.

Using the toiletries, Jain washed up as much as possible and combed his hair. He put on the clean clothes and ejected the garments he'd worn in captivity. He absolutely never wanted to see those things again.

Then there was nothing to do but wait. Without tools to repair the communications console, he could make no contact with the outside world. He couldn't even check the time.

He sat back on the bench seat and tried to relax. After a minute, he picked up the recording sphere. Balancing it in his palm, he stared at his warped reflection on it. The black hair and silver eyes were exactly like his father's. The only thing to set him apart was the huge bruise purpling his face from hairline to jaw, a souvenir from Raena slamming his head into the bulkhead. He supposed he ought to thank her for that. At least it looked like he had tried to capture her.

What had Raena recorded on the ball? Was it the video of the interrogation where she shamed him? Was it a message for Jain, or for his father? Jain wished the comm were working, so he could check the ball before he turned it over to the family.

Funny how she'd taught him to learn as much as possible about a situation before he leapt into action. She'd made him question his father's motives, his father's love: things he'd never doubted in his life. If Jain had been engineered to cry, he might have—except for the fear that his rescue party would find him weeping.

He wondered where Raena was. Had she managed to escape?

Maybe his father was chasing her even now.

Jain was ashamed to find himself hoping he'd have some respite before he had to face his father and lie about having lost control of Raena Zacari.

*　*　*

As small as her tomb had been big, the space inside the comm console was surprisingly cozy. Raena listened to Jain rustling around the escape pod, but as long as she kept quiet, there seemed to be no danger that he'd break into the console and discover her.

The whole pod oscillated, buoyed by the ocean outside. Raena didn't know much about the Thallian homeworld, not even what they called it among themselves, other than that water covered most of what survived of it. Jimi's photo of the sabershark had given her enough information to identify the planet. From there, she was able to find its scientific designation, thanks to an old encyclopedia that referenced the environmental devastation rained down on it after the War in retribution for the Thallian family's crimes. When the criminals themselves couldn't be located, their homeworld had been executed in their stead. No one seemed to suspect the mass murderers still inhabited the planet.

Raena didn't know where on the planet they had hidden. She was relying on the family's reduced circumstances to have made all their possessions precious. They wouldn't destroy the pod or abandon it if they thought there was anything they could salvage from it. Besides, she was certain that Jonan would want to analyze the pod's external recording of the final moments of Revan's transport. She hoped that Mykah's crew had been able to pull off the escape sequence as planned.

If not, she might find herself chasing Thallian across the galaxy after the transport. The thought grimly amused her.

Although her cubbyhole was dark inside, Vezali had done a good job with the ventilation. The air blowing on Raena's face felt fresh and slightly cool. All in all, she found it a very comfortable little space. The rocking made her sleepy. Smiling, Raena let her eyes close. This might be the last rest she got for a while.

* * *

Voices woke her. The helmet and the mag shielding on her hideaway made the words hard to decipher, but their tones seemed excited and happy. Jain's homecoming was apparently welcoming. She was glad, for the boy's sake. Let him enjoy it while he could.

After the initial gabble of voices, she could not mistake Jonan's. He stomped into the pod and flung himself down on the bench seat. Raena held her breath and willed her heart to stop bashing its way out of her chest. She wanted to hear what he said.

"You alone escaped?" Thallian demanded. The sound of Jonan's voice raised goosebumps on Raena's skin. Her body remembered how to fear him.

"Yes, Father," Jain said. "I'm sorry. I got careless. She attacked me, and when I woke, I was in this pod."

"So you don't know what caused the *Raptor* to explode?"

Surprised by the casually dropped news, Jain stuttered, "N-no, sir."

"Did you bring me anything of hers?"

Raena couldn't make out Jain's response, but she had the feeling he wouldn't give his father the recording ball. Kid was learning to be cautious.

* * *

"This was hers," Jain said, pouring the blue dress into his father's lap. He watched his father rub the silken fabric between his fingers, play with the shimmer of the diamond clips, raise the bodice to his face, and breathe deeply.

"You had her," his father sighed.

"Yes, sir," Jain said cautiously. "Please forgive me for not bringing her to you." He realized belatedly that there was no way to lie his way out of this.

The silence stretched uncomfortably. Jain didn't dare look up from the toes of his father's boots. The bruise throbbed across his temple. He hoped it looked as if he'd struck his head hard enough to damage his memory. He didn't want to admit that Raena sent him away to cover her escape.

His father stood suddenly, jerking upward like a puppet. "First we must get you home," he said cheerily. "The boys will certainly have traced the other escape pods by then. Merin can collect them from the meteor belt."

* * *

Raena heard a series of clangs, which sounded as if cables were being clipped to the pod. Shortly afterward, it was winched aboard some kind of oceancraft. It felt like flying to be hoisted into the unseen vessel's hold. There the pod was lashed to the deck. After the voices went away, the ship began to move. Eyes closed in her private darkness, Raena tried to determine the direction of their movement. They seemed to be going…down?

That would make sense, she supposed. If the surface of the planet had been scraped bare and its atmosphere poisoned—using Templar technology, just to make the justice that much more poetic—then the safest place for the Thallians to hide would be under the sea. Raena wondered if anything else still lived in it. Probably, to provide a cover against ships scanning for life from space.

Working as quietly as she could, Raena unscrewed the bolts holding the panel of the communications console in place. She eased the panel open to find herself still in total darkness.

She gently set the panel against the bench seat and felt her way across the pod. Its hatch gaped open. She leaned against the doorframe, listening. It was awfully quiet in the dark hold outside.

Raena was grateful for the darkness—very conservative, these Thallians—since it meant that they hadn't felt it necessary to post a guard over the escape pod. They honestly had no idea she'd stowed away. Meeting Vezali through Mykah had been a stroke of the purest luck.

Raena pulled back the padding on the pod's walls and armed herself. Her years in the tomb had given her the skills and sensitive fingertips to do the job while completely blind. She quickly discovered she'd taken more from Mykah's horde than she could carry, which meant more than was probably necessary. She filled her holsters, the sheaths in her boots, the back of her belt, and the rucksack she'd brought along. Anything more than that and she would clank as she walked. Still, one never knew when she'd need concussion grenades or a sharpshooter rifle.

She collected everything else and stuffed it inside the communication console. It was fairly easy to disassemble a grenade and rig a tripwire. Then she gently replaced the comm console's plate. Anyone who poked into her hiding place was going to get a surprise.

She crept out of the pod to explore her immediate surroundings. The cargo hold stood otherwise empty. The tricky part then would be to leave the hold without attracting notice. She'd need to find a hole to hide in somewhere on the submarine until they reached Thallian's base. And it wouldn't hurt to find something to eat if she could. No telling when she'd have another opportunity.

✳ ✳ ✳

The younger boys crowded into the mess to talk to Jain. He kept one eye aimed down the passage toward the cockpit and his father as he pulled the men's magazine from his rucksack. He'd swiped it from the grave-robber's apartment on Brunzell, but he felt so ill now that he didn't want to keep it for himself.

Jin frowned at the slippery pages with their photos of naked human girls, too young to understand their appeal, but Jarad snatched it away, eyes aglow. "Got any more of these?" he whispered.

"Not like that," Jain said. "There's some inter-species stuff…"

The boys stared at him like he'd turned green.

"They still have tits," he hissed in his own defense. He decided to keep the bottle of Old Kentucky Home to share with Jamian and Jozz. Maybe his older brothers would understand him better.

* * *

Wedged behind the controls inside a disabled gun turret, Raena got her first view of Thallian's home. The city was larger than she'd hoped. A collection of domes clustered on the ocean floor. The central dome contained a sort of castle, its crenellated security wall overlooked by narrow towers. That would be her primary target.

Other domes held barracks, workshops, and, undoubtedly, the cloning lab. After her initial dread, Raena noticed how few lights burned in the buildings. Most people were either asleep—she had no idea what the planetary hour was—or else much of the city was vacant. In fact, on closer examination, one of the darkened domes sported a web of ominous cracks. Money certainly seemed to be running out for the Thallians.

Perhaps her presence wasn't even necessary here. In another decade or so, they'd be forced out into the galaxy, scattering to survive. Maybe what she planned to do was more of a mercy than she'd suspected. At least they would all die together.

Oh well. She was here. Jonan was here. Might as well finish the job. Priority one had to be to evacuate all non-essential personnel. Raena had some ideas about how to go about that, using one of Jonan's own schemes. She wondered if he'd recognize it and see it as the tribute it was meant to be.

* * *

The boys lined up as an honor guard to meet the *Predator* when it returned with Jain. Eilif took her place at the end of the line beside Jarl, the youngest boy. She would have preferred to hide somewhere less conspicuous, but her absence might be noticed. She had learned not to invite trouble.

She anticipated seeing her rival marched off the submarine in shackles, but only Jain escorted Jonan down the gangway. Jonan halted beside Merin and leaned close to whisper orders, but Eilif was too far away to guess what they were.

The pause granted her a good long look at Jain. He had grown since he'd left home. His ankles and wrists showed white beyond the cuffs of his dress uniform. He seemed more gaunt, but maybe it was just that the large bruise gave his face a hollow, hunted aspect. He looked beaten.

Eilif wondered what had happened to her husband's favorite son. She wondered if anyone else could see the transformation, or if the boys, crowding around Jain now with scuffling hugs and resounding slaps on the shoulder, were merely so relieved to have him back that they'd overlooked the change.

She was startled when Jain's eyes met her own. She saw that her assessment had been correct. Then she stepped briskly forward. "Let's have Dr. Poe look at that bruise."

The normal Jain would have shrugged off the injury and worn it as a badge of pride. This Jain looked grateful for the excuse to flee the homecoming commotion.

"Jamian, Jarad, Jimi, with me," Merin commanded.

The rest of the boys lined up again beside Jozz, at attention as the others marched off to their new duty.

"I think Dr. Poe will be in the kitchen," Eilif said to Jain, leading him away. She knew better than to ask what was wrong.

* * *

The cloning facility wasn't abandoned, as Raena first thought. It was merely short-staffed, scarcely warded by a skeleton crew that seemed to be janitors more than guards.

Curiosity drew her from one deep, narrow tank to the next. Most were empty, but six held clones of Jonan, small black-haired boys curled forward with knees drawn up. They were so pretty that it was a shame she'd have to destroy them all.

It looked easy enough to pull the cords that kept them warm and nourished, that circulated their bathwater and carried away their waste. Unfortunately, someone might discover her sabotage and be able to re-engage everything before serious damage was done. She kept moving through the lab, looking for a permanent solution.

After she passed several rows of empty tanks, she came across a handful more that were occupied. These clones were younger, almost full-term human infants. Female. As she watched, one of the clones opened its night-black eyes and looked up at her.

Raena's reaction was visceral. Hot anger quivered through her until she trembled like a struck bell. He had cloned her.

Now her search for poison took on new urgency. She surged forward in a fog of horror and disgust, determined that these abominations would be spared what he had done to her. Her clones could not survive to have him touch them. The only mercy she could offer was to wipe them out.

Just beyond the lab, Raena found a broom closet stocked with just the sort of thing she needed. Sodium hypochlorite should do the trick.

* * *

It took longer for Jain to find a moment alone than he expected. The boys buzzed around him, relieved that he was home, but also curious about the galaxy beyond their confinement. Not that he'd really seen all that much, between the week on the desolate Templar cemetery world and all the transit time on the *Raptor*. But he'd had his hours on Kai, marveling at the spectrum of creatures shopping in the market. And he'd had his days conversing with Raena Zacari. Even Jamian and Jozz, who had gone on supply runs before, could not claim to have spent as much time alone with a woman.

Between the weeks on the hunt and the hours spent in confinement, Jain's days and nights had gotten turned around. After the other boys turned in for the night, he lay wide-awake. Eventually, he crept out to a terminal. He slipped Raena's recording sphere into the player, plugged in his earphones, and hunched close.

Raena Zacari filled the screen. She wore crimson hands'-breadth bands across her breasts and low on her hips, but the rest of her skin was bare. She had turned away from the camera and looked back over her shoulder. Her back was ridged with old scar tissue. A starburst scar scrawled over her ribs where she'd been shot protecting his father. A rope of scars encircled one ankle.

"Yes, this was consensual," she said in her sweet, low voice. "When I consented to be beaten bloody, your father allowed me to continue to live. I knew the price of saying no, of begging him to stop, would be paid with my life. I bought my life with blood and pain. What have you paid for yours, Jain?"

Jain froze the image, sat back from the computer, and closed his eyes. What was she doing? As far as everyone knew, she'd been killed in the *Raptor*'s explosion. He was sure his father didn't believe that. Even now, Uncle Merin was out searching the minefield for evidence that the ship had not been destroyed. If his father saw this video, he'd be after Raena like a dog after a bitch in heat.

Despite his revulsion, Jain wasn't immune. Like the other boys, he'd watched his share of degrading entertainment online. This was the first time he'd seen a woman he knew basically undressed. It didn't matter that she was scarred or old enough to be his mother. As ashamed as he felt, he could make no apologies for his reaction to her.

But what did she want from him? Even though he'd enjoyed hearing her stories aboard the *Raptor*, he knew she hadn't confessed to him by accident. She'd chosen him to listen, chosen what to tell. Why had she chosen him to see this?

He couldn't figure it out. He knew he was being manipulated, but to do what?

He shook his head and tried to look at the problem from another direction. What was she asking him? What had he paid for his life?

What made her think that he'd paid any less than she had? He didn't have the visible scars to show off, but he had the mended bones, bad memories, and the knowledge that his father was older, stronger, more ruthless, implacable...

Ice trailed down his spine. Was that her point? That the price they'd paid was comparable? That he was a slave, just as she had been?

Jain leaned back again, rubbing his eyes, and wondered what she wanted him to do. He wouldn't betray his family. They were all he had in the universe. And yes, he understood that was because they were protecting his father's generation for war crimes that had occurred before the boys were born.

He tore the sphere out of the player, unwilling to see if there was anything else she wanted to say. He was tempted to deliver it immediately to his father.

Then the sphere slipped in his hand and Jain scrambled to catch it before it could roll away and escape. If he turned over the recording, he would have to make up new lies about how it had been made. How had he undressed his father's girlfriend and why. Jain knew with clearer certainty than anything else in his life that one did not lie to his father. That was why Raena made sure Jain was unconscious when the *Raptor* exploded. He honestly had no idea what had happened and that might keep him safe. His father was usually sane enough to recognize honesty when he saw it.

Jain changed his mind, bent down, and rolled the recording sphere under the desk. He knew he should destroy it; that if anyone else found it, he was doomed. But destroying it wasn't going to be a silent process, and he didn't want any sleepy boys asking questions. Later, after things had settled down, he could retrieve it, watch it one more time if he had to, and then find a way to lose it permanently.

CHAPTER 16

Raena stood amidst the vats holding the latest crop of Thallian boys. She tried to feel a touch of pity for them before she dumped the bleach in, but really, the pity was that they would grow up to be Jonan's sons, part of his army. It was kinder to spare them that future. They would die for him either way.

She moved on and dispatched all the baby Raenas. She turned her back on them, unable to watch as her clones thrashed and perished. Even though she'd had no connection to them other than genetically, their deaths still chilled her. She stood guard until she was sure nothing could be salvaged to start the process again.

After the job was done, it was easy enough to steal the appropriate cleaning supplies to evacuate the city. Raena traced the building's air supply until she found its connection to the dome nearby, where the proles lived.

It wasn't until the chemical spill spread its fumes throughout the ventilation system, when she could finally see the city's inhabitants coughing and shouting, fleeing—they thought—for their lives, that she noticed women seemed a rare luxury on Thallian's world. The men had an eerie similarity to each other: all human, all dressed in black, and all pallid from their lives under the sea.

They were even all roughly fortyish. Her suspicion was confirmed when she saw a man she recognized. Leuwis had served Thallian during the War.

These were the surviving crewmembers of the *Arbiter*. Thallian's warship had been large, with a complement of over a thousand. As Raena watched the men streaming toward the lifeboats with remnants of their military precision, she counted a fraction of that. Had the others died in service? Defected when a chance presented itself? What were the remainder still doing serving the madman twenty years after the War was over? Didn't they have anywhere else to go?

The lifeboat station had armed guards, but they put up minimal resistance to the hysteria. One soldier who opened fire on the crowd was quickly swarmed, disarmed, and beaten to death. The rest of the guards could smell the corrosive air and feel it in their eyes and sinuses. Perhaps if any of Thallian's clones had been stationed there, there would have been less of a rout. As it was, Raena was pleased by the efficiency of the evacuation. It left her only the people in the castle to handle.

* * *

It was more difficult to get into the castle than she'd expected, which was to say that its defenses were actually online. Raena watched a crew of sleepy boys follow their father down to try to stanch the flood of refugees. Thallian had grayed, but she knew that from the family photos she'd found on the family's private channel. He was also smaller than she remembered. She shook her head, amused. Her memory had built him up to be a towering figure, even though she knew logically that couldn't be true. He was only a man with a penchant for snappy dressing and an air of command predicated on a total disregard for anything other than his own agenda. Kind of pathetic, now that she thought about it.

She turned back to the scanner she hoped to ghost past.

Someone who worked for, or was part of, the Thallian family was a mechanical genius. He'd rewired the security system so that it was full of elegant redundancy. He'd probably been the one to keep the transport flying decades after it had gone out of date. Whoever he was, she expected to see more of his work before she left the city.

* * *

"Come back," Aten told his younger brother Merin on the comm screen. Since the chair regulated his breathing, he couldn't force the words to sound more urgent. He explained, "We're under attack."

Merin glanced sideways, checking a monitor Aten couldn't see. Looking for spaceships, probably. When he didn't see any, Merin stared at the viewscreen as if his gaze could penetrate it. "Attacked by whom?"

"Jonan's phantom, it seems. Someone contaminated the air supply down in the city domes. The men are fleeing en masse. Jonan has taken most of the remaining boys to try and re-establish some sanity."

"Jamian—" Merin began, but the boy interrupted him.

"I'm turning us around, sir."

"All possible speed," Merin ordered unnecessarily. Then to Aten he said, "The men know they won't survive long on the surface."

"It's a full-scale panic. I doubt there's logic involved."

"How did she get into the city?"

"My best guess is that she somehow stowed away in Jain's escape pod. I'm going to take the youngest boys and see what I can find out about that now."

"Do it. We'll be home as soon as possible."

* * *

Ariel tugged her braid out from under Kavanaugh's shoulder so she could get up out of bed. As she crossed the cabin, she pulled his shirt over her head. If she sat close enough to the monitor, it shouldn't be obvious she had no pants on.

When she was situated, she turned on the computer. Its screen filled with a Shtrrel, who clicked his beak disapprovingly. "Miss Lex? Sorry to wake you."

"That's all right." She brushed her hair back toward its sloppy braid, trying to come awake enough to place him. Then a poster over his shoulder—showing a sail race past a familiar set of stone arches—made her realize this was Kai's Head of Planetary Security. "Did you find Fiana?"

"It's rather more complicated than that." He shuddered slightly, resettling his feathers. "We have Gavin Sloane in our custody now."

The change from pseudonyms to real names jolted Ariel awake. "Go on," she encouraged.

"Sloane ingested a large dose of some form of human truth serum. Apparently, he came back to Kai under false pretenses, intending to, shall I quote? 'Beat the truth out of Thallian's goons.' Kai City Prison Security captured him in the process of doing just that."

Ariel put her forehead in her hand and hunched forward so she could prop her elbow on the desk. "Is anyone injured?"

"Not permanently." He resettled his feathers again, evidently feeling awkward. "Ms. Shaad, your party has brought nothing but trouble to Kai. As no lasting damage has been done beyond a spate of negative news reports, we are willing to release Mr. Sloane to your custody, effective as soon as you can return to Kai to claim him."

That wasn't where she'd thought this conversation was going. "Commander, I'm not interested in paying Sloane's bail."

He hooted in surprise.

"After we left Kai together, Gavin Sloane attacked me. In fact, I was forced to stun him. It's not my habit to be armed on my own ship, but I was lucky to have been able to stop things when I did. I put Sloane off my ship at Mallech and consider myself lucky to have been armed at that time. I do not, under any circumstances, take responsibility for Sloane or his behavior after we parted ways."

"Ms. Shaad, you understand that Sloane has been under a truth serum. You understand he's told us everything about your stay on Kai."

Ariel gave him a wry smile. "I'm sure he gave you much more detail than either of us is truly comfortable with, sir."

The Shtrrel inclined his head.

"Then no doubt he's told you who Thallian is, who Fiana is, and why I don't want to have anything more to do with what's going on between them. I am in hiding, Commander, until I'm sure Raena's vendetta has been carried out."

"If you won't take Mr. Sloane off our hands, we will be forced to have him bound by law."

"Understood, Commander." She relented a little. "I'm sorry we have been so much trouble for you."

He made a gargling noise that she recognized was a laugh. "It's been much more excitement than we are used to on Kai."

* * *

An hour later, poking around the Thallian family's transportation yard, Raena found a hopper parked in a bay apart from the family's other ships. The antique hopper had hoses hanging out its undercarriage. Tools lay spread out nearby. They were polished clean and very orderly in their arrangement, but the implication was that someone had been repairing the hopper and might get back to work on it soon.

She crawled around and under it, approving the modifications Jimi had made. It appeared ready to go. The sprawl of hoses was merely well-done camouflage.

While she was occupied, something exploded not far away, a boom so loud that her head rang. The deck beneath her back flexed. The overhead lights flared twice, struggled, then went out. A fuse somewhere had been asked to carry too great a load.

Raena lay in the darkness listening to the basso profundo groan and grumble of the dome holding back the ocean overhead. Her reaction to the ominous sound was primal: take the hopper and get out now.

She lay still a moment, exploring the way her body felt as panic coursed through it. Then the dome held, the sounds calmed, and reason reasserted itself. She knew she'd stay. Perhaps she should have used less explosive on the escape pod. While breaching the castle's dome would solve the problem of the Thallians' continued existence, it wasn't the way she personally wanted to go out: crushed by a wall of black water. She would keep the lesson in mind.

The emergency lighting finally kicked into gear. Dim red lights filled the room with ominous shadows. She heard voices shouting and feet running as the fire squad mobilized.

One pair of footsteps peeled off from the others and ran into the bay where she lay hidden. Something landed inside the hopper with a thud. All around the little ship, maintenance hatches were being hastily slapped shut as the unseen person prepared to leave.

Raena did her part by disconnecting the unnecessary hoses. When the boy pulled one lose, she came with it.

He jumped back, silver eyes full of pupil in the semi-darkness. He looked exactly like Jain, the same arch to his eyebrows, same smooth black hair, and the same strong chin. He was obviously an even younger clone of Jonan. "You're Jimi, aren't you?" she asked.

"Yes." He swallowed. "Your name's not really Fiana, is it?"

"That was my mother's name."

He struggled to decide which question to ask her next. He settled on, "What are you going to do here?"

She smiled. "You're leaving. What do you care?"

"I don't want them coming after me," he spat with startling vehemence.

"I'll do what I can about that."

He nodded once, a sharp jerk of his head that she recognized as one of his father's gestures.

"I need to go now," he said. "While they're busy. I've been waiting for a distraction like this to cover my escape."

Raena helped him finish the rest of the preflight prep. When he climbed up to get into the cockpit, she followed him up the ladder.

"I want you to understand something," she said quietly. "Your father taught me never to leave an enemy alive. He made a mistake when he didn't come into my tomb to finish me off. I want to know that I'm not making the same mistake in letting you go."

"I want you to kill them. I want you to kill them all. I'll be watching the news to hear that the ocean has swallowed the last of the Thallian murderers. I want to know this place has been washed away."

Raena smiled at his loathing. "Don't you want to stay to make sure the job is done right?"

"I'm too much of a coward," he admitted. "My father, my brothers—they've never liked me. They've always known I'm not like them. I don't see the family's hand in the Templar genocide as anything glorious."

"I don't want you to change your mind someday, Jimi. I don't want to find you on my tail, ready to avenge your family."

"You won't."

"If you so much as think about coming after me, I'll kill you in your sleep."

"I won't. You're doing the right thing here, Raena. Kill them all. Kill Father last."

She nodded and slid back down the ladder. The hopper's canopy whooshed closed. The boy watched until she'd gotten beyond the blast shielding to power up the engines.

Raena slipped out into the corridor outside, curious to watch the fire suppression activities. Would they work together as an integrated team, or was there yet more dissent among the family?

* * *

Merin dove into the flames with his fire extinguisher upraised, spewing foam indiscriminately over everything. The boys scrambled into the hangar behind him, protecting his back as much as mastering the fire.

Standard procedure for fire was to close off the affected area and drain its air. Looking around at the inferno, Merin suspected he should have done that here. None of the equipment was going to be salvageable. But his older brother had been in here, searching the *Raptor*'s escape pod. Merin had wanted to rescue him, if that were possible, although Aten might not necessarily thank him for it.

Merin managed to carve an oasis of calm out of the flames. A foam-draped shape hunched in front of him. He reached out to brush aside some of the foam to confirm it was Aten's chair.

His brother slumped in it, clearly dead. The chair continued its wheezing, forcing air and now fire suppression foam in and out of Aten's burned lungs. The chair had undoubtedly sucked the fire into Aten's chest after the initial explosion, cooking the poor cripple from the inside.

Merin shoved the chair hard enough to face the obscenity away from him.

Around the pod bay, the boys were making headway at last. Merin stepped carefully through the slick foam to peer into the escape pod. The metal walls radiated heat that he could feel even through his gloves, so he didn't touch them. After leaning inward, he could see two bodies, one curled on the floor and the other on the bench seat. Their crisped skin looked like burnt paper. Nothing remained to identify them.

Merin did a mental count, looking around at the boys behind him. The dead boys must be Jarl and Jin. Where was Jimi? Merin roared the boy's name, but got no response.

Later, after the inferno was completely subdued, Jimi remained missing. Merin considered whether the boy might have had some connection to the blaze. Jimi was smart enough to rig a firebomb, but not ruthless enough to use it. If he had tried to kill anyone, it wouldn't have been Aten, who'd treated the boy gently. Jonan's harlot must have done it, but why hadn't Jain, the last occupant of the pod, set her trap off? More was at work here than was immediately apparent. Normally Merin loved a good mystery, but this one had cost too dear.

It was time to demand answers from Jonan.

* * *

Thallian's hands shook as he snapped the final cuff on Jain's wrist. He winched the boy upward until his toes just brushed the floor. "We will discuss this again," Jonan said with dangerous calm.

"I don't know what's going on," Jain protested. He sounded surprised and hurt, but not as angry as he should have been. The other boys might have collapsed immediately at the slightest discomfort, but not Jain. Jain, if he'd been innocent, should have been stronger than this. Disappointment tightened around Thallian's throat.

"Let's start again. Tell me about going to the 'pleasure planet' and capturing Raena."

So Jain confessed the embarrassing truth: that Raena had destroyed their attack squad. She'd trapped Revan in a net taken from Jain and then killed the man with her foot. She'd chased Jain back to the *Raptor* and imprisoned him in the cell meant for her. She'd stolen the transport, strapped him into the escape pod, and sent him home. If the *Raptor* exploded after Jain left it, he couldn't guess what had happened to it or to Raena. He hadn't betrayed the family or given her the location of the homeworld. She told him one of his brothers had already done so.

Thallian watched the litany pour from the lips of his favorite son. Sick dread twisting in his stomach, he demanded, "What did she *do* to you on the ship?"

"Nothing," the boy said. "Mostly she left me alone. She told me stories about what it was like to be your aide."

There was more to that, Thallian was certain. "What did she tell you?"

"That you never had any sense when it came to her," Jain snarled.

Thallian heard that Jain spoke the truth to the extent he knew it. Still, he didn't realize his blow was in motion until he saw Jain's head rocket backward away from his hand. Pulled off balance, the boy lost his purchase on the ground. He swung crazily, suspended by his arms. He was smart enough not to fight the motion, to let his weight hang until it pulled his pendulum swinging to a stop. He would feel the suspension now.

"Did she fuck you?" Thallian asked.

Jain's eyes jerked up to meet his father's. He opened his mouth, but no response came out.

No, Thallian understood. And the boy was horrified that his father even considered the possibility.

Good.

"How did you smuggle her down to the planet?" Thallian asked.

"I didn't know she was in the pod. The comm didn't work. She must have been hidden inside the console," Jain guessed. "The comm console wouldn't have been big enough for a normal person, but..."

Thallian nodded. "So. You brought Raena to me, as you were charged. But you lied to me, Jain. If you'd told me you'd been her prisoner, I would have been disappointed in you. I thought I'd trained you better than that. To be honest, though, it doesn't surprise me. Raena was the best pupil I've ever trained. Revan was a fool to underestimate her."

Jain watched him working it out. He wriggled, trying to adjust the strain in his shoulders.

"You shouldn't have lied to me, Jain."

"I'm sorry, Father. I was afraid."

"You have every right to be afraid. Because of your dishonesty, the lower city is empty. Some of the men are dead. The rest are struggling to survive on the planet's surface. It will take a while to round them all up again, bring them back down here. The explosion of your escape pod weakened the dome in the hangar, putting all our remaining ships at risk of flood. Aten is dead, and Jin and Jarl. Jimi is missing. The new clones have all been mutilated and poisoned. And Raena is out there, up to who knows what kind of mischief now."

Jain's face composed itself as the boy prepared to take his punishment.

"I'm curious to see if Raena grew attached to you when she had you in her cage. So you will help me set a trap for her."

Jain laughed. He lost control enough that he laughed hard and long, throwing his body into another swing. "She won't come after me. She's here to kill you, Father. She's here to take away everything you have and then kill you."

"You don't know her as well as you think you do," Jonan assured. "Maybe she sees a lot of herself in you. You're about the same age as she was when I took her in. She'll want to spare you some of whatever she thinks I put her through."

"We're nothing alike," Jain argued. "She was a slave. I am your son. I am a prince."

"Funny how a little betrayal can change that," Jonan said. "Now you're nothing to me, but bait."

"One more thing," Jain said quickly. "She gave me a recording that she made on the *Raptor*. It's hidden under my desk."

"I'll get it," Merin offered.

Jonan nodded sharply. To Jain, he said, "You can't buy your way out of your punishment."

"I wouldn't dream of it, Father." The boy's voice was so cold, so haughty, that it made Jonan proud.

* * *

Eilif brought a cup of tea to Merin as he searched below Jain's desk. They didn't go through the tasting ritual as she did with Jonan. Merin was confident enough in his strength that he trusted no one would poison him. He believed that anyone who had a problem with him would face him with it.

Eilif respected that. Surreptitiously, she tasted his tea before she brought it to him. Part of her hoped—prayed almost, if it were possible there were deities to hear—that someone would attempt to poison one of her masters. She wished to die badly enough that she'd be grateful to go in their service.

As she set the teacup on the desktop, she asked, "Any sign of Jimi?" She asked softly enough that Merin could choose to ignore the question if he didn't want the interruption.

"One of the hoppers left about the time of the explosion in the shipyard. I doubt our nemesis left with her job half done, so it must have been Jimi running away at last."

Eilif closed her eyes and nodded. One of her sons escaped, at least. Two others were delivered from their misery. And Jain was being punished by his father. It was enough to drive a woman mad, she thought, if a woman had the luxury of going mad.

"Was there something else?" Merin asked.

To her surprise, Eilif asked bluntly, "Why is this happening to us?"

Merin crawled up off the floor and shoved a silver recording sphere into the player. On the computer screen, a tiny woman glowed in the darkness, luminous and scarred and shameless. Her voice was musical and soft.

Merin spoke so that Eilif could not make out the black-haired woman's words. "She booby-trapped the escape pod that brought Jain back to us. She didn't know who she'd catch in the explosion, but she must have known it wouldn't be Jonan. It appears she helped Jimi escape. I don't know yet what he gave her in return. Probably he was the one who betrayed our location. I do know that one of the boys tampered with the news viewers and kept us blind to what had happened to Revan and the *Raptor* crew, some of whom continue to survive in captivity on Kai. I'll attend to that soon enough. For now, Jain has been compromised. Either he led her to us, or he's a fool that she's used. Either way, I'll be very surprised if Jonan doesn't kill him for his complicity…"

"Why is she doing this to us? Jonan loves her."

Merin looked away from the half-naked woman on the monitor to Eilif, still kneeling beside him. He was too shocked to answer.

"Where is she now?" Eilif asked contritely, her eyes downcast.

"It's my job to figure that out," Merin reassured.

"But she's here? Somewhere in the castle?"

"I'll find her," he promised. A smile bared his teeth like a skull's. "It's what I do."

* * *

Raena sat on a rooftop, watching creatures swim past the other side of the castle's dome. The leviathans were enormous, as big as spacecraft, with mouths full of teeth as long as swords. Apparently, all the excitement when the lifeboats fled the city had drawn the big predators' attention. She wondered how they would react if they smelled blood in the water.

Jonan and several of his sons had been busy. They marched Jain out in shackles, then hoisted him up to dangle from the highest parapet. He had a tiny ledge to stand on. A noose ringed his neck. If he lost concentration—fell asleep, let his mind wander—or lost courage, death was but a step away.

Bait.

Jonan was crazy if he thought Raena would climb the tower to rescue the boy. All those stairs and no exit? Or maybe Jonan had been watching her video from Kai. Maybe he hoped to see her fly. Whatever. The boy had chosen to come home. Whatever his issues were with his father, she wouldn't get involved in sorting them out. Their relationship… their problems.

Still, she found it uncomfortable to see the boy up there on the precipice. She respected him, in some strange way. They were very similar. He just didn't have a sister like Ariel, who could put his feet on the path to escape.

Once the lynch mob had retreated into the building, Raena reassembled the sharpshooter rifle from her rucksack. She braced it against her shoulder and sighted down the scope. If she were as good a shot as Ariel, she could probably shoot the rope above Jain's head. If the surprise didn't kill him—and his hands were free—Jain might be able to pull himself back onto the tower and save himself. But where could he go if he wouldn't leave home? Back on the transport, she'd already done the math about saving him.

When she brought the sight down from the thread of rope, Jain's face was very clear. His gaze fixed in her direction. She read her name on his lips. Then she realized he had an open communicator collar around his neck. He'd seen the flare off her scope and was reporting her location.

She smiled, grateful that he made the decision for her. Let them come, she thought. Time to get this over with.

* * *

Jaden watched his brothers put on their armor. Usually, when they prepared to spar with their father, there was teasing and wrestling and fun in the locker room. Now everyone was concentrating, making sure their straps were tightened down and their staves were charged up, playing out the attack in their heads. Suddenly, they were no longer facing a game where one of them might be injured. In the back of their minds, they'd always known that their father wouldn't really kill any of them. He held them too dear. They were nearly irreplaceable.

But there was no guarantee with this madwoman. She had already killed Revan, the crew of the *Raptor*, the men in the avalanche on the Templar world, the new clones, Aten, and their two youngest brothers. Jarl and Jin had only been six years old. Their childhood hadn't protected them.

Why, oh why hadn't he told anyone about the news from Kai? If they'd had any warning, they might have been able to prepare…

Jaden broke that thought off. They had been preparing. Their whole lives, their father had been training them for just such a moment as this: when the sins of the fathers finally came home, fully armed and murderous.

No one had seen Jimi since the explosion in the hangar, but he wasn't being listed among the dead. Jaden wondered if they just hadn't found his body yet. Maybe the woman captured him somewhere in the castle. Maybe she'd tortured him. Jaden had never really liked the little whiner, but he was a brother. He had to be avenged.

Jamian worked his way down the line, checking all the boys' staves and banging the butts against the floor to set off their charges. The boys were supposed to capture Zacari, bring her unharmed to their father. Merin, when he set them to the task, reminded them to work together. Jozz wondered aloud if they were expendable. Merin's answer had been, "Don't give her an opening."

Their father bustled into the locker room, smiling like a saber-shark, his silver eyes alight with strange fire. "You make me so proud," he said by way of greeting. "Look at you! My fine young soldiers. Thallians, all. Remember, Raena is fast and she won't stay her hand. It's up to you to out-maneuver—out-think—her. You've been well-trained and constantly drilled. You can do this. And whoever strikes the blow that captures her will take Jain's place as my prime son."

Jaden exchanged a glance with Jarad. His twin had always wanted only that: to take Jain's place.

Jaden could only picture their brother standing proudly atop the tower with a noose around his neck. Jain had been shamed in a way he would never be able to survive. A similar fate awaited any of them who disappointed their father now.

CHAPTER 17

Before long, five boys converged on Raena's rooftop. Two came from the stairway she'd taken to the roof. The other three came roaring over the walls with jetpacks on their backs. Each one was armed with a stun staff.

The meter and a half long staves were tipped with two sparking prongs. The butt was capped with a durable nonconductive porcelain, the same material from which Ariel's family used to make their rifle stocks. The staves' butt ends were heavy enough that they could be used as bludgeons.

They wanted to take her alive. She shook her head.

Raena shot the boy who'd risen directly into her sight. His hand slipped from his jetpack controls. He rocketed upward to smack hard against the dome. The rockets continued to roar, bashing him upward like a fly against a windowpane. Raena aimed carefully; one missed shot might shatter the aged dome and drown them all. She fired again and pierced one of the rocket tanks.

Before she saw the boy fall, she heard a staff whistling toward her. She dropped to the rooftop and rolled.

All the weaponry she was carrying slowed down her somersault and made her awkward. Another staff came plummeting down toward where she lay. She quickly reversed her hold on the rifle and caught the staff against her stock. The rifle's impact-resistant butt absorbed the blow, but the scope might be rattled enough to make the gun useless.

She kicked upward, flipping onto her feet. That put her within striking distance of one of the boys who'd come through the door.

Raena turned her back to him, stepped inside his reach, and pulled his staff across her chest. He had the staff strapped to his right wrist so that she couldn't pull it free as planned. Problematic.

Then the others attacked, three on two. She didn't expect any of them to pull their blows just to protect the brother trapped behind her.

The fight was textbook, attack and parry. She could have fought it in her sleep. And yet these were Jonan's sons. She had expected better of them. Had they ever faced a real opponent, one not bound to them by blood or payroll? She doubted they'd ever beaten their father with moves like this.

In fact, the boy at her back was enjoying his opportunity to press up against a real woman all too much. He hadn't yet realized that if he stepped back from the fight, he could draw the Stinger on her left thigh with his off-hand. She wanted to get out of his way before the strategy filtered past his hormones.

Unfortunately, the three boys closing in on her hadn't given her enough room to regroup. The hero at her back wasn't giving any ground. Finally, she was able to dodge left, dragging his arm into the position recently vacated by the staff they were both holding. When the next blow came, his arm caught it. Raena heard him groan as the bone shattered.

She continued on around, putting the injured boy between her and the attackers. She dropped her hold on the staff and left him to fend for himself. That gave her a second to draw the Stinger. As she came around, she opened fire at point-blank range.

The boys never stood a chance. She wondered if Jonan had ordered them to their deaths, or if they'd volunteered. Or if they'd been intentionally betrayed by Jain.

She looked up to where Jain stood on the ledge, but without the rifle's scope, he was too far away for her to read his face. While she watched, he deliberately stepped forward off his platform.

The rope had very little slack to it. His feet scrabbled against the stone, but they didn't regain purchase. Raena watched until he'd stopped kicking. She wished there had been another way for Jain, but she still couldn't imagine what it might have been.

She looked down at the dead boys in front of her. The oldest pair were maybe nineteen. The youngest twins seemed no more than ten. Children. She tried to feel something for them. She had never known a mirror like that, nor the sense of something she loved growing inside her body, an autonomous possession that would adore her as the god who had created it. Children meant nothing special to her.

Now Thallian's sons were dead. She had destroyed him in all his reflections: nine clones gone, all the creatures in the vats contaminated, and no mirrors left.

No one else came for her. Apparently, she was going to have to hunt Jonan down herself. She left the rifle and took one of the jetpacks. It would be a faster way down than taking all those stairs.

* * *

. Because Raena was flying, she was high enough in the air to see the cloning laboratories explode. All of that dome's air suddenly bubbled upward.

She paused to watch, immensely surprised to find someone had the courage to fight on her side. She wondered who it could be. If she'd counted the boys correctly, and if Jimi's photo had contained them all, there should be none left to betray their father. Was her assistant one of Jonan's brothers? Someone from the *Arbiter* who'd stayed behind when the city was evacuated?

The ocean poured in through the broken dome to smother the fire raging inside the complex. Goosebumps shivered over Raena's skin and she laughed at her own horror. At least that kind of death was quick.

Anyway, she'd seen the security precautions between the domes and knew she was safe here near the castle. The breach of one dome didn't necessarily threaten the others. Still, the destruction, when that dome cracked, rained in inescapably fast. The breather she'd packed in her rucksack would give her a scant moment to get out of the crush and cold of the water. Survival was an outside possibility. She could never swim to the surface before the pressure or the leviathans killed her.

While she tried to slow her racing heart, another explosion split the dome covering the city. Then the vacant dome beside it collapsed, followed by others farther away, the farms and factories, washing away everything the Thallians built under the sea. Somebody meant to leave them with nothing. Who?

Raena wondered if Jonan was standing somewhere at a high window, watching the devastation of his kingdom. Or had he ordered it himself, to drive her toward him?

She took the breather from her bag and looped it over her head to dangle around her throat. Then she used the jet pack to change her trajectory to aim for the shipyard. Her cursory examination earlier had shown that all the ships had been adapted for travel underwater as well as through atmosphere and into space. She had an escape vehicle picked out. Maybe it was time to make sure it was gassed up and ready to go.

* * *

Sickened, Merin watched the devastation, too. His first thought was to blame the girl, but then he saw how she panicked and fled toward the shipyard. She hadn't set these explosions. The possibility of being trapped underwater terrified her.

Good. He could work with that.

At full speed, he cut his rockets. As he dropped, he made no sound. His feet caught her hard in the small of the back, but his angle was slightly off and he didn't snap her spine. Still, he had no doubt that it hurt enough to get her attention.

She rolled into a little ball—and she was small enough that it was a very little ball—then pulled out in time to kick off the upper lip of the security wall. She'd cut her own rockets, so she wasn't fighting their thrust.

Merin launched himself at her again. He body-slammed her into the dome, but she squirmed away before he could get a hold on her. Her size made her tricky. He was used to pulling back when fighting the younger boys. Jonan had approved of injuring them, but killing them would have crossed the line. Merin didn't want to kill this girl either, although she deserved it. Still, he did want it to hurt as he incapacitated her.

She ran along the curved surface of the dome gingerly, as if she worried how much pressure it could withstand from within. Even with those ludicrous heels, it wasn't a concern. The domes were built to withstand a lot of abuse, if not explosives. He'd deal with the saboteur as soon as he had the girl subdued.

Merin drew his pistol, but he didn't want to fire on her while she kept close to the dome. She spun toward him, still moving fast, and drew her own sidearm. It seemed to be one of the Stingers from Revan's transport. As she ran toward him, she aimed in his direction.

Merin hit his rockets and blasted toward her. She dropped the Stinger, wiping her left hand along the top of her boot. When he hit her, she hadn't quite gotten the knife up. It glanced off his jet-pack harness and jammed into one of his ribs.

She was watching him, not her hands, so she got her right arm up under his and forced his pistol across his body, aiming straight into the dome. Then she turned across him, jabbing the knife into his back, missing a kidney by sheerest luck.

Merin hit his rockets, flying backwards hard and fast. He drove her into the parapet, felt the breath whoosh out of her past his ear. She'd angled the knife, so the impact stabbed it into the kidney she'd missed before. The pain sent a white jolt throughout his body.

She left the blade in place, pinned between their bodies. Her left leg wound around his hips. She pulled another knife from her other boot.

Merin slammed his head back, hoping to break her nose or crush her skull—anything to make the pain in his back stop. She was turned awkwardly on his back to avoid the hot jets of his rockets, so that his skull missed hers. His head snapped back, baring his adam's apple. Very obligingly, Raena grabbed hold of his graying hair and slit his throat.

* * *

Raena reached around the dead man's body and turned off his jetpack. His body suddenly took on its full weight. She let it drop.

Blood soaked her legs and slicked her arm, cooling rapidly. She used her jetpack to ease herself down to the ground. Nothing else had exploded. Had the demolition simply been intended to chase any stragglers into the castle dome? Or to erase anyone who'd stayed behind?

Nothing moved. The only sounds she could hear were regular mechanical noises—the air exchangers humming, water circulating in the pipes, the heaters and lights making life livable kilometers below the surface of the sea—sounds that she'd tuned out because she'd heard them since her arrival. Raena felt as if she was already walking through a ghost town.

Maybe Thallian, like Jain, had chosen to take his own life, rather than face the loss of everything he loved. She needed to see his corpse to make certain. She wondered if she would feel relieved or disappointed to be cheated of her victory.

Something boomed nearby. A projectile slammed into her shoulder, knocking her off her feet. The pain was surprising, but manageable. There were doorways around her, but no sense in taking cover until she knew where the sniper hid. She got to her feet and leaned forward into a run, trying to make herself harder to hit.

Pure electricity jolted through her, unstringing her limbs. She missed a step and toppled forward, unable to even get her arms out in front of her. Her head crashed against the pavement. Her teeth closed on her tongue. She lay in the dust convulsing, trying to force her hand upward to dig the electric bullet out of her shoulder. No. It couldn't happen like this. She was so close to accomplishing everything she'd hoped for, everything she'd lived for. She couldn't go down like this.

After an excruciatingly long time, a pair of lovingly polished black leather boots stepped into her field of vision.

"At last," Thallian purred. "Welcome home, my dear."

Raena felt unstoppable tears spill from her eyes. Thallian knelt beside her, rapt and adoring. He reached out to wipe a tear from her cheek like he was examining a diamond. She noticed he'd replaced his velvet gloves with rubber.

"What have you done to your hair?" he growled. "You had such lovely hair. I suppose it will grow back before too long." He stroked her head, setting off a chain of sparks across her scalp. That made him smile.

"Don't try to speak, my love. The charge is enough to disrupt your muscle control, as no doubt you've noticed, and it will garble your speech. Wait and tell me later. We'll have eternity to catch up."

He hauled her onto an anti-grav cart, which was also shielded by a rubber mat. The convulsions weren't strenuous enough to beat her up too much, but the constant jerking and twitching made her ache. Black spots flickered at the edges of her vision. She wondered how much blood she was losing.

As if reading her mind, Jonan clucked and stuffed gauze into the wound. That pain was alarming, white and sharp. It roused her from her swoon, for all the good that did her.

Where was her accomplice now? If someone was going to go to all the trouble of blowing up the city for her, the least they could do is rescue her from this madman.

Thallian escorted the cart as if it was some sort of palanquin and she some sort of returning queen. "The family can't wait to meet you," he promised.

There were more of them? Raena couldn't even shiver at the thought. Her tongue throbbed where she continued to bite it. Blood drooled from her mouth.

"Of course, we'll have to clean you up before I present you," he said. "At least, we'll have to see to your bleeding. But then, not all of that blood is yours, is it? Does any of it belong to my sons, or is it all Merin's?"

He looked at her as if expecting an answer. Raena didn't even attempt to respond. It didn't matter. Thallian's thoughts zoomed off in a different direction and he said, "I have such a dress for you! It was my wife's."

He paused, disturbed by some fleeting thought. When he continued, he was gazing off into the hallways of the castle. "It was her bridal dress. When I returned home after the War, I married her." His laughter echoed from the metal walls. There was a brittle ring to it. "I thought I'd never see you again. I thought I could replace you. I hope you will forgive my lack of fidelity."

On one level, Raena was relieved that he'd taken away her ability to converse. His madness made him much less fearsome. Part of Thallian's power over her had been that he had always set up every experience so that he could test and control her responses. He had been fascinated by taking her apart psychologically, stymied only by her silence. Eventually, he'd decided that the silence was a result of her damage rather than the source of her strength.

But where *was* Thallian's wife? His rant stumbled when it came to her. Interesting. Raena felt nothing but pity for the poor creature.

"Here we are," Thallian announced as he nudged the cart into a room near the bottom of the castle. Raena felt her eyes widen as she realized it was kitted out as an operating room. Jonan smiled down at her, displaying his pointed teeth. "This is Dr. Poe. He's been with the family for generations."

The antique medical robot rolled toward her, a scalpel upraised.

"He's going to remove my bullet and suture your wound." Thallian raised a mask connected by a hose to a canister of some kind. He held it above her face. Raena could smell the anesthetic. Normally, she would be able to control her breathing, but with the electrical interference jamming her nervous system, she had no defense. She couldn't even huff the drug and pray it put her out forever.

✳ ✳ ✳

When she woke, she was confined in a dress built like a steel cage. Her arms were forced behind her, bound from elbow to wrist in cold metal. Her shoulders were bare, so she could see the needlessly baroque dressing taped over her shoulder wound. Below that, from bosom to ankle, she was encased in metal. Perhaps Madame Thallian had been able to move in her bridal gown, but Raena was locked in place. Her feet didn't even touch the floor.

Before her stretched a banquet table. Arranged around it were the Thallians she had killed: the brother she'd stabbed in the back, a scorched cripple in an ornate rolling chair, and an empty place for Revan, whose anonymous corpse lingered unclaimed on Kai. Jain, with his broken neck, was propped up close to hand. Two charred boys were too fragile to be uncurled from their death poses. Toward the outer ends of the table slumped the young boys she'd shot on the rooftop. She noticed there was no empty place for Jimi. Perhaps he'd already been disowned. There was no vacancy for the wife either.

"My family," Thallian announced proudly. "They're thrilled to have you become a part of us."

He wore an elegant suit of black velvet, embroidered with ropes and coils of gold. It clung to his body like a second skin, revealing how obsessively he had preserved himself beneath the sea.

Raena knew from the burning between her thighs that he'd raped her while she was unconscious on the operating table. After quickly assessing whether there were any significant injuries, she locked her disgust down. This was just one more reason to kill him as soon as she was able.

Thallian turned slowly in a circle, eyebrows stitched together in puzzlement. "I don't know where the servants have gone. I ordered a feast in your honor."

"I'm sorry, my lord." A woman scurried into the room. "There's only me left."

"Eilif," he purred. Raena's hackles raised at the sound. Thallian grabbed the woman's arm and dragged her closer to where Raena stood imprisoned. "This is my wife," he said.

Raena couldn't find words to express her sympathy, so she merely nodded.

It didn't matter. Thallian's wife didn't raise her head to see. "I brought some of your father's wine to celebrate," Eilif said. She lifted a sealed bottle in her right hand. Her other hand clutched two glasses and a bottle opener.

"No glass for you?" Thallian wondered. "Don't you want to toast my new bride?"

"I—"

"No matter," he said, cutting her off. He took the bottle and proceeded to draw its cork. Eilif presented the glasses, which were thin as paper and glowed with a sheen like the surface of a soap bubble.

Thallian poured generous glassfuls. He handed one to Eilif, kept the other, and stepped back to gaze at Raena.

Eilif, without being told, held the second glass up for Raena.

"Decades I have dreamed about you," Thallian toasted. "In all the galaxy, I knew there was only one woman who was my equal. I knew one day you would find your way home to me." He lifted his glass and drank deeply.

Eilif mimed holding the glass up for Raena to drink, but even if Raena had felt the desire to join Thallian, the glass remained just beyond her reach. She looked down at the woman who cringed before her. Eilif lifted her green eyes to meet Raena's. A smile flickered across her lips.

Thallian's glass dropped from his hand, shattering on the polished stone floor. He followed it to the floor and collapsed amidst the glass and spilled wine, the curse frozen on his lips.

"You can drink the poison if you wish to join him," Eilif offered.

"Thank you, but no," Raena said. "Is he dead?"

"Not yet," Eilif said. "I'd like your help with that."

"My pleasure," Raena said. "Can you help me out of your dress?"

* * *

Thallian woke up as the last cuff snapped around his ankle. At least, it felt like he opened his eyes, but the blackness was absolute. Where was the emergency lighting? He strained to hear anything in the darkened sleep chamber. Nothing moved.

He tugged experimentally and felt metal bite his wrists. The bonds had almost no give. His limbs were stretched to their full extensions so that if he struggled, he would break his own skin. He thrashed anyway, until he smelled his blood on the air.

His head felt fuzzy. It was hard to think. How had his assailants gotten through the family's security? Why, after they had him immobilized, had they abandoned him? In the total darkness, the room echoed as if empty.

Something cold struck his chest. Wetness soaked his clothing until it clung clammily against his skin. The liquid lashed out again, drenching him.

Fear threaded through him. "Eilif?" The hope in his voice embarrassed him.

"Yes, my lord. I'm here."

"What's happened?"

"I poisoned you," Eilif said matter-of-factly, as if it was something she did every day.

That made no sense, so he chose to ignore it. "Where's Raena?"

"I'm here, too," an all-too-familiar voice replied. Raena Zacari struck a match. Twin flames sparkled in her black eyes. Despite the ruin of her hair, she hadn't really changed, hadn't aged a day. She was still twenty years old, too thin for her tiny frame, and dressed in a black catsuit of his wife's.

A smile slipped across her face like a knife being eased from its sheath. Thallian felt his body respond to that smile. He shifted his hips to draw her attention.

"Goodbye, Jonan." Raena flicked the burning match at him. It tumbled through the air, arcing slowly above his sodden clothing. The fumes ignited with a whump that crushed him down against the bed. A rush of intense heat stole the air from his lungs.

His women stood beside him and watched him burn. Raena's face was impassive, but he barely recognized Eilif. Glee contorted her face.

In the fifteen years she had been his, Thallian watched the lines etch around her eyes, watched her body grow lean as it outlasted its youth. She was no longer the beautiful girl he'd taken for his own. Still, she was his. She was here. He loved her more in this moment than ever before.

Raena turned away to pour the accelerant around the room, leaving them together.

CHAPTER 18

Eilif walked Raena back to the hangar and helped get a hopper ready to fly. "I have the castle rigged to blow up," Eilif told her calmly. "I'll wait until I see you're clear."

Never in Raena's life had she ever rescued anyone. Occasionally— occasionally enough to have been a fluke—she'd spared someone. Usually, as in Jain's case, they found death soon enough without her help. Never, ever had she inconvenienced herself to save someone. This time she saw too much of herself in Eilif to let the woman choose death, even if that's what Raena would have done in the same position.

"Come with me," Raena said softly. "You don't need to die here with *him*."

"I don't have anywhere to go," Eilif answered, an aching, hollow statement of fact. "I don't know where I came from. I don't remember anything before Jonan married me. It's like I woke up and was already a prisoner."

Raena suspected Eilif was a clone, but of whom she couldn't guess. She looked vaguely similar to Raena in build, though taller, and she had those electric green eyes. She was a substitute, a facsimile, but not a duplicate.

"The galaxy is a big place," Raena said. "There are lots of holes in which to hide. Come with me and we'll find you somewhere that's safe."

"I want to erase this place," Eilif argued.

"I support that." Raena smiled. "We can trip it as we clear the airlock."

Eilif smiled back. "It *would* be nice to watch it explode."

* * *

The hopper's cockpit would be cramped for the two of them. At least Eilif didn't bring anything with her, preferring as Raena did to travel with only the clothes on her back.

Raena tried to reach Mykah on her comm bracelet, but the dome, the water, or the distance into space prevented her from getting through. That added a challenge. She would have taken a larger ship, but she'd stressed to the pirates that they should run if anything larger than a hopper came off the planet. If she took the time, she could modify one of the other ships to chase Mykah's transport, but both she and Eilif were ready to be on their way. Besides, Eilif never had any training that might have given her the skills to escape. She'd be no help as a copilot. Raena wasn't sure she could fly a larger ship alone and one-handed.

Raena warmed up the hopper's engines as she and Eilif settled into the pilot's chair, un-selfconscious about the ways their bodies touched. They'd had so little control over who touched them, and how, for so long that they were able to compartmentalize the contact, lock it away.

Which was good. Raena needed her right hand free to fly, but her left shoulder throbbed where she'd taken the bullet. She rested gingerly back against Eilif and fastened the crash web over both of them. She'd just have to deal with the pain. She'd had worse.

Raena eased the throttle forward and awkwardly pulled in the landing gear. As they were nearing freedom, she mistimed the explosion. It triggered when she opened the airlock instead of after the hopper passed through. The blast thrust them forward, bashing the hopper hard against the half-open hatch. Something gave a sickening crunch.

Both women looked upward. Before they could worry about whether the canopy remained watertight, the current whirled them out of the dome and into the ocean.

The leviathans she'd watched before swooped down on them. Raena flew evasively, slamming the little ship from side to side, accelerating and braking, making the hopper jump.

Eilif's head had slammed against Raena's bullet wound. Raena hissed, but kept flying. Sword-blade teeth snapped too close all around them.

One of the monsters bit another by accident. Suddenly the churning water was veiled with blood as the creatures set upon each other. Raena saw her opening and gunned the hopper forward.

"Turn the running lights off," Eilif advised. "They've learned to track the lights."

Raena did so. The ocean ahead was illuminated by the glow of the castle burning behind them. The eerie blue flicker revealed the underwater topography ahead. Raena turned the hopper enough to clear a submarine mountain. That gave the women a better view of the fall of the house of Thallian.

Eilif's demolition had split the dome and flooded the castle. The accelerant Raena had chosen continued to burn, even without oxygen. Every stone seemed afire. Wicked sinuous tongues of flame danced as tall as the mountains. The black shadows of the leviathans swooped amongst them, scrounging up meals.

"I'm sorry about your sons," Raena said quietly.

"They weren't mine, of course," Eilif answered, just as softly. "I mothered them, when they let me, but they were Thallians. Clones of Jonan. They had been created to die for him. They never stood a chance."

Raena said quickly, "Jimi escaped. I told him how to adapt a hopper and he told me enough about his point of origin that I could bring Jain back home. Jimi's already on his way to a new life."

Eilif's smile was watery, but grateful. Then she turned her face away to watch the castle collapse in on itself.

* * *

Blood trickled into Raena's armpit, ticklish and annoying, where her stitches had torn open. With her left arm in a sling, she couldn't do anything about it.

How much blood had she lost already? She wasn't sure if the medical robot had topped her off with cloned blood or if anything else might be washing around in her system. Either way, her head felt woozy. She rushed to get them to the surface before she blacked out.

"See the bracelet on my wrist?" she asked, keeping her voice level. "It's keyed to a channel on Jain's transport. If you press the black button, it will connect you to the transport's crew. Tell them Fiana needs help."

"Who's Fiana?"

"My code name."

The proximity alarm shrieked and Raena slapped it off. A leviathan was on their tail. She leaned forward toward the controls, trying to coax more speed from the hopper's little engines.

Eilif hissed as she saw the blood slicking the front of her flight suit now that Raena had moved away.

"We're gonna make it," Raena promised. "I didn't survive this whole nightmare to be eaten by a fish."

She spun the hopper, firing off the charge meant to thrust meteorites out of the way. The leviathan took it in the eye and turned tail, swimming for its life before its brothers scented blood.

* * *

The hopper reached the ocean's surface without the speed it needed to leap into the air. It crashed back into the water. Eilif had a panicked moment of trying to figure out the releases for the crash web, but she got herself free at last and hit the right buttons to power down.

She could see land a couple hundred meters away. They could make it. She grasped Raena's wrist, hit the black button on her comm bracelet, and relayed the message she'd been given.

"We're on our way," someone told her.

Raena was out completely. Eilif reached around her, gathering the emergency supplies. She took a very deep breath. Then she popped the hopper's canopy. As water poured into the ship, Eilif pulled Raena free.

The ocean was icy in the planet's perpetual winter, but Raena didn't react. Eilif swam strongly for the shore, towing the smaller woman and the gear. For the first time, she was grateful that Jonan had insisted that she learn to swim.

Eilif hoped the gelid water would slow Raena's blood loss, but hypothermia would soon be a greater concern. She had to get the shelter up before long.

She pushed herself to swim harder.

* * *

Eilif listened as a ship landed nearby. Every cell in her body wanted to run, slip through the back wall of the shelter, and vanish into the ashen drifts outside. But that was suicide. There was no longer anything to eat on the planet's surface and no water she could drink. She refused to die now, after everything.

Besides, Raena needed her. Eilif curled close around the little woman, trying to keep her warm despite their sodden clothes. Raena had to live. Who else could protect her now?

"Raena?" a man called. His wasn't a voice Eilif recognized. She shivered. She'd never met a stranger, an off-worlder, before.

"She's here," Eilif called back. "She's been shot."

The shelter door slammed open. Three figures stood there, training all manner of mismatched weaponry on her. Behind a young man with a crazy bush of beard stood a hulking figure covered in long lavender-blue fur and a slim creature that made Eilif think of a squid.

Her head swam at the sight of them—aliens!—but she blinked hard and forced herself to say calmly, "Thank you for coming for us."

The man stepped forward, sheathing his gun, and peeled back the crinkly thermal blanket to look at the mess of blood saturating Raena's clothes.

"Who are you?" the blue girl demanded.

"I was a slave," Eilif said, still clutching Raena. "She rescued me."

"Looks like you're returning the favor," the man said. He was gentle as he pulled her away and handed her toward the tentacled creature. Eilif let herself be directed, watching as he picked Raena up in his arms. "Let's get her onto the transport."

"Are they coming after you?" the blue girl wanted to know.

Eilif didn't have to ask who "they" were. "They're all dead," she assured her.

Belatedly, now that escape was so close, triumph surged through her. She felt as if she'd never smiled before in her life.

Eilif followed the man and the aliens onto Revan's stolen transport. She didn't even feel the cold of the planet she was leaving behind.

* * *

Mykah had more experience leaking things to the media, so Raena asked him to arrange the rescue of the last survivors of the *Arbiter* from the surface of the Thallian homeworld.

She watched the news coverage from the darkness of her cabin aboard Mykah's transport, now renamed *Veracity*. Overall, the *Arbiter*'s men seemed grateful to be retrieved from their long exile. Some of them even looked forward to standing trial, so they could spill the details of the Thallians' responsibility for the Templar genocide.

Mykah was thrilled at being allowed to break the story.

Raena sipped some kind of herbal tea that Haoun had brewed for her, something supposed to aid her body to heal. Her shoulder was still stiff, but Eilif seemed to have done a masterful job of stitching it up. The weakness from the blood loss seemed slower to dissipate. It seemed as if the memory of what had almost happened to her did not want to leave her flesh.

Still, dead was dead. Raena had stayed until the fire consumed the contents of Jonan's room. Then, wearing a borrowed fire suit, she'd waded into the inferno and smashed what remained of his skeleton to splinters. She wanted to see for herself that there was nothing left to clone. The last agent of the Empire—the last scion of the Thallians—had been erased.

She hoped that somewhere safe, Jimi—or whatever he had chosen to rename himself—was watching the news that the last of the Thallian murderers had been assassinated and their secret base swallowed by the ocean. She pictured the boy at work in some shipyard, applying his uncle's elegant solutions to aging spacecraft. She hoped he would find peace.

Raena felt entirely exhausted, but sleep would not come. Whenever she closed her eyes, she kept seeing Thallian's funeral pyre. She wasn't sure why Jonan's death stayed with her more than any of the others. She'd loved him less than Jain. Still, the expression on Jonan's face, as the flames caught his clothing and started to burn him, made her shiver. She'd expected to see hatred when it finally penetrated his madness that she refused to be his. Or perhaps to see some kind of acknowledgement of the pain, some kind of struggle against his fate.

What she never thought she'd see was the ecstasy he felt. Jonan not only surrendered to the pain, he embraced it. He craved more. He wanted to be devoured.

That level of masochism shocked her as deeply as anything Thallian had ever done in life.

Then, in his final moments, to see him turn to Eilif: knowing she had betrayed him in retaliation for all he'd made her suffer; knowing that in the end, she chose freedom rather than joining him in death.

Raena wondered if Jonan had ever loved his wife as much as he did at the end. Only her final act made clear to him what had been true all along. She hated him as thoroughly as Raena had herself.

Raena's thoughts spiraled to Gavin and Ariel, to the love they proclaimed for her that she could not return. Both of them loved the person she had been before the tomb, not the one she was now or wanted to become. She could envision no future with either of them that she would call freedom. She didn't want to be a possession or an adornment, another in a string of wives, or a companion and bodyguard. She didn't want to be the mother, even the co-mother, of anyone's children. She wanted the ability to come and go as she liked, something she had never yet experienced in her life.

Even so, she envied the easy camaraderie between Mykah's crew. Celebration was just beyond the door of her cabin, but Raena could not bring herself to join it. She was just too lonely.

So she poked around the interweb, struggling to find distraction. Eventually she washed up on the Shaad family channel. Ariel's message to her still waited to be picked up. Her defenses were low, Raena admitted. It was time to see what Ariel had to say.

Lean and full of character from all the years that Raena had not known her, her sister's face filled the screen. "Hey," Ariel said by way of greeting. "If you view this, I will take it as confirmation that you killed that bastard, that you survived and escaped him again. You don't need to respond if you don't want to. Of course, I'd love to hear from you, but...I understand. Or I think I do. You need your own life, not the past you'd be living with me or Gavin. Your body's only twenty, Raena. You have decades ahead of you. You need to find your own way. And I promise I will not hunt for you again." Ariel smiled, bitterly amused. "I can't make the same assurances about Gavin."

An encrypted string appeared at the bottom of the picture. Ariel explained, "I've set aside a fund for you. Use it to start your new life. Take it in a lump, move it somewhere safe, and don't worry about paying it back. Call it my way of making restitution for the years you spent as my family's slave."

Ariel smiled again and Raena almost felt as if their eyes met. "I love you, Raena. I hope you find happiness. The galaxy owes you."

Raena reached out to touch her sister's face, but her fingers found only the smooth surface of the computer screen.

Nodding to herself, she leaned toward the computer screen to record her reply. She knew she looked like hell, but that didn't matter. "Hey, Ari," she said hoarsely. "Thanks for the money. I'm gonna do what you said and start a new life. But I need one last favor. Thallian's wife helped me escape. Her name is Eilif. She's a clone, although I don't think she knows it. Looks to me like they tried to mature her too fast and something went wrong in the process. I don't know if she has long to live. She doesn't remember anything except being Jonan's slave."

Raena paused, giving Ariel time to understand what that meant. "Eilif's a survivor. She's clever. She understands how things work. I know she's not a cuddly orphan, but she needs help, Ari. Can you find her a place? Some decent work and a safe home? She … she makes me think a lot about how I might be, if it hadn't been for you. You saved my life, Ari. More than once." Raena smiled in apology. "I hope you can save her, too."

She sat back and pressed send, unable to play the message back and endure the pain in her own voice again. Ariel would help. Raena knew she would.

She started to stretch, then thought better of it. Instead, she powered down the computer and wondered what there was to drink on this boat. Petting her hair up on end, she went out to join the party.

ACKNOWLEDGMENTS

I've been dreaming of seeing Raena's story in the real world outside my head for so long that I have many people to thank for making it a reality. First off, thanks so much, Mom, for taking me to see *Star Wars* the summer it opened, long before it became *A New Hope*.

Thanks to Mart, who read every draft and published the first stories about Raena, Ariel, and Thallian in her zine *Tales of a New Republic*. Thanks to Brian, Paul, and Kelly, who contributed to the depth of the backstory. Thanks to the members of MediaWest, who wrote my first fan letters and let me know my story was connecting with people I didn't know.

Thanks to everyone who helped me finish this book, especially Seth Lindberg, Claudius Reich, and Lilah Wild in their roles as the Paramental Appreciation Society. Thanks to Dale Bentson and the members of the Writing Salon's Round Robins, under the direction of Jane Underwood, who encouraged me when I needed it. Thanks to Nanowrimo, which lit a fire under me to get it done.

Thanks to Mason and to Sorrell, who talked me down from ledges as I wrote and rewrote this novel.

Thanks especially to Jeremy Lassen, the best editor I have had the pleasure to work with. His clear eyes, probing questions, and imagination added so much to the final draft. Without his help, you would not now be holding this book in your hands. Thanks also to Jason Katzman and Cory Allyn for holding down the Skyhorse side of things and being very patient with my questions.

Photo courtesy of Ken Goudey

ABOUT THE AUTHOR

Loren Rhoads is the co-author (with Brian Thomas) of *As Above, So Below*. She's the author of a book of essays called *Wish You Were Here: Adventures in Cemetery Travel* and editor of *The Haunted Mansion Project: Year Two* and *Morbid Curiosity Cures the Blues*. Her science fiction short stories were collected into the chapbook *Ashes & Rust*. She remembers the Christmas there were men on the moon and looks forward to the New Year's Day there will be women on Mars.